Birt

A Novel
by

Sive Haughey

Lonnra Press

Published in 1998 by
Lonnra Press,
Muff,
Co. Donegal
Ireland

ISBN O 9531707 0 5

Cover Illustration by Ken Drakeford

Printed by Colour Books Ltd.,
Baldoyle Industrial Estate,,
Dublin 13,
Ireland.

Acknowledgements

The encouragement, help and advice which I received from many people made the writing and publication of this novel possible. I am greatly indebted to them.

Patrick Boland was extremely generous in sharing the knowledge he had acquired in publishing "Tales from a City Farmyard."

Bridie Burns was always available to help with the computer work. Her patience was amazing!

Maura Johnston, Rosie Mouton, Myra Dryden, Maimie Donoghue and Mary Egan gave encouragement and help in different ways.

I extend my thanks to them all.

For
Eddie and Eimear

PROLOGUE

HUGH

Hugh Staunton sighed. He looked out through the glass front door of his bungalow. It was a sunny spring day. The shrubs were bright and colourful with the year's new growth. The lawn would soon need to be cut. His neighbour, John Monks, would arrive any day now, wheeling his lawn mower.

It was Hugh Staunton's eighty-sixth birthday. The tenth of March, 1993. He sighed again. Birthdays were a drag. Shortly the family would arrive, fussing and scolding, unduly solicitous about his health and well-being. It was half past eight. They would come at ten, and stay until five, and it would be a tense, anxiety filled day.

He noticed the cat outside the front door, trying to attract his attention. He let her in, and led her through to the kitchen, where he fed her some scraps of bacon and a dish of milk. Then he let her out the back door, remembering to place her dish outside.

Last year Margaret had been horrified.

'A cat in the house, Dad?' she had yelped. 'That's very unhygienic. Cats carry germs, you know. You could get anything if you let that animal have the run of the house!'

He noticed, as always, the meaningful glances she had exchanged with Philomena and Kevin.

He went to the sink and washed his breakfast dishes, one mug and plate, one knife and fork. Normally he wouldn't wash any dishes until evening. There was no need, as by evening there would be exactly ten items of crockery, which he would wash and leave to drain. On his birthday last year Margaret had spotted his breakfast cup and plate in the sink. She had done a noisy, splashing washing up, followed by a noisy, rattling drying and putting away.

'Did you not get your breakfast dishes washed, Dad?' she had demanded. 'He's not coping,' he had heard her loudly whispering to Philomena. 'He didn't even know where the drying cloth was.'

'You can't talk to him,' Philomena had answered, while nodding her head, repeatedly, meaningfully. 'He never listens to anybody.'

****

'Here's your paper, Mr Staunton,' called Mrs Monks from the hall, handing him the Irish Times. 'I came early today, I know you'll be having visitors, so I thought I'd get the paper early, and be away before they arrive. I wouldn't want to intrude. And, by the way, happy birthday.'

She handed him a flat, bottle-shaped package.

'Thanks, Mrs Monks,' said Hugh. 'You really shouldn't have.'

'And why shouldn't I?' demanded the little bird-like woman. 'It's only a little something, nothing like a wee jorum to make you sleep well at night. See you later, bye ....'

She flitted out the front door and disappeared.

****

'That woman just walked in without knocking,' Margaret had complained last year. 'Did she not know your family was visiting? And, in any case, you shouldn't have the door on the snib like that. Anyone could walk in!'

Hugh had attempted to explain to Margaret that Mrs Monks called with the paper every morning, that she came once a week and cleaned the house for him, that she did messages for him, that her son John kept the lawn mowed and the hedge trimmed. But, as he talked, he realised that none of his visitors was really interested in what he was saying. Philomena had interrupted to say that Mrs Monks was a common little woman. Margaret had asked how much he paid for the cleaning job, and, without waiting for an answer, said that she was sure it was far too much. Kevin had said that you couldn't be too careful about letting people into your house these days.

****

A green van drove up to the front door.

'Hello, Master,' said Vincent the postman. 'Grand day for the time of year.'

He handed Hugh a large envelope with a French stamp.

'Looks like a day for celebrating, Master,' he remarked cheerily. 'I suppose the family will be coming?'

'Yes, Vincent, they will indeed,' replied Hugh.

'Well, have a good day, and stay sober,' called Vincent as he drove off.

Hugh took the card inside and opened it. It was, as he knew, from Angelina and Claire.

Dear Angelina! She was the youngest, considered by her siblings to be the black sheep of the family. Living in Paris, she could not come for the birthday visit. But she would come in August, with her teenage daughter Claire. They would hire a car, and spend a fortnight with him. They would go out driving, and have dinner in restaurants. They would call with friends. They would talk a lot, laugh a lot. Angelina would not advise him or fuss him or lecture him. At the end of the fortnight, she and her daughter would regretfully leave, promising to come again soon, always saying that they hoped, one day, to come back and live in Ireland.

Hugh knew that today, his birthday, would not pass without merciless criticism of Angelina by the other three. She had got above herself, that one. Who did she think she was anyway? There she was, living abroad, full of airs and graces. And the nerve she had, getting married at the age of nineteen, and just before Philomena. Not that it was a proper marriage, of course, and when that awful Frenchman walked out on her before Claire was born, it was only to be expected. It had been such an embarrassment to the family, especially to poor Mother, who might have lived longer if she hadn't been dealt this fateful blow.

And Hugh knew that life in Paris was far from glamorous. Angelina had told him about the tiny fifth floor flat for which she had to pay about half her wages in rent. She had told him about the cost of living in Paris, and about the rush and tedium of city life. But it never got her down. She always made the best of things, and was always good company when she came in August.

****

It was nine o'clock. Hugh went out to the front door and strolled towards the gate. He heard the familiar rattle of crates as the milk van stopped. By the time he reached the gate, Gus the milkman was standing, holding his bottle of milk, while staring fixedly at the ground.

'Hello, Master,' he said. 'See the ants? They're moving colony.' Hugh followed his gaze to the ground, where there was a procession of ants emerging from under a bush at the right hand side of the gate. They made their way in a straight line across the gateway, disappearing under the hedge at the far side. There must have been hundreds of them, walking purposefully in the same direction.

'Ants have only one queen in the colony,' said Gus. 'Did you know that, Master? When the queen gets too old to lay eggs, the whole colony ups and away to set up a new pad. Amazing, isn't it?'

It certainly was amazing. Hugh and Gus watched intently until the last of the ants had straggled away out of sight.

'And do you know something else, Master,' continued Gus, as he climbed back into his van. 'They're out of season. You normally don't see ants moving until June. The old people used to say that when the ants moved at the wrong time of year it was a sign that the day wasn't going to end as it had begun.'

He said goodbye and drove off, wondering if he had been indiscreet in suggesting to a man in his eighties that the day might not end as it had begun.

Hugh returned indoors and put on the kettle. He would have a leisurely cup of tea and read the paper before the invasion. Then they would come, swooping and yammering, criticising and fussing. Margaret would bring a casserole for the lunch. She would ask him what was a medium heat in the oven. He would suggest a hundred and eighty. A couple of years ago he had not known this. He never used the oven. Margaret had been shocked.

'You don't know what's a medium heat?' she had demanded incredulously. 'Well, I suppose it would be about a hundred and eighty.'

She had darted glances at the others. He was senile, definitely senile, the glances had said. He didn't know how to use the oven. He wasn't safe in the house.

Since that day Hugh had stored this piece of information, though he still never used the oven, nor had any intention of using it. Medium heat was a hundred and eighty.

****

Today again, Margaret, Philomena and Kevin would inevitably return to the topic that came up every year. They would try to persuade, to coerce him to leave his comfortable house and go into an old people's home. They wanted him to leave his house, his books, his cat, Mrs Monks, his milkman, his postman, his afternoon walks to the pub, his carryouts, and his lunches in front of the television. They would try, united in effort, and he would not respond. But he would have to be very careful. Their eagle eyes would be watching for one slip, one memory lapse, one unwashed cup in the sink, one whimsical remark, any of which would be interpreted as impending senility. They would talk, full of gentle concern, about residential homes, about the lovely one they had visited last week, about the nice meals that would be served, about the company he would have.

And then they would move into the hall, whispering and muttering angrily among themselves. From their urgent and not too silent whispers, Hugh had got occasional hints about how their concern was less for his welfare than from how they might benefit from his move. He had once heard Philomena say angrily, 'Why should we have to wait for our share? It'll be more use to us now than it would ever be to him!'

And he could have told them that they were wasting their time, that his worldly possessions, while adequate for his needs, would be of little value to anyone. But, until now, he had said nothing.

It's not important, he told himself. Let them come, let them make all the fuss they want. I don't have to go along with their suggestions. Let it slide, don't get irritated.

For the duration of these visits, that was exactly how Hugh responded. He let it slide. Occasionally he considered letting them know the true state of his finances. But he put it off, preferring to avoid the arguments that would inevitably follow.

And occasionally, when someone made a more than usually insensitive or personal remark, Hugh felt silently enraged. In those moments, he felt tempted to tell them that he knew what they were planning, that he was not deaf, that he could hear their sotto voce comments, that he was fully aware of their interest in the sale of the house. He felt wicked and mischievous, and seriously wanted to tell them a story, going back some fifty years, that would be certain to shake them out of their self-righteous complacency. But it was a story so amazing, so incredible, that it would have given them further reason to doubt that he was in full possession of his senses.

And yet, the story was true. And he was the only living human being who was aware of those most unlikely happenings that had taken place half a century back. His wife Teresa had known, and one or two other people, sworn to secrecy in their lifetime and now deceased. And Father O'Lorcan, long deceased, had known. In fact, he was the man who had masterminded this highly irregular sequence of events.

So, in spite of the serious annoyance and provocation that accompanied the family visit, Hugh remained cautious and silent.

Eventually, after a day fraught with anxiety, Margaret, Philomena and Kevin would talk about avoiding the evening traffic, and grumpily take their departure. They would stand at the gate talking agitatedly to each other for a few minutes before finally leaving.

Then Hugh, breathing a sigh of relief, would saunter over to the pub for a contemplative pint before settling down for tea in front of the television.

MARGARET

Margaret Gillen sighed. She sighed most mornings. There was always, every day, some source of exasperation, something that was going to annoy her. She stirred her coffee, lit a cigarette, and sighed again.

What was annoying her this morning, she tried to remember. Yes, it was the tenth of March, her father's birthday. She would have to start getting organised for the visit. In fact, she would have to leave shortly. What a bore this was! And the extra work it gave her! Yesterday evening she had made a casserole to bring for lunch, as if she didn't have enough to do already. Things weren't as easy as they used to be. She was now forty-nine, and with her varicose veins, and the trouble she had with gallstones, she couldn't be expected to be running round like a young one.

And yes, there was something else annoying her. That conversation with Philomena last night had just been the end. Philomena had had the nerve to opt out of today's visit. She was going to have a perm, and then in the afternoon she was taking Natalie to her riding lesson. She had even asked Margaret what was the point of this birthday visit, which had become a routine for the past six years. Their father was so ungrateful. He didn't show any appreciation of all they did for him.

Yes, of course, thought Margaret, their father showed no appreciation. But he was always welcoming, she had to admit. He was talkative, interested, and full of news. He always enquired after all his grandchildren. He would tell them the local news, who had got married, who had died, who was starting up a new business. This was such a bore. How could he expect any of them to be interested in what was happening in a backward little village like Kincade?

He really shouldn't be living there, she thought. He should be in a proper home, in a decent sized town. But every time they broached the subject, he became silent and withdrawn. A few years ago he had told them quite emphatically that he did not intend to move. Since that, he had refused to discuss the matter.

This time, Margaret was determined that they would have to persuade him. Living in an old people's home was, of course, expensive. But one of the less expensive ones would do. After all, it was pointless to expect luxury at the age of eighty-six. He could use his pension, and, with the money he'd save on other things, he could easily afford it. There was that woman who did his cleaning, for example. He paid her far too much, and he also paid her son to do some gardening. And those evening walks to the pub used up a lot of money. This time, they were going to have to make him see sense.

It had really enraged her when Philomena had just decided to opt out and leave it all to herself and Kevin. It was the responsibilty of all the family, but it seemed to Margaret that she was left with an unfair share. Of course, you couldn't really expect Kevin to do much, being a priest he couldn't really get involved in the family scene. But Philomena never offered to make the casserole. It was left to her, every year, to prepare a dinner to bring. She often intended to make this point, but never got round to it. Philomena should understand that Margaret was now finding things difficult, with the gallstones and varicose veins.

And, on the subject of sharing responsibilities, what about Angelina? What had she ever done to help the family? Wasn't it well for her, flying her kite in Paris, nothing better to do than live it up in a foreign country. She would, as usual, come in August, travelling round in a hired car, taking their father gallivanting round the country. Of course, Angelina never had a scrap of sense. It was pointless to expect any support from her now.

Margaret's husband, Peadar, had not accompanied her on the birthday visit for the last two years. She had at first discouraged him, then insisted that he should not come. Peadar got on very well with Hugh Staunton. They always got involved, first in serious conversation, about what was on the news and in the papers. Then they talked in lighter vein, joking and telling amusing anecdotes. They had even, on the second last visit, taken an afternoon walk to the pub. This had enraged Margaret and Philomena and Kevin. It had made it totally impossible to follow up their plan about an old people's home.

'Why don't you let him be?' Peadar had asked Margaret, in the car on the way home two years ago. 'He doesn't want to go into a home. He enjoys life where he is. I can't see him being happy in an institution.'

'If we could get him into a home,' pursued Margaret, 'he could sell the house and we could have our share now.'

'But it's his house,' Peadar had pointed out. 'It's his right to live in it as long as he likes.'

Margaret had said that that was a typical man's attitude. She had not brought up the subject again. But she had insisted that Peadar would not come on the next visit.

Sighing again, Margaret carried the casserole out to the car, and placed it carefully in a cardboard box on the floor at the passenger side. She went back and lifted from the sideboard the birthday card and the gift-wrapped package containing two pairs of socks. She lit a cigarette, pulled the front door behind her, and set off on the twenty mile journey to her father's house.

PHILOMENA

Philomena Murray sighed. She would need to hurry. She wanted to get over to Margaret's house, to catch her before she set out. She took a birthday card from the mantel piece, a picture of an old man with a fishing rod, sitting beside a river.

The children had laughed at it.

'Grandad never fishes,' they had remarked, so infuriatingly logically.

But she had to buy some sort of card, and it was so difficult to get something for an old man. She hastily wrote on it, stuffed it in its envelope, and lifted the plastic package containing two pairs of socks. By way of making it a bit tidier, she folded over the top and sealed it down with sellotape. She got into her car, and drove round to Margaret's house, just three streets away.

Margaret had been in bad form last night. She had been full of reproaches when Philomena told her that she couldn't go on the birthday visit. She had gone on at length about the casserole she had made, and about her varicose veins. But Margaret should have understood. She knew that Philomena had to have a perm, and if she missed her appointment today it might be ages before she could get another. And anyway there was Natalie's riding lesson. It was all right for Margaret, her children were grown up, past the stage when you had to chauffeur them here and there.

14

And Margaret had made such a fuss about their father. He would have to go this time, she insisted. They would have to persuade him to see sense. And was Philomena really leaving her to do all the dirty work herself? She had reminded Philomena that it was in her interest also that their father should go into a home. They could all, Kevin included, do with their share of the price of the house now. So wasn't it up to all of them to pull their weight in getting it settled? Philomena had answered that she could add nothing to what Margaret and Kevin would say anyway, and as their father was such a pig-headed old man what would it matter? He almost certainly wouldn't listen anyway.

As Philomena approached Margaret's gate, Margaret was driving out. When she stopped, she saw a distinctly what-do-you-want look on Margaret's face.

Philomena jumped out of her car, gave Margaret the card and the package, saying, 'Here's Dad's card and present ....'

'Oh, good of you to think of it,' said Margaret sarcastically. 'Isn't it well I'm going, so I can do your delivering for you?'

'You know how it is, Margaret,' Philomena answered. 'I'd go if I was free. But you know how busy I am ....'

'I do,' said Margaret. 'And I know how busy I am. Don't worry, it's well that I'm prepared to take on the responsibility.'

She rolled up her window and drove off.

Philomena turned her car, and set off in the direction of the hairdresser's.

KEVIN

Father Kevin Staunton sighed. He was preparing to set off early, to make the sixty mile journey to his family home. He would spend the night with Margaret, and return the following day.

His parish priest had encouraged him to stay a couple of days. 'Your father lives alone?' he had said. 'Why not stay until the weekend? He could maybe do with the company.'

Kevin had turned down the suggestion. He gave no reason. He could give no reason. He could not have expressed clearly his reasons for wanting to keep the visit as short as possible. Family reunions did not appeal to him. He felt ill at ease, and, as often as not, there was some

15

friction or argument. No, he would not stay one moment longer than was necessary.

There would be the inevitable talk about their father moving into a home. Of course he should be in a home. A man of his age should be looked after. And that house was not secure, with the glass front door where you could see right into the living room. Anyone could break in, and there was so much of that sort of thing nowadays.

Kevin would have to try seriously this time to persuade his father to see the sense of moving to a more suitable place. He could not for the life of him understand why he wanted to stay in the bungalow. He had no one to cook his meals, and, even though that cleaning woman came in once a week, it was not a satisfactory arrangement. Suppose the house went on fire? Suppose he had a heart attack? Kevin would have to explain all these possibilities. In his mind, he rehearsed the conversation he intended to have on arrival.

'I'd better buy him a birthday present,' Kevin thought as he approached the next town. It was difficult to know what to buy. The only presents he ever received himself were from his two elder sisters. Each year they got together to buy him something. Last year there had been a golf bag, on other occasions there had been a radio and a camera. But what could you buy for a man in his eighties? He stopped at a chain store, went in and purchased two pairs of socks. He chose a shade of dark navy, as he felt conspicuous being in a shop at all, and buying anything but black socks might look peculiar.

With a quick glance at the time, Kevin resumed his journey. He hoped to be the first to arrive. Maybe, if he got a chance to talk to his father alone, man to man, he might have the whole business settled before his sisters arrived. In this very positive frame of mind he sped forward.

ANGELINA

Angelina Lemoine sighed. It was her day off work, and she glanced dolefully round her small flat. Normally she made use of a free day to clean and tidy the flat, and to catch up on chores like ironing, or visits to the launderette. But today the sun was shining. She would have loved to take the day off and just go out and stroll around. And then she thought, no, I'll clean the flat. It's a dingy hole anyway, and it's far worse when it's not tidy. To come in on a sunny day, to climb the stairs to the fifth floor and find the place in a mess would be just too much. It would be depressing for Claire, too, coming home from school. She would make an effort, and do a speedy clean up.

She thought about her father. It was his birthday today. She wondered if her birthday card had arrived in time. She would try to phone him later. Yes, Angelina thought, I'll phone him this evening and see how he's getting on.

As Angelina swept and tidied the small cramped area that served as kitchen and living room, she planned the rest of the day. She would gather up a load of clothes to take to the launderette. She would leave them to be collected later, and then she would walk round to the convent near the Etoile to visit the nuns.

She always enjoyed these visits to the nuns, a small community of Irish sisters who ran a hostel for students. The convent was like a haven, a pleasant airy building that was amazingly quiet considering it was on a busy main street. There was a shady garden at the back, where, on sunny days like today, the students would sit and drink coffee. Angelina always enjoyed the cup of tea that Sister Aine made for her. You could never get a good cup of tea in Paris, except here, in this little Irish enclosure, where the world seemed to stand still.

Angelina was aware of a niggling disquiet, with the knowledge that her present job was nearing its end. But the nuns would help. In the eighteen years she had been in Paris, they had, from time to time, helped her find a job. They had numerous contacts, and Angelina had had several child minding jobs, as well as work in small cafes and hotels.

Bringing up a child in Paris had not been easy. When Claire was small, Angelina often had to work late hours, leaving her in charge of one of the students from the hostel.

Her present job was the longest she had ever had. For four years now she had been looking after Jean Louis Lambert. She had understood from the start that the job would be finished when Jean Louis reached school age.

Jean Louis was due to start at the ecole maternelle in the autumn. Just yesterday, Madame Lambert had reminded Angelina that her contract was coming to a close. But, Madame continued, Jean Louis had grown very attached to Angelina. Could she continue to work with them on a part time basis, coming in the morning to take Jean Louis to school, and then come back in the afternoon to look after him at home until his parents returned from work? Naturally she would not have the same pay. But she would get half of her present wage.

Angelina had explained that this was impossible, as things stood she had to spend half her wages on the rent for the flat. Madame had been quite irritated. Could she not get another part time job? Or a smaller flat? Or could her daughter, now sixteen, not get a weekend job to help out? It was going to be very difficult for Jean Louis to have to get used to a new person. The atmosphere had been slightly strained.

Angelina tried to put all these worrying thoughts out of her mind, as she hurried on with her chores.

Be positive, she told herself. Don't let things get you down. She would shortly be ready to go out, and she looked forward to having a pleasant chat and a cup of tea with her good friend Sister Aine. Anyway, it was nearly the middle of March. She allowed herself the luxury of starting to think about the summer holiday, the annual trip to Ireland which was the highlight of the year for herself and Claire.

It wasn't easy, arranging this holiday every year. When they returned to Paris at the end of August, Angelina would immediately start saving for next year. Other things might be put off. She would do without new clothes, she would wear an extra cardigan rather than put on the electric fire. When Claire was a small child, Angelina often went to bed shortly after her daughter's bedtime, just to save electricity. But it was always worth it in the end, when they took the overnight boat to Rosslare and their adventure had started. They never took a cabin on these overnight crossings. The boat journey, with all its trappings, was the start of the holiday. They would watch the entertainment, have a go in the competitions, see a film. In the evening they would join in the disco dancing. By midnight, exhausted, they would fall asleep in the lounge. When morning came Ireland would be in sight.

Claire, since early childhood, had loved the Irish holiday. When she was a small child, she had always cried when it was time to pack up and go back. As time went on, she constantly begged her mother to let them go back to Ireland to stay. And Angelina dearly wished that this was possible. Claire, as a teenager, had much better holidays in Kincade than she could ever have had in Paris. She had made friends with some of the local girls, and during their visits they often went cycling, swimming and playing tennis. The last few years, their visit had coincided with the local festival in Kincade, which provided plenty of entertainment for the young people.

After the holiday, Claire always kept in touch with her friends, with letters and Christmas cards, and they always looked forward to meeting again.

Angelina also budgeted in her holiday expenses for the hire of a car. It was important to be able to take her father out. He didn't go out much for most of the year, so in the summer it was a good idea to arrange a few outings. They would visit old friends, and have dinner in restaurants. They would visit other members of the family, who would be unwelcoming and critical.

'Isn't it well for you,' Philomena had said last year, 'living it up in Paris, and then coming over here splashing out money on a hired car! I tell you, if you had three children to bring up as I have, or five like Margaret, you'd have to cut your corners a bit.'

Angelina had tried to explain that she was not at all well off, that she had to scrimp and save to make the holiday possible.

'Well, if that's the case,' Margaret had pursued, 'why don't you do something sensible with the money you save? You know, you shouldn't be driving Dad all round the country like that. He's not fit for it, you know, most men of his age should be in a proper home where they'd be well looked after.'

Kevin had followed the argument. 'I think it's quite irresponsible,' he said, 'to have Dad out running around at his age. He could have a heart attack while you're out, and what would you do then?'

Angelina had tried to point out that their father could, of course, have a heart attack while they were out motoring. He could also have a heart attack at home. Any of them, for that matter, could have a heart attack. But why spend your life sitting indoors waiting for the heart attack that might or mightn't come?

Kevin had said that Angelina was, as always, a bit above herself. Margaret had said that she was just not making sense. Philomena had said that anyone who was living away in a foreign country could have no idea of a proper sense of values. And Angelina, normally bright and enthusiastic, felt, as always, a sense of awe at the older members of the family, and said no more.

She had always been in awe of Margaret, Philomena and Kevin. When she was a small child, they were comparatively grown up, so they had very little in common. And as she had been away from home, living in Paris since she was seventeen, she had had little opportunity to get to know them better.

She was aware that they had never approved of her marriage, and had made known their displeasure when, aged nineteen, she had married Bernard Lemoine. Philomena, twelve years her senior, was getting married that same year. The rest of the family had made it clear that if she was going to do such an irresponsible thing as to marry a foreigner in a foreign country, she should at least have had the decency to wait until after her older sister's wedding.

When within a year her marriage broke up, she had received no sympathy. She knew, and had known ever since that summer sixteen years ago, that she was not welcome with her brother and sisters. Every August when she came on holiday, she was subjected to their merciless taunts. They showed no interest in Claire, and even tried to keep her apart from her cousins.

Angelina had always got on well with her mother, who was kind to her and her daughter. And with her father she had always had a very special relationship.

In the winter of 1986, her mother had died. Angelina had come home for the funeral. She had left Claire, then ten years old, in the care of Sister Aine in the hostel. She had found her father devastated by events. Margaret, Philomena and Kevin were more than usually hostile. It was her wayward behaviour, they led her to believe, that had accelerated their mother's death. And, heavy-hearted, after the funeral, she had taken the boat back to France.

'Stop daydreaming!' Angelina told herself sharply. 'You've more to do than getting yourself annoyed moping about the past! You've to start thinking of a new job. It's only a few months until Jean Louis goes to school, and, to survive, you need to find something better than Madame Lambert is offering. And you need to check your bank account, to see how things are shaping up for the summer. And you'd better go and see Sister Aine, and find out what's on the job scene for September. And you've to see what new clothes Claire needs. And, for a start, you've got to clean up this disgusting flat!'

CHAPTER 1

On a sunny June morning in 1937 Hugh Staunton got up from the breakfast table in his Edinburgh digs. He glanced at the time, and thought of the day ahead. Within minutes he would be on his way, just as on any other Monday morning, to catch the train for Cowdenbeath, to the primary school where he worked. Today he would be back, full time, in the classroom. For the past month he had, in addition to his own work, taken on the duties of acting principal, while Mr Murphy, the principal, was convalescing after an operation.

Now, in mid June, the summer holidays were approaching. The next few weeks would be very busy, finishing off the term's work, planning next year's syllabus, organising sports day and other end of term activities. The letterbox rattled, and his landlady, Mrs McCormack, came in with a handful of mail.

'Your paper, Mr Staunton,' she said cheerfully as she handed him the packaged Western People from home.

'Thank you, Mrs McCormack,' he said, on his way to the door. He walked out into the summer sunshine, and made his way to Waverley Station, with his Western People, still packaged, in his pocket. He might have a glance through it during the twenty minute train journey, but at lunch time he would peruse it in detail and catch up on news from home.

When he reached the station, the platform was crowded with early morning travellers. In the train there was standing room only, so he did not have a chance to read his paper. He promised himself the luxury of an undisturbed read at lunch time, and then let his thoughts stray to the coming day at school.

He had been acting principal for a month. Older teachers had warned him, 'It's an exhausting job. You're so young. I wouldn't take it on for anything. Imagine trying to teach your own class, and cope with administration, visitors to the school, inspectors, parents. You'll never stick it.'

In spite of their gloomy predictions, Hugh had enjoyed the responsibility. Well, of course it was demanding. But the challenge had brought out the best in him. And he quickly realised that not only was it work that he liked, but that he did it extremely well. He found it exhilarating. Within a short time he found himself actually looking

21

forward to what the day might bring. And, even though he was a young man, barely thirty, he felt that here was an area where he had a natural flair.

Arriving at the school, he first went to the office, where Mr Murphy was sitting at the desk. Hugh welcomed his principal back, and gave him a brief run down of all that had happened in his absence. He then went to his classroom, where the morning was spent in the usual routine of arithmetic, grammar, essay writing and religious knowledge. At twelve thirty, the bell sounded for lunch, and the pupils filed out.

Hugh sat down at his desk in the empty classroom. Before joining his colleagues for lunch in the staffroom, he would have a quick glance through his paper. His sister Catherine, a teacher in a country school in County Galway, always remembered to send him the paper. He glanced through the headlines, and read quickly through a few items that caught his attention. He read the deaths column, and noticed that old John Lavelle from his home town had died. Well, he was old and he had been ailing for a long time. There wasn't really much news of interest in the paper this time. He glanced absent-mindedly through the classified ads.

In the Situations Vacant column, he read: Principal wanted for two teacher school, Kincade, County Sligo. Apply with references to Rev. P. O'Lorcan. Hugh took about one minute to consider. Kincade was a small village. He had never been there, apart from passing through it on the Belfast train on his journeys to and from Scotland. His recollection was of a rather drab railway station, with a straggle of houses in the background. It could be a bit of a dead end. But, he told himself, any place, be it town, village or countryside, is what you make of it.

Hugh was acutely aware of the fact that he wanted to be a school principal. Life was good at the moment. The work and the camaraderie of the school in Cowdenbeath were very agreeable. But his future career was important. He was thirty years of age. This was, by normal standards, young to be a principal. But when an opportunity presented itself, you did not pass it by.

He folded his paper and went straight to the principal's office. He showed Mr Murphy the advertisement he had just read.

'I think I'll apply for that,' he said.

Mr Murphy showed no surprise.

'So you'll be wanting a reference,' he said. Hugh nodded, and Mr Murphy continued.

'It'll be a pleasure. Make no mistake about it, I'd be very sorry to lose you. But since the first year you were here, I spotted that you were a fellow who had all it takes to be a principal. And, young as you are, it would be foolish to let a chance go by.'

In the course of the afternoon, Mr Murphy wrote a reference, in which he described, in glowing terms, Hugh Staunton's dedication to his work, his excellent exam results, his rapport with his classes, his involvement in sport and other school activities, and the proficiency he had shown during his spell as acting principal.

Back in his digs in Leith Street that afternoon, Hugh was busy. He wrote out his application to Father O'Lorcan, describing in detail his qualifications and experience. He read, with some satisfaction, Mr Murphy's reference. And then he thought, I should get another reference, maybe from the head of the training college in Waterford. Yes, he thought, I'll write to Brother Hanley, and ask him to send me a reference. And then he thought, no, that would take time. He immediately wrote a letter to Brother Hanley, explaining what he needed, and asking for it to be sent directly to Father O'Lorcan in Kincade. Decisive as ever, he sealed and stamped his two letters, and took them out in time for the evening post. They were on the way now, Monday evening, he thought. They will be in Ireland by Wednesday. Maybe next week I'll have an answer.

On Thursday evening, when Hugh arrived back from school, there was a telegram waiting for him. He tore open the yellow envelope and read: Appointment confirmed. Come at once.

****

Hugh stuffed the telegram into his pocket, and went out for a long walk. As he walked, he thought. He had felt optimistic about getting this job. But he had thought that it would be for the coming term, the new school year, in September. He had not anticipated leaving Cowdenbeath as abruptly as this.

Still, if this was the way it happened, this was the way it was meant to be. This Father O'Lorcan sounded like a man who was accustomed to getting his own way. Hugh did not see this as a serious problem.

During his nine years in Scotland, Hugh had got to know many of the Irish community. He knew older teachers, nearing retiring age, who made the tedious journey home to Ireland every Christmas, Easter and summer. On retirement, they would eventually return to live in Ireland, where they no longer had any social life, as most of their friends and relations were dead or gone elsewhere. There were other Irish teachers who had married and settled in Scotland. But life wasn't kind to them either. Salaries were

23

not great, mortgages were high. The cost of living was high, they seemed to have a constant struggle to make ends meet. So often he had heard the regretful words, 'If only I had gone back to Ireland when I was young ....'

And here he was now, with the chance being handed to him. He knew what he wanted to do. The next morning, before the start of class, he was in Mr Murphy's office.

'So you've got the job?' asked Mr Murphy, before Hugh spoke. He had guessed, by the younger man's confident demeanour, that all had gone well. 'Congratulations, Hugh.' It was the first time he had addressed Hugh by his first name. He rose from his desk, shook hands with Hugh, and earnestly wished him well.

'Thank you, Mr Murphy,' answered Hugh. 'But I'm afraid there's a complication. Father O'Lorcan wants me now. I thought the appointment would be for the beginning of next term. But,' and he took the crumpled telegram from his pocket and passed it over the desk, 'he had more or less ordered me to come at once.'

Mr Murphy studied the telegram, while Hugh continued. 'I feel that my duty lies with you in Cowdenbeath, and I can't walk out on you. I should write to Father O'Lorcan and explain this, and tell him I'll be ready to start in the new term.'

Mr Murphy thought for a moment.

'Parish priests are a cantankerous breed,' he observed, 'and nowhere more so than in Ireland. This man seems to like to have his own way. I seriously think you should go. You can't be sure that he wouldn't give the job to someone else if he was kept waiting.'

'Well, this occurred to me,' said Hugh. 'But, on the other hand, would it be wise to jump to his bidding? I wouldn't like to start by giving him the impression that all he had to do was click his fingers and I'd come running.'

'There's little chance of that, as you well know,' answered Mr Murphy. 'You're very much your own man. If you go now, you'll go because it suits you. And when you get there, you'll start as you intend to go on. And now, don't worry about your class here. They're very well through the year's syllabus, as you know, and we're nearly into the holidays. We'll manage all right. This is too good an opportunity for you to take any risks.'

After some further discussion, Hugh decided that, subject to the approval of the school manager, he would accept Father O'Lorcan's offer, and start on his new career immediately. Mr Murphy made immediate contact with the manager, who was very understanding. In the course of the day, Hugh said goodbye to colleagues and friends, and to his class. All were sorry to see him go, and wished him well in his new venture.

That night, he was on the overnight boat to Belfast. On the journey, he had the leisure to think of the unexpected turn of events. He thought about his mother, a frail elderly lady on the home farm in Mayo.

One of her favourite sayings was, 'You can't tell in the morn how the day's going to turn.' She would come out with this comment when anyone was making plans, as a warning that all might not turn out as expected. On this occasion, her saying was right.

Who would have thought, last Monday morning, that Hugh would be now, on Friday night, on his way to a new job in an unknown village? He had no misgivings. Once a decision is made, he told himself, stick with it. Don't look back at the alternatives.

On the next day was the long and tiresome journey from Belfast, down through the large sprawling towns of Lisburn, Lurgan and Portadown, and then Omagh, where he changed trains, and went on through the farmland and small towns of Tyrone and Fermanagh. After another change at Bundoran, he was on the Sligo train, and soon found himself approaching the village of Kincade. For the first time ever, this village meant something. Until now, it had been nothing more than a railway station that he passed through, a rather neglected railway station, with nothing more memorable than the name in large white lettering on an overgrown grassy bank overlooking the platform.

As the train slowed and stopped, he was aware that he was the only passenger alighting. The platform was deserted apart from a portly middle-aged priest, who was pacing up and down impatiently. As Hugh gathered his cases and descended, the priest approached him briskly.

'Ah, Mr Staunton, so you've arrived. I thought you'd be on the train today.'

Genuinely surprised, Hugh asked, 'How did you know I was coming today?'

'How did I know? Wasn't it Thursday I sent the telegram? And it would have been too late to get the Thursday night boat, so I knew you'd take the Friday crossing ....'

Hugh found himself silently observing that here indeed was a man who was accustomed to getting his own way.

'Now, don't bother with those cases,' continued Father O'Lorcan. 'Joseph!' he shouted, and a drab looking man in uniform appeared out of the station master's office. 'Joseph,' he said, 'get those cases brought over to the master's house. And now, Mr Staunton, we'll go over to the parochial house and I'll tell you about the school.'

Hugh accompanied Father O'Lorcan out of the station, and across the road to the parochial house, a fine two storey building with bay windows. They entered, and went into a comfortable sitting room, where, although it was a warm June evening, there was a turf fire burning. They were immediately followed by the housekeeper, who had obviously anticipated their arrival, and was carrying a tea tray laden with freshly made scones, sandwiches and toast.

The evening passed pleasantly. Sitting at the fire, they drank tea, ate sandwiches, then had a glass of whiskey, as Father O'Lorcan described the village, the community, the school, the post left vacant by the sudden death of the Master McGivern, the last principal. Master McGivern was approaching retiring age, but had died suddenly of a heart attack. His children were grown up and living away from home. His wife, a Dublin woman, had gone back to live in the capital. She had left the school house furnished, and would be back in the near future to see if the new master would want to buy any of the furniture.

Then, in the gathering dusk, they went round to the house. A few people they met on the road greeted them. 'Good evening, Father. Good evening, Master.' Hugh could see that his arrival was already known in the village. On reaching the teacher's residence, he saw his cases stacked tidily at the door.

Father O'Lorcan handed Hugh the keys of the house and the school. He pointed out a farmhouse, across a field, where milk could be got. He showed him the village shop, where most day to day necessities could be purchased. The school, a long low building, was directly across the road from the house. He told Hugh about his assistant, Miss Margan, who was, in his opinion, a 'silly bat.' She actually had the temerity to apply for the post of principal.

After bidding the priest good evening, Hugh let himself into the house which was to be his home for many years to come.

He found an oil lamp, which he lit and carried around, as he surveyed the house. Compared to some of the cramped city flats and digs he had stayed in, it was a palace. There was a large sitting room to the right of the hall, and a kitchen with a range to the left. Upstairs there were four bedrooms, with sheets, blankets and quilts folded and stacked. There was no water or electricity, and the toilet was out in the back yard. But the space was such a luxury that Hugh felt well satisfied with his surroundings.

In a shed at the back, he found some turf and sticks. He lit a fire in the living room, and by the light of the oil lamp he read a newspaper he had bought at the railway station in Belfast. Tomorrow he would go out and get bread and milk and other necessities. Just now, he was happy to read, and shortly to sleep, after the exhaustion of the two days travelling. He sat contentedly at the fire, thinking about all the changes that had taken place since last Saturday night.

****

Last Saturday night! He had been with friends and colleagues at the Palais, a popular dance hall in Edinburgh. He had been dancing with Teresa McKinney, as he did on many Saturday nights. He had arranged to meet her the following Saturday, tonight! And he had completely forgotten! Well, he would write to her and explain what had happened, how things had taken this unexpected turn.

He must get a radio, he thought. And books. He had always been interested in books, but until now had no place to store them. He looked with satisfaction at the long empty shelves along the back wall of his living room.

****

Teresa McKinney sat disconsolately in her parents' living room in Marchmont Crescent. She was alone, as her parents had gone to visit friends, and her young sister Patricia was at the dance in the Palais, the dance where she was supposed to go with Hugh Staunton. She had gone to their usual meeting place, the cafe near the Palais, but Hugh had not been there. This was most unlike him. She couldn't understand it. Last Saturday night it had been a firm arrangement. From the cafe window, she had watched as others of the crowd who met regularly at the dance made their way into the hall. After a long wait and three cups of tea which she didn't really want, it dawned on her that Hugh was not coming. Angry and disappointed, she returned home.

Teresa was twenty five years of age, and had a good job in the Civil Service. She was a pretty young woman, fair haired, blue eyed, rather stoutly built. She was lively and popular, and for years had been very keen on the social life and the dance hall scene.

Recently, she was becoming aware that many of her friends were either married or engaged. And she was beginning to feel the urge to settle down. So the friendship that had developed with Hugh Staunton over the past few months was, she hoped, likely to continue. He was, without doubt, the most eligible bachelor on the scene. In fact, Teresa was well aware that she was the envy of the dance hall on the evenings she spent with the tall, handsome, rather flamboyant Irishman with the shock of thick, black straight hair which always looked as if it had fought against being combed.

The previous night, Teresa had taken a lot of trouble with a hairdo for the dance. She had bought a new summer dress, and had gone out in high good spirits. And then Hugh had just not shown up. She waited, hopefully, over the weekend, in case he might call with some explanation.

Two days later, at work on Monday, she was dismayed to hear the news that Hugh had left, suddenly, to go to a new job in Ireland.

CHAPTER 2

Sunday morning dawned bright and clear. Hugh woke up early, feeling refreshed. He got up, and, in daylight, took a better look at his surroundings. From the stair landing window, he could see across the field the whitewashed walls of the farmhouse where he would later go to purchase milk. The garden was quite neglected, a tangle of weeds and overgrown shrubs. There would be a lot of work needed to put it right. Inside the house, the wallpaper was shabby and stained. But there was space, plenty of space, and, in time, he would refurbish the entire house and garden.

In the kitchen, he had a look at the large black range. He would need to light a fire in it before he could make his breakfast, or have warm water. There was enough coal in the shed, and shortly he had a fire going, and a kettle on the hob, filled with water from a barrel outside the back door. Briefly he wondered where the drinking water would come from, knowing at the same time that he had all day to find out. He unpacked his cases and hung his clothes in the wardrobe, and when the water in the kettle was warm he washed and shaved.

Then he put on his good suit, and as soon as he saw people in their Sunday best walking towards the chapel, he joined the crowd and made his way to Mass. On the way into the chapel, and later on the way out, people greeted him. 'Good morning, Master. You're welcome, Master,' many of them said. Children clung to their mothers shyly as they took a peep at their new teacher. And, as he returned to his house, Hugh was aware of the eyes following him, appraising him, in this little village where a new arrival was a major event.

He later walked across the field to the farmhouse. Mrs Brennan was standing in the doorway, as if she was waiting for him.

'Good morning, Master,' she said. 'You'll be wanting milk.'

As she spoke, she poured out a small can of milk from a much larger can behind the kitchen door. She also gave him four fresh eggs, and a loaf of home made bread. Hugh thanked her, and asked about payment.

'It's all right, Master,' she said. 'We'll settle the account once a month.'

This seemed to be a satisfactory arrangement, and Mrs Brennan went on to tell him about the spring water he could get from the well just at the end of the hedge, and about Durcan's, the village shop, where most groceries could be purchased, and about the butcher's van which came on Tuesdays.

Hugh thanked her and returned home. After depositing his purchases on the kitchen table, he went to Durcan's, where he bought bacon, butter and tea. Again he was greeted and welcomed by everybody.

Back in the house, he made himself a substantial breakfast of bacon and eggs, feeling very much at home in his new surroundings.

This was strange, he thought. Less than twenty-four hours he had been here. And yet this was home, in a way that neither the farmhouse of his childhood in Murgintra, nor his lodgings in Edinburgh had ever been.

Here life was simple, uncomplicated. You could get everything you needed within walking distance. And he was more than gratified at the friendliness of all the people he had met so far.

He spent the afternoon writing letters. He wrote first to his mother, on the home farm with his eldest brother Timothy, and let them know about his return to Ireland, promising that he would come to see them at the start of the summer holidays. His mother, in poor health, never left her home nowadays. Timothy, a hardworking bachelor who spent his entire days working on the farm, rarely travelled further than to the nearby town to purchase groceries.

Then Hugh wrote to his brother Dominic, who was a solicitor in Dublin. Dominic and his wife Una had lived in Dublin for many years now, with their three daughters. And he wrote to Catherine, a teacher in a country area in County Galway, who returned home to the farm every weekend to tend to their ailing mother.

His next letter was to his sister Anne, a nun in a County Wicklow convent. He knew that she would not get his letter immediately. She had once told him that the nuns were allowed to receive letters only on the first day of each month. Letters that arrived at other times were put aside until the start of the next month. Relatives of the nuns had been informed that if there was an urgent message, such as a death in the family, they were to make contact with Reverend Mother. But for ordinary family news, only once a month could mail be received. And they could have only four visits in the course of the year. These visits were confined to family members. A friend who was not a close relative could accompany the family on a visit, but could never come alone.

Hugh found himself wondering about these rules. Who made them? And why? And did the nuns know, before entering the convent, that they were going to be subjected to this regime? In his letter to Anne, Hugh let her know about his new job, and said that in the near future he would accompany Catherine or Dominic on a visit, rather than use up a whole visit himself.

Finally, Hugh wrote to Teresa McKinney, explaining the unexpected train of events that had prevented him from keeping their appointment on Saturday night. And, as he sealed his last letter, Scotland seemed far, far away.

****

Early on Monday morning, Hugh crossed the road to the school, and unlocked the heavy green painted door. A few pupils had already arrived, keeping discreetly to the far end of the schoolyard as they observed their new teacher. Hugh went inside, and from the large desk with the slanted hinged top, he took the roll books. He noticed that on the roll there were fifty-three pupils, who were divided between infants and first class in Miss Margan's room, and the remainder of the classes in his room.

He then lifted a pile of copy books, and was flicking through the pupils' most recent work, when he was distracted by the sound of a car at the school gate. Looking out, he saw a small battered car screeching to a halt, and a small dark haired woman jumped out. Immediately she started, in a strident monologue, to harangue the children who had now gathered in the schoolyard.

'What's this?' she demanded. 'Mary Kelly crying again? I declare to God you'll turn into an onion on us one of these days! And Joseph Garvan, you've got your hair cut at last. About time too! I was beginning to think it was a wee girl you were! What's that you're saying, Bernadette?'

'Please, Miss, can we have handwork today?' a small voice asked.

'Handwork, is it? We'll see. And only if you get all your sums right, do you hear me, all of them! And then, maybe, we'll think about handwork. Now, inside, everybody! Do you think we've nothing to do but stand in the yard all day?'

'Please, Miss, the new master's here,' another voice ventured.

'He is, and if he sees you lot standing around the door he'll have something to say. Into line, quickly, move on!'

As Miss Margan ushered her class indoors, Hugh left his desk and went through the connecting door between the two classrooms to meet her.

'Good morning, Miss Margan,' he greeted her. On seeing her at close range, he noticed that she was very small, and would have been in her mid forties. She was wearing a brightly coloured floral print dress, and was heavily made up with rouge and bright lipstick. She wore bangles and earrings, and the overall effect was somewhat dramatic. The children sat, awe-struck, wide-eyed, as their two teachers met.

'Good morning Mr Staunton,' she answered. 'Father O'Lorcan told me you'd be here today. You're very welcome.'

They had a brief conversation about the school, the pupils, the syllabus, the materials available, before settling into the day's work. Miss Margan told Hugh about Anne Hyland, a girl in sixth class who had always been subject to fainting fits.

'Let me know if she faints,' she said. 'I'm well used to her. I'll look after her.'

Hugh asked if there were any problem pupils, any pupils who were reluctant to work. Her answer was brisk.

'Reluctant? I don't know. Reluctant or not, they do their work. I have yet to meet the pupil who will not work.'

Hugh liked this answer, and he liked Miss Margan. As he started organising his own classroom, he heard her authoritative tones as she gave out slates and chalk to her infant class to do their sums, while first class had to get on with the business of writing an essay.

Father O'Lorcan had described Miss Margan as 'a silly bat.' Hugh could see nothing silly about this woman. She seemed to be a competent and dedicated teacher, sensitive to her pupils' needs. But she did not dress in the conventional dark grey or navy blue suits favoured by most lady teachers. She drove a car. She was very independent. Perhaps too much so for Father O'Lorcan.

CHAPTER 3

Within a few days, Hugh and Miss Margan had established a good working relationship. Miss Margan took the girls for sewing and cookery, while Hugh looked after sport and other outdoor activities. The girls were often discontented as they sat working at their specimens of hemming and backstitch, while they listened to the shouts of the boys at their sports lesson outside. But the boys were no less displeased when they had to join in the singing lessons, which Miss Margan taught with great gusto.

'You know, I applied for the job of principal,' Miss Margan told Hugh one day. 'Not that I had any chance of getting it. Himself up the road,' nodding in the direction of Father O'Lorcan's house, 'wouldn't have a woman principal, not in a thousand years. But I applied, just for badness. He didn't even acknowledge my letter.'

'Why not?' asked Hugh, bemused.

'Oh, he's totally old-fashioned. A woman's place is in the home, and all that. A woman teacher is alright, in the infant class. But a principal, never! And it's not just women. That man has respect for nobody. There's no bishop, cardinal or pope will tell him what to do. And he thinks he invented the Catholic church.'

'Still, he seems to be good company,' said Hugh.

'He is, he's all that, and very well-read and cultured,' answered Miss Margan. 'He's interested in music and art, and, would you believe it, in botany. Just take a look some day at the exotic shrubs he has in his garden. But you need to watch him. He cannot tolerate any situation where he is not totally in control of everything.'

****

Over the following weeks, Hugh became quite well acquainted with Father O'Lorcan. The old priest was very sociable and hospitable. He regularly invited Hugh to visit him in the parochial house, where they had lively discussions on many topics. There were areas where they disagreed, as Father O'Lorcan held very conservative views on many issues, but in some areas he held surprisingly unconventional, even radical opinions, and he was no respecter of the hierarchy, nor of Rome. They both enjoyed the discussions, and indeed the arguments.

Sadie the housekeeper always arrived in, as on the first day Hugh had arrived, supplying them with tea and scones. Later there would be a glass of whiskey, as they drew their discussions to a close.

****

At the start of the holidays, the first week in July, Hugh prepared to visit the various members of his family. He said goodbye to Miss Margan and Father O'Lorcan. He locked up the school and the house, and set off on the train to his home townland.

He spent the first week at home on the farm in Murgintra. His mother, ailing for some time, was now practically immobile. Catherine, on holiday from her Galway school, was tending her. Timothy was, as always, totally taken up with farm work, appearing indoors only for meals and at nightfall. He spoke little, being mostly preoccupied with his work.

It was not an enjoyable week. Hugh found it depressing to see his mother so feeble, and Catherine was also finding it very difficult. They discussed the possibility of having someone to come in and help with the housework and nursing. On Hugh's last day in the house, they had reached an arrangement with Mrs Devenney, a local woman whom they had known all their lives, to help out where necessary.

Hugh then went on to Dublin, where he spent a fortnight with his brother and his family. This was a more active and lively holiday. They played golf, went to the cinema, visited friends. Towards the end of Hugh's stay, they decided to go out to Wicklow to visit Anne in the convent. And that visit required the most elaborate preparations.

****

'Maeve, would you come down out of there!' Una shouted up the stairs. 'And I hope you're looking decent. Remember, it's a convent we're going to.'

Maeve appeared at the top of the stairs, nearly causing her mother to have a seizure. 'What in God's name is that you're wearing? Get back into your room and put on your pleated skirt.'

'But, Mammy, this is the dress I wore to Auntie Eileen's last week. What's wrong with it now?'

'It has short sleeves, for a start. And a V neck. Have you no sense at all? You can't go to a convent dressed like that. And put down your hair. You know the nuns wouldn't approve of a girl of your age putting her hair up. Here, give me a ribbon.'

Una fixed her daughter's hair in a demure style with a band of ribbon, and sulkily Maeve returned to her room, from which she shortly appeared wearing a pleated skirt, a plain sweater and an exasperated expression. Her mother was by this time checking that the two younger girls were properly attired.

'Why can they wear short sleeves when I can't?' shrilly demanded Maeve.

'Because you're fourteen, that's why,' answered her mother.

'So I'm too old to wear short sleeves, and too young to put my hair up?' pursued Maeve.

'Oh, don't argue,' said Una impatiently. 'It's a convent we're going to, not a party. Now, hurry up, we're late enough as it is.'

And Una pulled on her modest cream coloured cardigan over her short sleeved summer dress before they set off on their visit.

They drove through the Wicklow countryside to the convent. Anne, whose name in religion was Sister Assumpta, greeted them joyfully. They sat in a spacious parlour, with a highly polished table and tall straight backed chairs. Large, heavy-framed pictures of the saints adorned the walls, and bright brass fire irons hung by the empty grate.

'So how are you all?' demanded Anne excitedly. 'And how is Mother?'

'Poorly, poorly enough,' said Dominic. 'We haven't seen her since Easter. But Hugh has just come from home, and the form wasn't good at all.'

'No,' added Hugh. 'She's not well at all. In fact, we had to get help in the house. Mrs Devenney is coming in for a few hours every day. She'll give Catherine a bit of a rest. Poor Catherine was working day and night, she was exhausted.'

'Yes, that's good that you've got Mrs Devenney in. A good woman she is, she'd be hard working and honest. How much is she being paid?'

Hugh explained that they had not agreed a wage, but that he had left money with Catherine, and Dominic also was going to send some. Catherine could then decide on how to use it.

Anne's expression showed surprised disapproval. 'You mean you didn't settle an hourly rate? And Catherine would need to keep a notebook to write down the hours day by day.'

Hugh immediately dismissed the suggestion. Catherine was running the house, he pointed out, and she was surely capable of organising a home help without the rest of them breathing down her neck. Dominic and Una agreed.

Anne smiled, unconvinced. 'Well, maybe you're right. Catherine will always do her best, we can be sure of that. A saint she always was, our Catherine. She always looked after all of us. And do you know, there was some saint, Saint Bonaventure I think it was, or maybe Saint Benedict, who said that the spinster had more to contribute to the church than even the nun. And I always thought that about our Catherine. A saint she was, always.'

Dominic and Una exchanged despairing glances, as Anne went on and on. Having exhausted the topic of the saintliness of single ladies, she went on to question the three girls about their school life, their subjects, their teachers, their leisure activities. She congratulated Dominic and Una on having such a good family. Then she turned her attention to Hugh.

'So you've come home at last,' she said. 'Well, it was only to be expected. You couldn't have stayed in Scotland forever. I've been praying for you for ages, that you would get a job in Ireland. In fact, I've had the whole community praying for you. And here we are, our prayers have been answered, and you're back in Ireland. Scotland is so far away. And you could so easily lose your faith there. It's a pagan place, I've so often heard Sister Aloysius saying. She used to live in Scotland before she entered.'

At this moment Hugh thought wistfully about Scotland, about the golf club, about the dance halls, about Teresa McKinney. His recollections were not of a pagan place. But his sister Anne, long sheltered from the world, could not see Scotland as a normal place. He did not try to explain.

After about an hour, other nuns looked in to greet the Staunton family. There was tea, and when, at six o'clock, a bell rang, they were invited to benediction. When they eventually left, the girls were relieved. For them it had been an excruciatingly boring afternoon. In the car on the way home they giggled a bit about the nuns, and were told by their mother not to be disrespectful.

A few days later, Hugh said goodbye to his brother and family, with an invitation to them to come and spend a few days with him in his new home. He took the train across the country, and returned to Kincade.

On arriving home, he found two letters waiting for him. One was from Teresa McKinney, six pages of lively news about all their friends, and activities in Edinburgh. The other letter, in unfamiliar handwriting, had a Dublin postmark. Hugh opened it, and read a brief note from Mary McGivern, widow of his predecessor in the primary school. She said that she would call with him in the autumn as she wanted to sell all the furniture in the house, and would give him first choice of anything he wanted.

Hugh spent some time over the next few weeks painting the doors and window frames. He bought some rolls of wallpaper, and papered his living room. He took a detailed look at the furniture, and decided that since Mrs McGivern wanted to sell it, he would buy the lot. It was adequate for his needs, and would save him the trouble of shopping.

He bought a bicycle, and turned his attention to tidying the garden. He joined the golf club in Rosses Point, where he became an active and enthusiastic member.

CHAPTER 4

On a bleak, blustery day in November, Hugh heard a knock at his front door. He opened it to see a tall, gaunt, sad looking woman, with grey hair, grey face, grey coat.

'I'm Mrs McGivern,' she introduced herself. 'I wrote to you in the summer.'

'Hello, Mrs McGivern, you're welcome, come on in,' said Hugh.

Before entering, she glanced around the wet, windswept road, where winter winds were sweeping the last of the fallen leaves along.

'A right dump, this place, isn't it?' she said. 'The end of nowhere. I never thought when I came here thirty years ago that it would be for a lifetime. It's a pity for you, coming to this God-forsaken place. I suppose it's as well you're not married, it would drive a woman mad living here.'

'Well,' answered Hugh, 'so far I've no complaints. The job is grand, and the neighbours are very friendly.'

'Wait till you've spent a winter here, and you'll change your tune,' said Mrs McGivern. 'Nothing to do, no social life. You're mad if you decide to stay. Not that my Thomas ever intended to stay here, but time went on and nothing turned up for him. We always wanted to go back to Dublin, and he was due to retire next year.'

Hugh offered to make tea, which Mrs McGivern declined, saying that she had a few calls to make, and was expected for tea with some friends down the road. She immediately brought up the topic of the furniture she wanted to sell.

'If you want to buy the lot, Mr Staunton,' she said, 'it would suit me well. I've got a small flat in Dublin now, and this country style of furniture would be out of place in it.'

Hugh readily accepted her offer to sell all the furniture, including kitchen equipment and utensils. They settled on a mutually agreeable price, and he wrote a cheque. Then, with a last baleful glance around, she was gone.

****

Miss Margan was preparing her pupils for the Christmas concert. Every year, on the Saturday evening before Christmas, there was a parish concert at which Miss Margan's singers always performed. In the course of a school year she taught a truly amazing repertoire of songs. As well as the usual songs recommended on the school syllabus, she did many more demanding pieces. Her singers could all give tuneful renderings of the Ash Grove, Sweet Lass of Richmond Hill, the Battle Hymn of the Republic, Loch Lomond, and many others. Somewhere in the archives of disused school equipment she had found two pairs of cymbals, two triangles, a little drum and a tambourine. Several members of the group were instructed to bang or shake these instruments, providing a substantial backing to the singing.

Miss Margan also trained the chapel choir. The members of the choir were mostly girls from fifth and sixth class, who also sang with the school group. Choir practice, with Father O'Lorcan's permission, was held in the chapel on Thursday afternoons, so that the girls could practise their hymns to the accompaniment of the organ. And while you were in the chapel, Miss Margan thought, why not do just a wee practice of the songs for the Christmas concert? It was so much easier to practise with the accompaniment of the organ.

****

One Thursday afternoon in November, Hugh was at his desk in the classroom. The pupils in third class were doing multiplication sums. Fourth and fifth classes were writing essays. A group of sixth class boys stood round the master's desk, while he explained to them the rudiments of algebra. Miss Margan was at choir practice in the chapel.

He was interrupted from his work as the postman appeared in the doorway. The postman usually came in the morning, and delivered the letters at the house. This time, he was carrying a telegram, and Hugh knew from his expression that it was something urgent.

'Thanks, Michael,' he said, as he opened the envelope and read: Mother very ill. Come now. Catherine.

Hugh looked at the time. It was five past three. The evening train would leave at five. He set his boys a few problems to solve, and went round to the chapel to look for Miss Margan.

As he entered the chapel door, he was amazed to hear, from the organ loft above, a loud and rousing rendering of 'What Shall we Do with the Drunken Sailor?'

He went up the stairs, and as he reached the gallery Miss Margan looked round at him, a shade startled. Then, regaining her composure, she beckoned him over and whispered.

'Thank God it's you. I thought it was Himself back again. He came over about ten minutes ago, complaining about the racket we were making. Fortunately I saw him crossing the path, and I had to change the music. I had them half way through the Adeste by the time he got up the stairs. And then he says -- what's that you're practising, Miss Margan? And I says, innocent as you like -- It's the Adeste, father. We're getting ready for Christmas. And he wants to know what we were doing just before the Adeste. And I told him that we had done about ten hymns today, the last one could have been Silent Night, or the new Tantum Ergo.'

Hugh came to the point immediately.

'I've just got a telegram, Miss Margan. It's bad news from home. My mother is very ill. They want me to go at once.'

'Oh, Mr Staunton, I'm so sorry to hear that. And there I was going on about hymns and songs and Father O'Lorcan. Now, you just go on, I'll get right back to the school and finish your lessons. And I'll look after everything for you until you get back. Does Himself know? No? Don't worry, I'll go over and see him, you'd better hurry to get your train.'

She turned to her singers, saying, 'Come on, girls, back to school, practice over for today.'

Hugh, grateful for her support, went home and got ready to make the evening journey to Mayo.

****

It was a wet, stormy evening when Hugh got off the train at his home town. He walked to the family home, about a mile from the station. He found the rest of the family gathered there, everyone tiptoeing around, talking in whispers.

'Father Martin has just been,' Catherine told him. 'She was barely conscious.'

The doctor had been in earlier, and had given the opinion that she wouldn't last much longer.

The night was spent with all family members taking turns to sit at the bedside. Outside, it was very stormy, and the heavy rain continued till morning.

About ten the next morning, as everyone sat, pale, tired, and worn out, old Mrs Staunton got out of bed. She washed her face, and brushed her hair. She put on her best cardigan, and came out and sat at the range.

Everyone was amazed. They offered her tea, they stoked the fire. They told her how well she was looking. And, without doubt, she was looking well. She looked calm and happy. Her complexion seemed suddenly devoid of wrinkles. She had lost the deathly pallor of the previous days.

But there was something distant about her. Dominic, wanting to appear jovial, started talking.

'Well, you're in grand form today, Mother. You'll be back on your feet in no time.'

Her answer was clear.

'You can't tell in the morn how the day's going to turn.' This had always been one of her favourite sayings.

Later in the morning, Mrs Devenney and her daughter Ellen, who had been helping a lot in the house lately, arrived. Mrs Devenney couldn't believe her eyes.

'So you're up today, Mrs Staunton,' she said. 'Isn't that great! And you're looking well. Lord save us, did you ever hear the likes of the storm last night? But thank God it's a fine day now. There's a great calm out there.'

'Yes,' added Ellen. 'It's calm, and the cold has gone. It's a very warm day for the time of year.'

'When it's calm and it's warm, look out for the storm,' declared Mrs Staunton enigmatically. Everybody in the room looked from one to another, startled, with a sense of foreboding.

Shortly, Mrs Staunton went back to bed. At three o'clock in the afternoon, she died peacefully.

In the following days, during the wake and funeral, the family told and retold the story of their mother's apocryphal remarks. They had often heard her say that you couldn't tell in the morn how the day would turn. Nobody knew whether it was a line from some old forgotten rhyme, or something she had thought up herself.

But the following comment was truly alarming. When it's calm and warm, look out for the storm. Again and again they wondered, they asked each other, and couldn't find an answer.

Was this something she knew, did she improvise the rhyme, did she know how the day would end?

41

It was Easter, 1939. Teresa McKinney was in very bad form. Life was passing her by, she thought. Her younger sister Patricia had just got engaged, and was to be married in the summer. Teresa, two years older, was to be bridesmaid. Most of her friends were either married or engaged, or had gone to work away from home.

She used to love the social life of the dance halls, but now this was wearing a bit thin. At dances nowadays, she was often invited to dance by the husband or fiance of one of her friends. And, of course, this was what was known as a 'duty dance.' Other men who asked her to dance were either too young, or in some way unprepossessing. Teresa was aware that at her age, twenty-seven, you did not go to the dance just for the music and the social life. You went in the hope of finding a man.

She thought wistfully of the handsome Irishman, Hugh Staunton, whom she had been dating briefly two years ago. She had great hopes at the time that the relationship might develop. And then he had disappeared without warning, to go to a job in Ireland. He had written to her at first, and she had enthusiastically answered his letters. But, of late, the correspondence had fallen off. It was months since she had heard from him.

Now, at Easter, Teresa had a few days holiday from the office where she worked. She found that the time passed slowly. She had no interest in going out, and as the days went by she became more and more depressed. When, on Wednesday, she returned to work, she was quite relieved to have something to fill her days.

On arriving home that evening, Teresa found a letter waiting for her. She felt elated, as she looked at the familiar handwriting and the Irish stamp. She quickly opened it, and read Hugh's letter, telling her that he intended coming to Edinburgh for the second fortnight in July. He hoped she hadn't planned on being away at that time, and asked if she would call with Mrs McCormack, his old landlady, to see if she could put him up.

Teresa nearly jumped with joy. Within a day she had everything arranged. She called with Mrs McCormack, and booked a room for Hugh. She arranged to take her own holidays the second fortnight in July. Then she wrote a letter to Hugh, telling him that his lodgings were arranged, and that he was invited to tea in her parents' house on the evening of his arrival.

After that she turned her thoughts to buying some nice clothes for the summer. Then, in very good spirits, she started counting the days until mid July, like an impatient schoolgirl waiting for the end of term.

****

On the fifteenth of July, Hugh arrived in Edinburgh as planned. He went straight to Teresa's home, where he spent a pleasant evening with the family. Then he went to Mrs McCormack, who was very pleased to welcome him back.

Hugh and Teresa spent the first week socialising, visiting their many mutual acquaintances. In the evenings they went dancing, or to the cinema. In the second week they moved out of the city a bit, and went hiking in the Pentlands, or walking on the beach at Portobello.

As the second week drew to a close, Hugh decided that he was not going home to Ireland yet. He was not tied to time, so he put off the return journey for a week, and then another week. Teresa was now back at work, and Hugh met her each day at five o'clock outside the office. They spent the rest of the evening together, sometimes dancing, sometimes in Teresa's home, but mostly walking and talking.

The first week in August, Teresa's sister Patricia was getting married, and Hugh was invited to the wedding. It was a very enjoyable day, after which Teresa and Hugh went on a short tour of the Highlands.

It was at the end of the third week that Hugh proposed, and Teresa accepted with alacrity.

The next day they went into town, and bought a ring in a jeweller's in Princes Street. They talked a lot about life in Ireland, about Hugh's house, the school, the village. Teresa thought it sounded like a dream. When it was eventually time for Hugh to leave, they arranged that Teresa, who had never been to Ireland, was to come over at Easter. She would stay in Sligo, a big town on the west coast. Hugh would bring her to his home, show her around, maybe arrange a get-together with some of his family.

The wedding date was not settled, but would be sometime the following summer.

CHAPTER 6

One fine spring morning as Easter approached, Hugh and Miss Margan were talking in the school playground. Miss Margan was doing a bit of gardening with first class. Each member of the class had been instructed to bring to school a trowel or gardening fork, or, if they couldn't bring a trowel or fork, they were to bring a good firm short stick. All ten children were industriously digging or scraping, and clearing a patch in the corner of the playground. They were then going to plant flowers, and watch the growth as spring went on.

'So you'll be getting married soon, Mr Staunton,' remarked Miss Margan.

'Yes, sometime in the summer,' answered Hugh. 'Teresa is coming over for a while at Easter. She'll be staying in Sligo, and she can see a bit of the countryside while she's here. I'll get her fixed up in a guesthouse.'

'Now, why would you do that?' asked Miss Margan. 'Can't she stay with me? I've a big empty house there. It would save you going in and out to Sligo every day.'

When Hugh thought about it, he agreed that it was a good idea. And so it was settled.

Teresa arrived on Easter Monday, exhausted from the long journey, but excited and enthusiastic about her first visit to Ireland. She was delighted with the house. Having lived until now in a small city terrace house, it seemed the height of luxury to have all these spacious rooms, and a garden as well. They talked about having water and electricity installed, and Teresa was already thinking about colour schemes for mats and curtains.

She noticed some rolls of wallpaper in the cupboard under the stairs. Hugh had purchased them the previous year, but, apart from the living room, he had not yet done any papering. Teresa was quite excited. She had a flair for home decorating. When she was a teenager, she had always enthusiastically helped her parents with papering and painting. As time went on, she had taken over this work in her home. Her parents were very pleased to leave her to it, as she had a good eye for colour, and could quickly and easily do any room in the house. And now, here she was, in her future home, surrounded by bare walls just waiting to be done. She was very happy.

The holiday was full of activity. Hugh and Teresa took several trips into Sligo, where they bought curtain material and kitchen equipment for their new home. They went to Strandhill and Rosses Point. They walked on the beach and they played golf. Then they spent the evenings back in Kincade, mostly in Miss Margan's house.

Miss Margan was an excellent and entertaining hostess. At any time of the day or night she would quickly throw together a meal, and cups of tea were always on hand. She was an enthusiastic theatre goer, and, in fact, was an accomplished performer herself in local drama festivals. She told many amusing stories about the activities of drama groups, about rehearsals, about mishaps or near mishaps. The evenings in her house were always enjoyable.

'What on earth is that?' asked Hugh one evening, indicating a military style overcoat that was on a hanger behind Miss Margan's front door.

'That? Oh, that's a coat. Someone left it behind, I think it was the Kilkean crowd. They stored their stuff here during last year's festival.'

'That's all right, then,' said Hugh. 'When I saw the coat, I thought for a moment that you had a man stored away up in the attic!'

'Have sense, Mr Staunton! If I did have a man stored up in the attic, it wouldn't be a fellow who'd wear the likes of that. Here, try it on!'

She pulled the coat from its hanger, and held it for Hugh to put on. They all laughed hilariously as he modelled the long, belted, wide-skirted coat, with its epaulettes, braid, and double row of brass buttons.

For further good measure, Hugh burst into a chorus of 'The Bold Gendarmes,' and sang lustily while marching up and down the living room. By the time he got to the line, 'We'll run them in, we'll run them in,' Teresa and Miss Margan were also marching and joining in the song. A few minutes later, they all collapsed into armchairs, laughing with exhaustion.

'A great song, that,' said Miss Margan. 'It would do well for my school choir. I wonder why I never thought of it before.'

'Well, if you do, don't practise it in the chapel,' warned Hugh. 'You don't want to give Father O'Lorcan a seizure.'

'What's this about practising in the chapel?' asked Teresa, and, more than pleased to relate yet another funny tale, Miss Margan told at length about her choir practices, and her near skirmishes with Father O'Lorcan.

As midnight approached, Hugh got up to leave, and Teresa and Miss Margan went to the door with him. They saw a figure approaching, wheeling a bicycle. It was Espie Coyle, a little man who lived about a mile further up the road. In his present state of inebriation, he had wisely decided to wheel his bike instead of riding it.

'Good evening, Master,' he said. 'Evening, Miss Margan. Evening, Ma'am,' he addressed each one of them, as he propped his bicycle against the wall, obviously in a mood to talk.

'I was in Sligo today,' he started. 'Me and the German.'

Espie's sister was married to a rather exotic and irascible German who had appeared some years ago, from nobody knew where, had decided to stay, and married a local girl. Nobody was sure what his name was, he was simply known as 'the German,' and addressed by everyone as German. He had once tried to explain that he was not German but Latvian. This did not matter at all, he was foreign, and German was a more familiar and manageable title than Latvian. So he remained the German.

'The German,' went on Espie, 'is the divil to please. He wanted to buy a coat. And I declare to God that he tried on every coat in town. And not one coat would please him. This one was too short, another one had the sleeves too wide. And most of them were too ordinary, he says. And I says to him, what do you want anyway, German? If a coat keeps the cold out, isn't that all you need? But he keeps going on about the style and the cut, if you don't mind. I'm telling you, you couldn't please him.'

'Wait a minute,' said Miss Margan, as she went into the house and came back carrying the coat left behind by some theatre people. 'Here's a coat, and I'm telling you, the German won't be able to say it's too ordinary. Do you think this would please him?'

She held it out at arm's length for Espie to view.

Espie looked earnestly at the coat. He touched it, almost reverently, then took it and looked at it admiringly.

'Tell me, Miss Margan, are you giving away this coat?'

'I am, Espie,' she answered. 'Someone left it behind here, a good while ago. It's no use to me, the German may as well have it.'

Espie continued to gaze at the coat in total fascination, said, 'Miss Margan, if you're giving away this coat, there's no fuckin' German is gettin' it! Sorry, Ma'am, excuse my language.'

Slowly, he put it on, and rolled the sleeves up a full six inches to fit his arms. He closed the brass buttons, and fastened the belt. Unconcerned that the coat nearly reached his ankles, he thanked Miss Margan profusely, saying over and over again that not only was it the best coat he had ever had, but it was the best coat anyone round here had ever had.

Then he wished them all goodnight, mounted his bicycle, and wobbled off into the night.

As he disappeared into the darkness, Miss Margan told Hugh and Teresa that Espie's real name was Sebastian Peter. Not being very bright, as a child, he had difficulty in writing or saying his name. But he was shrewd enough to hide the fact that his name gave him trouble. He never wrote more than his initials, SP. He became known ever after as Espie.

That night, after Hugh had left, Teresa asked Miss Margan if it would be all right if, instead of returning to Scotland, she stayed another while. She wanted to make curtains, and do a few things in Hugh's house.

Miss Margan agreed. Of course, Teresa was to stay as long as she liked. She offered the use of her sewing machine for the curtains. She said that they might even take in a play or two before Teresa would go home.

****

The next evening, Hugh and Teresa were sitting at the fire in his house.

'I'm not going home yet, Hugh,' she told him. 'I'll write to my boss, and tell him I'm staying here a while. Miss Margan has said it's all right with her. And I want to get these curtains made.'

'That's fine,' said Hugh. 'We'll do a bit of touring around next weekend. We might go to Dublin, or Murgintra. Or we might have a look at Donegal.'

****

That night, in the spare bedroom in Miss Margan's house, Teresa wrote a few letters. She wrote to her boss, giving her resignation. She wrote to her parents, telling them she was staying in Kincade for a while to do some work in the house and garden. And she wrote to her parish priest, to get her letter of freedom and baptism certificate.

Somehow, she knew that she was not going back to Scotland.

CHAPTER 7

The following weeks passed euphorically. Hugh and Miss Margan were back at work. Teresa, far from having time on her hands, found a lot to do. She cut out curtains for every window in the school residence. She went to Sligo, where she bought material for summer dresses. She also bought seeds. She had never done any gardening before, and had no idea of where to start. But she spent a long time studying the instructions on packets of seeds, and bought some nasturtiums and marigolds. Back in Kincade, she raked and weeded a small plot in a corner of the garden, and planted and watered the seeds.

She did the day to day shopping in Durcan's, the village shop, where she got to know many of the local people. After a short time, she began to feel that she had been there always. Every afternoon, she prepared a meal for Hugh and Miss Margan, sometimes in his house, sometimes in hers.

Sometimes Teresa wondered how she was going to tell Hugh that she had already decided not to go back home before the wedding. But as it happened, there was no need. She seemed to gradually merge into place in Kincade. She got used to being there. Hugh got used to having her. She developed a firm friendship with Miss Margan. In the village, she had made an immediate impression. She was lively, good-humoured, friendly. Everyone liked her, and the general opinion was that the master had made a good choice.

Every weekend Hugh and Teresa went off somewhere. They went first to visit Catherine, who had bought a small house near the school where she taught in Galway. She had recently finished furnishing her new home, and was proud to entertain her brother and future sister-in-law as guests.

'I got tired eventually of living in digs,' she told them. 'Mrs Gallagher, my landlady, was very nice, and her house was very comfortable. But there comes a time when you just want a place of your own. And what else would I do with my savings?'

Hugh and Teresa both agreed with her, admired her house and furnishings, and wished her good luck in her new home.

Catherine then told them that their sister Anne had been strongly opposed to this move.

'She told me that I should keep my savings for when I retire, and go back to the farm. But I've been here a long time, and I've lots of friends in this area. I know hardly anybody at home now. I really don't know what I'd do with myself if I went back to Murgintra.'

'You're quite right,' said Hugh. 'Of course you should have a place of your own. Anne sees everything from --- I suppose you could say --- a rarefied point of view.'

'And what about yourselves?' asked Catherine. 'Any plans? When's the big day?'

'Oh, sometime during the summer,' said Hugh. 'Possibly August. We'll let you know as soon as we set the date.'

At the end of the weekend, Hugh and Teresa returned to Kincade, having decided to visit Murgintra the following weekend.

'I think I'll get a car,' said Hugh, one evening that week. Once Hugh decided anything, he wasted no time. He got a licence, and went into Sligo and purchased a second-hand Morris.

It did not take him long to get used to driving. A few years ago, he had learned the basics of driving in a friend's car in Scotland. By the time he got back to Kincade, he was quite competent at the wheel. On Friday evening, they set off for Murgintra.

The weekend in Murgintra was enjoyable, though very quiet. Timothy, a silent, rugged, handsome bachelor, spent most of his time outdoors. Sometimes Hugh and Teresa accompanied him, helping where they could with whatever work he was doing. There was little conversation, but there was a pleasant calm about the place.

'We'll go to Dublin soon,' said Hugh in the car on the way home on Sunday evening. 'You'll love Dublin. We'll call and see Dominic and his family.'

'Yes,' said Teresa. 'I look forward to that. And how about Donegal? I'm dying to see Donegal. My mother's people were from Glenties, though they've been living in Scotland since my grandparents' time.'

'Good idea,' said Hugh. 'We'll go to Donegal next weekend. And maybe Dublin the following week.'

The following Friday evening Hugh and Teresa set off to Donegal. On arriving in Donegal Town, Hugh looked round for a hotel in the Diamond, where one of his colleagues had once stayed, and had highly recommended. They booked in, and had an excellent meal in the dining room. Then they drove to Rossnowlagh, a nearby seaside resort, where they walked on a long clear strand.

There was something almost unreal about the life they had been leading since Easter. Both solid, down-to-earth, practical people, they were now experiencing, for the first time in their lives, complete freedom and relaxation. They were happy in each other's company. The future looked good, the present was good. Life was extremely enjoyable.

To a casual observer, there was something settled and permanent about them. They were a handsome couple; he, tall, imposing, authoritative; she, fair-haired, stout, bouncy, with a lively personality.

When they arrived back later at their hotel, they went to get their keys at reception, and found that they had been mistakenly booked into a double room. They did not question it. It seemed the most natural thing in the world.

Their visit to Dublin was postponed, and they spent the next three weekends back in Donegal Town, having reserved the same hotel room, overlooking the bay.

****

Back in Kincade, on a June evening, Teresa was not her usual cheerful self. They had been to a play in a nearby town, where Miss Margan had been playing the leading female role. The play was hilarious, Miss Margan's rendering of the part had the audience rocking with laughter. Hugh was enjoying it immensely, but he was aware that Teresa was quiet and preoccupied.

Later, they sat in the house, drinking tea.

'Anything wrong, love?' asked Hugh. 'You've been very quiet all evening.'

'Hugh, I think I'm pregnant,' she said.

'Good God!' exclaimed Hugh. 'Now, let's see. We'll get married in Dublin. Immediately. Good thing the school holidays are starting soon. We can go to Dominic's and get married in his parish.'

Teresa was happy with this arrangement, and quickly regained her good humour.

The next ten days were spent in speedy preparation. Teresa wrote to her parents, telling them that she and Hugh were getting married in Dublin in the near future. Hugh wrote to Dominic, asking him to make arrangements with his parish priest. He wrote to Catherine and Timothy, telling them both that he and Teresa were going off on holidays, and would be married by the time they got back. He started a letter to Anne, but left it unfinished. They could, of course, call with Anne shortly after

50

the wedding. He wrote to the parish priest in Murgintra, asking him to forward the necessary documents to Dominic's address.

They told Miss Margan of their plans. She expressed the warmest of congratulations, and gave them a gift of a beautiful china tea set. On the eve of their departure, they walked round to Father O'Lorcan's house.

The priest invited them in, and Hugh came straight to the point.

'We're heading off tomorrow, Father,' he said. 'We'll be away for most of the holidays, and we'll be getting married. So you could give me my letter of freedom.'

'Certainly, Mr Staunton, no trouble at all. And since it's an occasion for celebration, we'll have a drink.'

From the cupboard he took two whiskey glasses, as he always did when Hugh visited him alone. He poured out two generous helpings, and handed one to Hugh. He then returned to the cupboard, and took out a bottle of sweet sherry and a very small glass. He half-filled the little glass, and handed it to Teresa.

'Your very best health,' he said, as they raised their glasses. He then wrote the required letter, and wished them well when they left.

****

The next day, during the journey, Teresa was again quiet and preoccupied. After some time she spoke.

'I don't know how to say this, Hugh,' she started, 'but it was a false alarm. I'm not pregnant.'

Hugh laughed heartily.

'Don't worry, love,' he said. 'We've the wedding all arranged, maybe it was just as well. We might have continued to put off setting a date.'

****

The wedding was a quiet affair, attended only by Dominic and Una, who acted as witnesses. The had a celebratory lunch in a nearby hotel, and then went off to spend a few days in Wicklow.

On the second day, they visited Anne in the convent.

'So this is Teresa,' started Anne. 'I've heard so much about you. All the nuns are dying to meet you. Aren't you the crafty ones, going and getting married quietly like that!'

She nudged Hugh aside, and spoke to him quietly.

'Well, isn't it great that you're married and settled. And thank God you got a good Catholic wife. But why didn't you let us know? The first I heard of it was when Dominic told me last week.'

'It was a last minute decision,' answered Hugh. 'We had decided to get married in August, but then we thought we'd bring it forward a bit.'

'And Teresa's parents weren't at the wedding? Or Catherine? There isn't anything wrong, is there? I wouldn't like to think there was anything the other nuns might hear about .... They'll think it very strange that I didn't know until the last minute.'

'Nothing wrong at all,' said Hugh. 'Everyone knew we were getting married anyway. We just decided to have a small wedding, no fuss. There's nothing for you or the other nuns to worry about.'

'Well, thank God for that. But now, what do you think about Catherine buying a house?' continued Anne, making no attempt to conceal her annoyance at the activities of her family members. 'I tried to talk her out of that notion last time she was here. Murgintra is her home, and it's where she should live when she retires. Timothy could do with her help, especially as he gets on a bit. He'd need to have a woman in the house. I don't know what the nuns will think, I haven't told them yet. But it's bound to come out, next time she comes to visit.'

'But why shouldn't she have her own house, if that's what she wants?' asked Hugh. 'It's all right to live in lodgings for a while, I really enjoyed it in Edinburgh, with the company and all that. But after a while you want a place of your own. It's nice to have space for your own things, and you can have visitors when you want.'

'Really, Hugh,' said Anne, 'sometimes I don't understand you at all. It's always been the custom that an unmarried sister in a family stays at home to look after the men. I know you'll get modern madams these days setting up their own homes. But our Catherine, I can't believe it.'

'But,' pursued Hugh, 'suppose Timothy were to surprise us all and get married? I mean, why shouldn't he?'

'Don't be silly, Hugh,' snapped Anne. 'Timothy won't get married now, he's forty-one this year. I don't know where you get your ideas, it must have been the time you spent in Scotland that has left you out of touch with reality.'

Completely unaware of the insensitivity of her last comment, Anne then turned her attention to Teresa. She asked her about her family, about her previous job, about her impressions of Ireland.

Hugh and Teresa did their best to keep the conversation equable, carefully steering away from thorny topics. Anne continued, doggedly, to advise, organise and criticise her family members about how they should run their lives and cope with the evils of the world from which she had escaped. Eventually they made their departure, and continued on their touring holiday.

CHAPTER 8

Hugh and Teresa returned to Kincade at the beginning of August. It was a busy month, largely spent entertaining. Teresa's parents came over from Scotland for a week. During their stay, Hugh took them on a tour of Donegal, where they visited Glenties, where Teresa's grandparents had grown up. After they left, Dominic and Una came with their three daughters to spend a few days. Catherine also spent some time with them, and they had regular visits from Miss Margan and Father O'Lorcan, both of whom would call informally in passing.

September came, and Hugh was back at school. But their social life was no less busy. They spent many evenings playing golf at Rosses Point. Teresa became quickly involved in parish activities, and always was available to help with the organisation of concerts and other functions.

As the weeks, months, seasons passed, everything seemed perfect in the Staunton household. But there was one small cloud on the horizon, a small cloud which spread and darkened with every passing month.

Teresa was a very maternal person. She was extremely anxious to have a family. When, during their engagement, she had thought she was pregnant, she had been worried. Then, as soon as they had made the hasty wedding preparations, she had felt happy, exhilarated. She had never admitted to Hugh, or even to herself, that she was bitterly disappointed when it had turned out to be a false alarm. But, being a practical, down-to-earth person, she told herself that everything would happen in good time.

In the summer of 1942, two years after their wedding, Teresa was becoming seriously worried. She was increasingly finding it an ordeal in the golf club, at the ICA, which she had recently joined, and even in the village shop. Other women of her age were talking excitedly and endlessly about their babies, what the babies were doing, what they were eating, wearing, saying. They told of the difficulties of sleepless nights, with teething and temperatures. They discussed their pregnancy symptoms step by step.

Frequently, someone would ask Teresa the tactless question.

'Nothing doing yet? You're taking your time, aren't you?'

Or what Teresa found more upsetting was the ill-advised remark, 'You're quite right to be in no hurry. You'll be long enough running after children.'

****

'I'm going to the doctor, Hugh,' Teresa said one evening as they sat together in the living room.

'Why? Is there something wrong?' Hugh asked, surprised.

Teresa explained what was worrying her, and said that she would like to have a check-up immediately. Hugh said not to worry, these things sometimes just take time, but if it would set her mind at ease, maybe the best thing would be to have a talk with the doctor.

Over the next few months, Teresa had a comprehensive series of tests and examinations in the regional hospital. On all counts she was told that she was in excellent health, that there was no reason why she shouldn't conceive. Doctors explained that sometimes these things take time, for no apparent reason. But all agreed that she had nothing to worry about. One doctor, however, suggested that she should get her husband to have some tests, just in case he had a medical problem.

At first, Hugh was not keen on the idea, but, knowing how much it meant to his wife, he agreed. He made an appointment in a Dublin hospital, comfortably far from home.

****

On the train journey back from Dublin, after his medical check-up, Hugh felt extremely perplexed. He was finding it difficult to come to terms with the result of the tests. At the clinic this morning he had been told that he could not father a child. It had something to do with mumps during childhood. But the outcome was definite, and there was no treatment that would correct the situation.

For the first time in his life, Hugh felt vulnerable. He was not even sure why, but he spent the entire train journey in a state of bewilderment.

How could he not have children? He, Hugh Staunton, who had coped effortlessly with every situation in his life so far, now found himself inexplicably at a loss. Espie Coyle, who couldn't write his own name, had six children. The cantankerous German had several boys of school age in Hugh's classes. Anyone could have children. At least, so he had thought, until now.

'Have you ever considered adoption?' one doctor had asked him in matter-of-fact tones. Hugh knew that this was not what Teresa would want. Teresa wanted motherhood, children, family. She wanted them passionately. She needed them. It was not just parenthood that she yearned for. She needed to be pregnant, to have a child herself, to bond with the child long before birth. Hugh got off the train at Kincade, knowing that she was going to be devastated by his news.

Deep in thought, he walked out of the station and turned towards home. Two local women greeted him as he crossed the road. He was so preoccupied that he didn't notice them. As he passed, they looked at each other, then at him, and shook their heads in bewilderment.

What would he say to Teresa, he asked himself, over and over again. As he approached the corner, he knew that she would be watching for his return. He immediately straightened up and hastened his step. He couldn't tell her yet. He had to get used to the idea himself first. But what was he going to say?

As he expected, Teresa was at the kitchen window. She greeted him happily when he reached the door, and asked him immediately how he had got on at the hospital.

He said the first thing that came into his head, that it would be a few days until the results of the tests would be complete, and they would then be sent to their family doctor.

****

For the next few days, Hugh was very worried. He had no idea about how he was going to cope with the crisis which was looming. He found himself avoiding Teresa, and spending most of his time working frantically in the garden. When he came indoors, Teresa would occasionally ask him when he would go to see Doctor O'Neill, just in case the test results would have arrived. He was evasive, saying that Doctor O'Neill would hardly have any word yet, but he would call with him tomorrow.

Teresa was beginning to suspect that everything was not right. She knew that Hugh was not his usual self. She hoped and prayed earnestly that her worst fears were not about to be confirmed.

On the fifth day after coming home, Hugh decided that he would have to do something. He told Teresa that he was going to call with the doctor. He left the house in the early afternoon and walked down the road, knowing that Teresa was watching him from the kitchen window, and would be waiting anxiously for his return.

As he turned the corner and left the main street, he saw the Father O'Lorcan's familiar figure approaching him.

'Ah, Mr Staunton,' the priest greeted him. 'Would you believe, I was just on the way round to see you. There's some business I want to discuss with you.'

Hugh managed to answer in his usual friendly fashion, as he noticed that Father O'Lorcan was motioning him towards the parochial house. What can Father O'Lorcan want to discuss with me, he asked himself. But in a way he was relieved. He was going to have to spend some time out of the house before going back to Teresa. He needed thinking time. Maybe a short spell in the parochial house would give him the break he wanted.

Together they entered the parochial house, and went into the large front sitting room with the bay window. As they sat down, Hugh detected an uneasiness in the older man's manner. There wasn't the usual scuttling entrance of the housekeeper with the tea tray, or the familiar clink of glasses and bottle from the mahogany cupboard. Father O'Lorcan appeared irritated, perturbed, anxious.

'I've been wondering about you and Mrs Staunton,' he started. 'Three years now you've been married, and no sign of a family. So I deemed it opportune to enquire if there was any problem in that respect.'

Could he have chosen a worse time to come out with this, Hugh asked himself.

'There's no problem, Father, no problem at all,' he answered. 'These things sometimes take time, you know.'

His usual confidence and assurance were diminished at the thought of the news he had received, a few days ago, in a Dublin hospital consulting room, and also by the sheer unexpectedness of the question.

Father O'Lorcan, sensing Hugh's discomfort, continued relentlessly.

'This will not do, Mr Staunton. I have my parish to think about.'

He paused dramatically, waiting for impact.

'Your parish, Father? What do you mean?' asked Hugh, uncomprehending.

Father O'Lorcan did not reply at once. He took out his pipe, filled it slowly, and lit it before answering.

'It has come to my notice,' he said, 'that some people in this parish have been using contraceptives. Now, Mr Staunton, as you know, this is not a sophisticated parish. These people are not at all wise in the ways of the world. Innocent and ignorant they are, and that's the way I intend to keep them. And now I find this new thing creeping in, this contraceptive thing, which, as you know, is contrary to the law of God. And, as I see it, there are two reasons for this evil having made its way into the parish.'

He paused, pulled at length on his pipe, then continued.

'The first reason, as I see it, was those missioners who were here in the autumn. It was against my better judgement that I allowed a mission in the parish. Those fellows do nothing but put ideas into people's heads. The word contraceptive would not have been known here until there they were, up at the altar, shouting about the evils of contraceptives. And what's the result? As soon as people know it's not allowed, some of them will have to find out what it's all about. So there you are, and we have a problem on our hands.'

He paused again and looked fixedly at Hugh, who still had no idea how this decline in parish morals should be his concern.

'The second factor in this deterioration of standards is, as I see it, yourself and Mrs Staunton.'

Hugh sat bolt upright on his chair, incredulous, outraged.

'Now look here, Father ....' he started.

Father O'Lorcan raised his hand for silence.

Hugh complied, partly in amazement, partly in total curiosity about what was coming next.

'You know the standing of the master in the community.' said Father O'Lorcan. 'The master is an educated man. He is a man on a level with the doctor and the priest. He is therefore a man whose example the people will follow. Now, if the master's wife has not yet produced a family, what will be said? A fine healthy looking woman she is, so why are there not two or three children by now? So, in the case of weak minded people who could be led astray, that will be their excuse. If the master and his wife can do it, I can do it.'

Hugh was enraged. He thought about Teresa, about her anxiety and disappointment about the continuing lack of a family.

'Teresa is very keen to have children,' he stated firmly. 'It has been a serious disappointment to her that nothing has happened so far.'

And won't happen ---- the quiet little voice inside his head reminded him, niggling unmercifully.

'Well, what's wrong?' demanded Father O'Lorcan. 'Has she seen a doctor?'

'Yes, she has, and she's all right. They said she was in excellent health, that things will happen in time.'

Nothing will happen ---- nagged the small inner voice.

Teresa didn't yet know the verdict from the Dublin hospital. She would be devastated. Pregnancy and motherhood were of primary importance to her.

'And further,' pursued Father O'Lorcan, 'being from Scotland, Mrs Staunton might well be considered to have different standards.'

'Now listen, Father,' interrupted Hugh. 'this is becoming slightly ridiculous, more than slightly. Being from Scotland isn't a crime, or a weakness.'

'As you well know,' Father O'Lorcan went on, 'Catholicism isn't the same in Scotland. There is not the same emphasis on the practice of religion. People over there couldn't care less what you say or do. I've known parishioners who spent some time working in Scotland, and never set foot inside a chapel while they were there. But back at home, those same people would not think of missing Mass. There's nothing like an Irish parish to act as watchdog over the conscience.

'Now, Mrs Staunton is not exactly involved in the Irish scene, is she? She plays golf, hardly in the Irish tradition. And I see she has joined that ICA crowd, which is an organisation which could well encourage women to get above themselves.

'I must say, Mr Staunton, that I am seriously concerned about the problem. There is so much at stake, the morality of the parish, for a start.'

If it had been at any other time, or on any other topic, Hugh would have countered these suggestions vigorously. He would have attacked the gross insensitivity and hypocrisy. He would scornfully have dismissed the idea that his wife, because she had grown up in Scotland, played golf, and went to ICA meetings, was a potential hazard to the morality of the parish.

But, at the moment, he felt under severe pressure, the pressure of the incomprehensible fact that he could not father children, the pressure of worry about Teresa's reaction when she would hear the news, and the pressure that Father O'Lorcan was at that moment exerting.

Shattered and mind-battered, Hugh found himself telling the priest about his visit to Dublin, and its outcome.

There was a silence of some minutes, which seemed like an eternity. Father O'Lorcan, without making any comment, pulled at length on his pipe. Then he got up, went over to the cupboard, took out the whiskey

59

bottle and two glasses, and poured out two large helpings. For several minutes more, not a word was spoken.

Father O'Lorcan held a firm view that the purpose of marriage was procreation. He had witnessed the increasing depopulation of the west of Ireland because of economic factors. He feared that if this society should grow to tolerate practices which frustrated what he saw as the primary end of marriage, it would be risking extinction.

A solution to the problem under discussion was taking shape in his mind. At first he resisted the idea. But slowly he was coming to the conclusion, that, irregular as his idea was, it could be justified on the grounds of achieving an end that would be good, that would be very beneficial, both for the individuals concerned and for the community in which they lived.

'There are five in your family, Mr Staunton, if I remember correctly,' he said.

Hugh nodded, and Father O'Lorcan continued.

'There's Dominic, the solicitor in Dublin. And Catherine, the teacher in Galway. They've been to visit you, and I've met them both. Fine upstanding people they are. And there's Anne, the nun in Wicklow. A very fine family you have, Mr Staunton.'

Hugh, tired and confused, but beginning to relax with the help of the whiskey, agreed.

'Now, that's four, yourself, Catherine, Dominic and Anne. Who else is there?'

'Timothy,' answered Hugh. 'He's the eldest. He never left home. He runs the farm.'

'Married?' enquired Father O'Lorcan.

'No, Timothy never married.'

'I've never met him. Has he not been here? The others, except the nun, have been here several times.'

'Ah, Timothy would never come. He has never been away from home in his life. He wouldn't leave the farm, not even for a day.'

'What's he like? I mean, what sort of a fellow is he?'

'A quiet fellow he always was. And very religious. In the early days the parents thought he would go for the priesthood. But he never had any interest in leaving home.'

Father O'Lorcan topped up the whiskey glasses. There was another long silence. A plan was emerging in his mind, a plan that was far from conventional, but somehow seemed very simple and obvious.

Hugh felt bewildered. Why was Father O'Lorcan expressing such an interest in his family? Did he think that since Hugh came from a family of normal size, there should be no problem of this kind? Did he seriously think that he and Teresa were deliberately avoiding having children? What was the relevance of his questions about Timothy, whether he was married, what sort of fellow he was? Was he trying to pinpoint some weakness, something in the Staunton family that was not quite as it should be?

'Have you considered adoption?' asked Father O'Lorcan.

'No,' answered Hugh. 'It's not something I would consider, and I know that Teresa wouldn't either.'

'If you're adamant about that,' said Father O'Lorcan, 'then we must think of another solution to our problem.'

What's he talking about, Hugh asked himself. Our problem? Hugh was acutely aware that he and Teresa had a problem that was going to be very difficult to resolve. Father O'Lorcan claimed to have a problem of some magnitude in his parish, but to merge the two together and describe them as 'our problem' was just going too far.

Could I seriously consider the solution I have in mind, Father O'Lorcan asked himself. He was in no doubt that it was a highly irregular proposition. But he was convinced that good people, taking the action that he was contemplating for them, would be doing no wrong.

It was all to do with procreation, he told himself. People were developing a materialistic outlook and losing their spiritual values. Societies that paid too little attention to procreation ran the risk of extinction. He had to fight this evil all the way, this evil of contraceptive practices which was threatening to insinuate itself into his parish. He was responsible to God for the moral and spiritual welfare of his parishioners. He would have to weigh carefully in his mind the arguments for and against the plan which had taken shape in his mind.

But how would Hugh react to his suggestion? Being a strong minded man, he could be difficult to persuade. And then there was Teresa who might refuse to have anything to do with such a scheme.

'There might be another solution,' he said, warily.

Hugh looked enquiringly at him.

Father O'Lorcan did not continue. He knew what he wanted to suggest, but before he would speak, he wanted to be sure of a favourable response.

'Look, Father,' said Hugh, rising from his chair, 'I think we'll leave it. I haven't yet told Teresa about what they said in the hospital, and I'm going to have to think how to break it to her. It's not going to be easy, you've no idea how much she has her mind set on having a family. But it's our problem, and we'll have to sort it as best we can.'

'Sit down, sit down, Mr Staunton,' said Father O'Lorcan. 'I think it's important that we talk the whole thing out before you go home.'

Once again, Hugh complied, completely at a loss about what could be achieved by further discussion.

'Your wife is a good woman,' said Father O'Lorcan. 'She is attentive to her religious duties. She is a good wife, and, you tell me, very anxious to be a mother. Now, we have to think what can be done about this. There may be a solution .... I know it's not exactly normal practice, but not unknown in the past. Now, your brother Timothy is not married, and he could be the solution ....'

'Good God!' exclaimed Hugh. 'You're not seriously suggesting that Teresa could ....? No! This is ridiculous! You have no right to make such a suggestion. And what about Teresa? She'd be horrified. If we can't have a family, we can't. We'll just have to adjust.'

'You say that you will have to adjust. Think about it, Mr Staunton. You, yourself, could well adjust. You are a dedicated and competent teacher. Your work is stimulating. I don't doubt for a moment that you would be very disappointed at not having a family, but you could adjust.

'Mrs Staunton, on the other hand, has a strong maternal instinct. She is going to be devastated. She isn't qualified to find a job outside the home, such as teaching or nursing, which could give her some fulfilment. She will continue cooking and cleaning, working hard for the two of you, and all the time growing more and more bitter. In the end she could grow to resent you.

'So, one way or another, you can see that you have a problem that cannot be treated lightly. You could end up, in middle age, with a discontented wife, disillusioned, probably angry at you, though you are in no way at fault.'

For several minutes more, not a word was spoken. Hugh was preoccupied, increasingly uneasy. The truth of Father O'Lorcan's statements was hitting home.

Teresa was a lovely woman. She was lively, loving, adaptable, competent. She was intelligent, understanding, devoted. Devoted, at this moment to her husband and home. Devoted, entirely devoted to her future, to their future, to their children, to their family. To the family they could never have.

What could the future hold for her? Would Teresa go sour, become bitter, lose her zest for life?

Hugh was under no illusions about Father O'Lorcan's interest in his future. Father O'Lorcan had a plan in mind. He was ruthlessly pursuing the reasons why his plan had to be considered.

After yet another long silence, Father O'Lorcan outlined his plan.

The continuing good of the parish was of paramount importance. The Stauntons must have a family. Mrs Staunton was desperate to have a family. Being a reasonable woman, she would accept a situation, maybe irregular, but which would solve the problem. Timothy was a good living man, and would respect the wishes of a priest. He would also respect the need for total confidentiality and secrecy. Timothy's offspring would carry the resemblance that people always look out for.

He said that he himself could go off in the near future, to drive to Murgintra and visit Timothy. On his return, they would discuss the matter further.

Weary and confused, Hugh stood up, took his leave and walked slowly homewards.

CHAPTER 9

Teresa was in the kitchen baking bread when she saw her husband walking slowly back towards the house. She had a sense of foreboding as soon as he appeared round the corner. His demeanour told her everything. Gone was the spring in his step, his bright and confident manner, as he trudged homewards, eyes on the ground.

In the three minutes, from the moment he appeared at the corner of the road until he came in the front door, a tumult of emotions crossed her mind. It seemed that in such a short space of time an unbelievable range of contradictory thoughts occurred to her.

She knew, without being told, that the news from the hospital was not good. And she realised that, deep down, she had known this from the moment Hugh had returned from Dublin. She felt suddenly, unreasonably angry and resentful at Hugh. Then she told herself that this was unfair, he was a good husband, that this was no fault of his.

Then she asked herself, had she married the wrong person? Maybe, married to someone else, this problem would not have occurred. She thought of her sister Patricia, married a year before her, with two children and another on the way. She thought of other friends and acquaintances from home, all of whom had got married and had shortly been blessed with families. But even as she asked herself this question, she remembered clearly, a few years back, how worried she had been that she might not get married. If she had not married Hugh, she would almost certainly be a single person, over thirty, considered to be on the shelf.

Then she suddenly felt trapped. And immediately she realised that this was irrational. It had been her choice to marry Hugh. She loved him. Nobody could predict in advance how things were likely to turn out. And, devastated as she was, she knew that he also must be shattered, must find this a serious blow to his ego.

And finally the ludicrous thought occurred to her. Could she have an affair? Could she, unknown to Hugh, of course, become pregnant by someone else? But the sheer impossibility of such a scheme struck her forcibly. In a small village, where everyone knew everyone else's business, this of course was not an option. And, to reach the stage when she could actually have an affair, she would have to establish a relationship with someone, to lead the other person on for her own ends, discarding him when her aim had been achieved. Given her own nature, conservative, organised, uncomplicated, she knew that she could not even entertain the idea.

Hugh arrived into the house, and they embraced, briefly, limply. He told her something about seeing Doctor O'Neill, but she did not hear a word he said. Then they sat together, silently, for some time, she had no idea for how long. She had never known him to be in such bad form. He was not normally given to moods, and she had never known him to be faced with a situation that he couldn't handle. As they sat in armchairs, on either side of the fireplace, she felt for a moment as if they were total strangers to each other.

'Father O'Lorcan made a suggestion,' he said tentatively.

Father O'Lorcan? Where did he come into this? Then Teresa remembered that Hugh had gone to visit the doctor, and had not come back for about two hours. So, on the way back from the doctor's, he had spent some time with Father O'Lorcan. What was it all about?

Hesitantly, tentatively, Hugh outlined the scheme proposed by Father O'Lorcan. Teresa's first reaction was one of complete disbelief. Then she remembered that, not so many minutes ago, the possibility of an affair had briefly crossed her mind. But it seemed highly irregular that her husband and Father O'Lorcan were actually discussing it as a possibility. Her thoughts turned to Timothy, the man whom until now she had never thought of except as her husband's brother.

Hugh looked at her, full of sorrow and concern.

'Don't consider it if it upsets you, love,' he said. 'I'm sorry I even mentioned it. I should have realised it was totally out of the question. And I know what a disappointment this is to you. But we'll cope ....' his voice trailed off unconvincingly.

'I'll need to think about it,' she answered.

****

Later, in the dead of night, she thought about Timothy. Would he agree, she wondered, and somehow she felt fairly confident that he would. She liked Timothy. He was a silent man, but she always experienced a sense of ease with him. He resembled Hugh, both of them being tall strong men, with grey eyes and thick black hair. Timothy was always tanned and weather-beaten, due to his outdoor life in all seasons. She found herself looking forward to their next meeting, which she earnestly hoped would be soon.

Briefly Teresa wondered about whether it was all right to embark on this venture. Back home in Scotland, she had known a few people who were involved in extra-marital affairs. It was considered to be totally wrong and immoral, and those people were the subject of the disapproval of all who knew about their activities. But this is different, she told herself. It is all for a good purpose. And, if Father O'Lorcan says it's all right, it must be all right.

She looked over at her sleeping husband. She loved him, and sincerely hoped that he would not feel in any way rejected in any way as a result of their plans. She would have to be especially reassuring on this point. And she looked forward to the day, hopefully not too distant now, when they would be a family rather than a couple.

****

Hugh woke at about six in the morning. He was normally an early riser, but on this occasion he was afoot much earlier than usual. He dressed and went downstairs, and in an agitated frame of mind he paced around the kitchen for a long time.

The idea of Teresa going off on this most unlikely errand filled him with disquiet. Had their marriage been a mistake? Could they have foreseen the anxiety that this problem was causing? How did Teresa feel about the proposed solution? When they had discussed it earlier, she had seemed alarmed at first, then had quickly regained her calm. She had said she'd think about it. In a way he wished that she had just refused to entertain the idea. But he could not forget her look of complete dismay when he broke the news to her about the diagnosis.

He thought with alarm about Teresa's possible feelings for Timothy. Could she prefer him, could it have a disruptive effect on their marriage? But even as this thought crossed his mind, he knew that Teresa was loyal and kind. She would never hurt him, or anyone else. She was an excellent home maker, a role which she would never leave. She was well-known and popular in the village, never showing for a moment any signs of her one cause for anxiety.

He knew that her maternal instinct was so strong, so overwhelming, that something had to be done. He knew that the continuing anxiety and disappointment would inevitably become destructive. And that was why he had gone along with Father O'Lorcan's plan. Hugh decided to go out for a walk in the fresh air, in an attempt to clear his mind.

****

Father O'Lorcan drove along in his little battered Ford. He always drove in the middle of the road, reluctantly pulling in to the side when he met other cars. He had an unusual style of driving. With his left hand always on the handbrake, his right arm rigidly extended and grasping the top of the steering wheel, he cruised along, leaning far back, his hat tilted on the back of his head.

It was a bright spring day, a good day for driving. Apart from an occasional horse and cart, there was very little traffic. In his mind, he planned the rest of the day.

He would see Timothy first. He did not anticipate any difficulty here. At this point, a shade of doubt crossed his mind. Was it really right, he asked himself, to ask, to tell people to embark on a line of action which was clearly in breach of the teaching of the church?

But he was not a man who entertained doubts readily. His doubts lasted no more than a few seconds.

'The greater good,' he told himself. 'If it's for the greater good, then it is certainly justified.'

He decided that after his visit to Timothy, he would call with his old friend Canon Greene in Westport.

****

'Timothy!' shouted young John Devenney, from the bottom of the lower field. 'There's a priest at your house!'

Timothy, who was up in the high field, left his work and came towards his young neighbour.

'He's at the house,' continued John. 'He knocked the door, and then he went round the back, and then he came back, and now he's walking up and down the street.'

In the distance, Timothy could see Father O'Lorcan's white head as he paced in front of the house.

'Run on, John,' said Timothy, 'and tell him I'll be right down.'

John ran ahead, and Timothy followed, with an unhurried step, thinking less of his unexpected visitor than of the work he hoped to complete before the evening.

As he crossed the low field, he could see Father O'Lorcan clearly. He was aware that this priest was a stranger, a man he had never seen. Who

67

is he, or what can he want, he asked himself. But he felt no anxiety. A man of the earth, he lived with the predictability and unpredictability of the seasons and outdoor life. Whatever came, whatever happened in everyday life, he handled as required. Whatever this priest had come about, he would also handle.

Father O'Lorcan greeted Timothy cordially, and introduced himself, adding that he was parish priest in Kincade.

'Is there anything wrong, Father?' asked Timothy, knowing as he spoke, that if there was something wrong, the news would hardly be transmitted by the parish priest in person.

'Nothing wrong, Timothy,' answered Father O'Lorcan, 'At least, nothing that we can't put right. Shall we go inside?'

Inside the house, Timothy hesitated. Should he bring the priest into the parlour? There had not been a fire in the parlour for months, and it would be very cold.

But as Father O'Lorcan was already sitting at the kitchen table, he abandoned the idea.

'Tea, Father?' he offered, moving the kettle over onto the hot plate on the range.

'Well, yes. Or whiskey, if you have it,' said Father O'Lorcan, looking enquiringly in the direction of the kitchen cupboard.

Timothy took out the whiskey bottle and two glasses, and served his guest.

At that moment there was gentle tap at the back door. Timothy opened it to find young John Devenney standing there.

'Mammy says if you've a visitor do you want her to come over and make tea?' he said.

'No thanks, John, it's all right,' said Timothy. 'Tell your mammy thanks all the same.'

In the Devenneys' kitchen, Mrs Devenney was questioning John.

'What were they doing?' she demanded.

'They were just sitting there,' answered John. 'They were drinking whiskey. And talking.'

'Well, what were they talking about?' she said impatiently.

'I don't know,' answered the child. 'I didn't hear.'

Ellen Devenney laughed out loud.

'You're so nosey, Mammy,' she said. 'You wanted to get making tea just to hear who the priest is and why he's there.'

'Hold your tongue, Ellen,' snapped her mother. 'You've too much to say for yourself these days.'

She was angry, more so because she knew that what her daughter said was true.

****

Father O'Lorcan came straight to the point. He explained the problem to Timothy. He outlined the reasons for needing a solution which would be acceptable to all concerned. He suggested the plan that he had in mind.

Timothy's expression betrayed nothing of the complete amazement he was experiencing as Father O'Lorcan continued to expound his plan. He made no attempt to comment or answer. He listened to what the priest was saying, and asked himself was this really true, this extremely unlikely proposition that was being put to him.

Incongruously, his thoughts strayed back to the fields. He thought of his day to day work, of the relentlessness of his daily routine, of the frequent urgency in getting things done. He thought of the hazards of farm life, of the difficulties that weather, disease or accidents could bring. He thought about the many things that could go wrong when working the land, and about how, as soon as something went wrong, there had to be an immediate contingency plan to follow. At this point his mind returned to focus on what Father O'Lorcan was saying.

Father O'Lorcan was saying that Timothy need have no anxiety on the religious issue. For as long as this arrangement was necessary, he had a dispensation, he was to attend to his religious duties as always. There was, of course, the need for complete secrecy and confidentiality in this matter. Nobody, except the people directly involved, must ever, either now or in the future, be told.

There followed a long silence, during which Timothy, without betraying the slightest emotion, got over the initial shock. He considered at length all the consequences of agreeing to such an unbelievable suggestion. He managed to keep his countenance devoid of expression, as he realised that he was actually looking forward to playing his part in the scheme.

'I'll do what I can to help, Father,' said Timothy, the first words he had spoken since the conversation had begun.

'I knew you would, Timothy,' said Father O'Lorcan. 'You're a good man. God bless you.'

More relaxed now, they chatted for a while about the farm, the weather, about what was recently on the news.

During the conversation, Timothy again found his mind wandering. A few times he had to concentrate, and make appropriate answers to Father O'Lorcan's comments. He was thinking of Teresa.

Teresa. Hugh's wife. He had liked her since their first meeting. A pretty girl she was, and friendly. She wasn't a bit like Dominic's Una. Una was all right, of course, but basically she was a city girl, and always seemed a bit out of place on visits to the farm. He found himself looking forward to meeting Teresa again.

He then found himself thinking further back, much further. He remembered the dance hall days of his youth, when he and his brother Dominic used to go out together. Dominic was a year younger than him, ebullient and extrovert by nature, had many girlfriends in those days, and, after the dances, was often in trouble about coming home late. He was frequently exhorted to follow the example of his quiet elder brother Timothy. Timothy smiled at the memory of those distant days, when, quietly and unobtrusively, he had had his own share of girlfriends, had had many pleasant interludes round the country lanes, but somehow was always home in time and never aroused any suspicion.

As time went on, his two brothers had married, his two sisters had gone to their chosen careers, and he had stayed at home. The farm was the love of his life. Family members, friends, occasionally asked if he had any thoughts of marrying. He never had an answer. He did not know himself, either that he would or would not marry. And then everyone decided that Timothy was just too quiet, and would certainly remain a bachelor.

Father O'Lorcan got up to leave, and then briefly returned to the topic that had brought them together, expressing the hope that things would be accomplished as soon as possible. Then he said goodbye, and set off in the direction of Westport, to visit Canon Greene. In a mood of satisfaction with a job well done, he drove along. He just hoped that Timothy had not suffered from mumps in childhood.

****

A few weeks later, Teresa set off on the train to spend a short holiday on the farm. On the journey she felt strangely elated, and not in the least apprehensive.

Her sojourn with her brother-in-law was going to need some explanation, to friends in Kincade, to neighbours at Murgintra. She told people that she was going to paint and decorate the parlour in the farmhouse. She had, in her suitcase, a pair of maroon coloured brocade curtains, nearly finished, which just had to be hemmed, pressed and hung.

Hugh threw his golf clubs into the back of the car, and went off to Rosses Point.

CHAPTER 10

Timothy met Teresa coming off the train. He had put on his good suit, and had cycled the mile from Murgintra to the station. They shook hands on meeting, he took her case, and they left the station. Together they walked back to the farm, Timothy carrying the case in one hand and wheeling his bicycle with the other. There was very little said on the way, but there was no awkwardness, each seemed already to feel at home with the other.

On arriving, they had a meal which Timothy had started to prepare earlier. The evening was spent talking about local and family history. Timothy, normally a silent man, was passionately interested in the farm, the land, his ancestors, his relations who had gone abroad. He was working on a family tree, which he showed to Teresa, explaining in detail all the connections. Teresa, who had only the vaguest knowledge of her own family more that one generation back, was intrigued.

They retired early, as Timothy had a heavy day's work in front of him.

The next morning, while Timothy was out in the fields, Teresa planned her day. She had thought that she would do some housework. But the farm house was very organised, clean and sparkling. Mrs Devenney and her daughter Ellen, Timothy had told her, came in every Friday, did laundry, and cleaned and polished the entire house.

So she went into the parlour, the room which she was going to refurbish. She moved all the furniture out into the hallway, and spent the rest of the morning stripping the walls in preparation for the new paper. She examined with satisfaction the rolls of new paper which Timothy had bought and stacked in readiness in a corner of the room. Decorating was a task she always enjoyed.

But she knew that she was going to have to find something more to fill the empty days. The parlour could be finished by tomorrow, if she worked at it all day. No, she would have to slow it down, to make the work last throughout her stay, which she anticipated being between a week and ten days.

Among the furniture that she shifted into the hall was a glass fronted bookcase filled with all sorts of interesting things. There were old novels, old school and college text books, volumes of poetry, books on local history, and loads of old magazines. Teresa made a mental note that she would find plenty of interesting reading when not working.

Towards midday, Timothy cycled into town, purchased the day's groceries and the daily paper, and came home for lunch. After that, he returned to the fields, and, as evening approached, Teresa turned her attention to preparing the evening meal. And that became the pattern of the next few days.

On Friday morning, when Mrs Devenney and Ellen were due to come, Teresa gathered her belongings and arranged them in Catherine's bedroom, taking care to leave the room with a slightly lived-in look. She spread one of the curtains on the ironing board, and sat down to work at hemming the second one. Then the three women had a cup of tea together, before starting on their various tasks.

A week passed like this, and at the beginning of the second week Teresa told Timothy that she would go home the following day. Apart from their long conversations on the ancestry and the family tree, they talked little. Other day-to-day issues seemed to be communicated with the minimum of words.

Timothy took the morning off to see Teresa to the train. In the farmhouse kitchen they kissed goodbye before leaving.

'You'll name me as godfather?' said Timothy.

'We will, indeed,' answered Teresa. 'And Catherine as godmother?' she added.

'Yes,' said Timothy. 'Catherine as godmother. That's good.'

They walked to the station, Timothy carrying Teresa's case, and wheeling his bicycle for the return journey. On the platform, they shook hands as the train pulled in.

'You'll be back?' Timothy asked quietly.

'I'll be back,' Teresa answered. The train pulled out, and she turned her attention to her return to Kincade.

****

During the afternoon, Teresa arrived home. Hugh was still in school, not knowing that she was to arrive that day. Through the classroom window, he saw her walk along the road towards the house. There was a lightness in her step, a happiness in her demeanour. Hugh realised immediately that the visit had been a success.

Shortly after three o'clock Hugh dismissed his class. But he did not go home. For about half an hour he sat at his desk, confused thoughts running through his mind. He had been delighted to see Teresa arriving home, looking happy and radiant. Then he immediately felt angry and resentful. He wondered what Teresa's feelings were for Timothy. For one brief moment he hated Timothy, then told himself that this was irrational.

He put aside the piles of copy books and other working debris of the day, then locked the school door and walked slowly across the road. As he opened the front door, Teresa greeted him joyfully, They embraced warmly, and despite his earlier misgivings, Hugh was gratified at his wife's obvious happiness.

Later that evening, they sat at the fire. They talked at length, about what was going on at the golf club, about an argument Miss Margan had with Father O'Lorcan over some trivial issue, about Timothy's work on the family tree, about some work that had to be done in the garden now that the Easter holidays were approaching. Both of them, respecting each other's sensitivities, kept clear of the subject that was uppermost in their minds, Teresa's pregnancy.

As the weeks and months went on Teresa blossomed. Pregnancy suited her. She stopped playing golf, she had too much to do at home preparing for the forthcoming event. She knitted little matinee jackets, and bought a cot and pram. While the subject was barely mentioned between herself and Hugh, she had excited conversations with other young mothers about all developments. And she learned to drive the car. You never know, she told herself, when you might need to be able to drive.

A few days after Christmas Margaret was born.

Now they were a family, rather than just a couple. Motherhood was all that Teresa had expected. Hugh was happy with the new arrival, and happy to see his wife so contented.

And it was a natural follow up, when, as spring approached again, Teresa said that Margaret would need a little brother or sister to play with. So she set off again, with the cot in the back seat of the car, for a short stay in Murgintra.

The following winter Philomena was born.

Life went on much as usual. Teresa rarely went out. With a one-year-old and an infant, she was quite housebound. But she was blissfully happy. Her time and energy were devoted to her two babies, and all the washing, changing and feeding, far from being a chore, was a joy. Hugh would have willingly shared the work, but Teresa preferred to do everything herself. So Hugh contented himself with his golf and his books.

When spring came again, it seemed the most natural thing in the world to go back to Murgintra. They had two girls. It would have to be a boy next time. Then, maybe, there should be a break of two or three years before the next one. Teresa planned to have a big family. She had grown up with one sister only, and had often envied the camaraderie that she noticed in large families. She was now thirty-three years of age. Yes, another one now, she thought, then a break, and she could comfortably have one or two more. It all seemed quite straightforward.

When she arrived at Murgintra this time, things were different. She sensed a change in Timothy immediately. Ellen Devenney, a young woman in her twenties, who used to come with her mother to clean the house every Friday, now was coming every day, sometimes staying quite late in the evening, seeming very much at home in the farmhouse.

At the end of her stay, as she prepared for the return journey, Timothy followed her into the spare room, where the two children had been sleeping.

'I'm getting married, Teresa,' he said.

'I know, Timothy,' she answered. 'I wish you well. And I'll miss you. But maybe it's the best thing, in the long run.'

They kissed goodbye in the bedroom, and, fighting back tears, Teresa hurried downstairs, lifted Margaret and Philomena into the car, and drove homewards.

On Christmas Eve, Kevin was born.

CHAPTER 11

It was early in 1947, shortly after Kevin's birth, that Timothy contacted his brothers and sisters. He gave them the news, known until now to nobody except Teresa, that he was going to marry Ellen Devenney. The wedding date was set for the last week in February.

Dominic and Una, Hugh, Teresa and Catherine were all pleased for him, and wished him well. But Anne was outraged. She wrote to each of the others, exhorting them to persuade Timothy to change his mind.

The Devenneys were not a good family, Anne wrote. Everyone knew about them. Mrs Devenney was, of course, a good woman, but wasn't there something about her husband? He had spent a lot of time in England. There were rumours about him, something about another woman. And if he was like that, who was to know whether his daughter Ellen was all she should be? The other nuns did not know of this yet, so it was essential that they would get the wedding called off before word would get out. And it could get out any time, Sister Jacinta came from Claremorris which wasn't all that far from Murgintra, and you'd never know what you'd hear from that nosey sister of hers who was likely to visit soon.

And if there was anyone she blamed for this, it was Catherine. If Catherine hadn't taken that notion of buying a house, Timothy would never have thought of looking for a wife, he'd have known that Catherine would eventually come back to Murgintra to look after him. In her letter to Catherine, Anne pleaded with her to sell her house immediately, and go back to her old habit of spending every weekend in Murgintra. If only she could do this before it would be too late, the unfortunate marriage could be called off.

And anyway, what was Timothy thinking of, getting married at his age? He was forty eight, old enough to be Ellen Devenney's father. It was so embarrassing.

Dominic and Hugh dismissed those letters without a moment's thought. But Catherine was devastated. She arrived the following weekend, unannounced, at Hugh's home.

It took Hugh and Teresa the entire weekend to persuade Anne that Anne's letters were nothing more than a lot of mischief, that Anne, from her secluded atmosphere could not possibly decide how people should live their lives, that she had chosen her own way of life which nobody begrudged her. They persuaded her that of course she was entitled to have her own home, that because she was single it must not be presumed that she must always be available to look after everyone else.

By Sunday evening, they had talked it out at length, and Hugh and Teresa had managed to reassure Catherine. Hugh would accompany her to the wedding. It would be impossible for Teresa to go, with three young children to look after. And Catherine returned home in better form.

On a frosty February day, Timothy and Ellen were married. The wedding was a small affair, which just a few family members on each side attended. They had a meal for visiting relatives in the Devenney household. Then the guests made their way home, and the newly weds returned to the farm.

CHAPTER 12

The following years passed quickly. Teresa was very busy with her young family, who had reached school going age. All three of them in turn went first into Miss Margan's class, then progressed into Hugh's class. Margaret resembled her mother, being stout and squarely built. Philomena and Kevin were growing tall, like the Stauntons. And all three children had the Staunton hair, thick, black and straight.

Teresa knitted jumpers and pullovers for her children, and made skirts and dresses for the two girls. She baked bread and cakes, made jam, and grew vegetables. She was always busy with some work, in the house or the garden.

****

'Are we very rich, Mammy?' asked Margaret, out of the blue, one day, at the age of ten.

'We are not,' answered her mother, laughing. 'Where would you get that idea?'

'The girls at school were saying,' explained Margaret, 'that we must be very rich because we wear shoes and socks all year.'

'That's right,' said Philomena, who tended to follow everything Margaret said. 'And they say we must be rich because we're going to boarding school when we're twelve, and boarding schools cost lots of money.'

'Now, don't talk nonsense,' said their mother. 'We're not very rich. We have enough to go on with. And I hope you two aren't boasting about anything, like going to boarding school.'

'No, we're not,' said Margaret, who was much given to boasting. She liked to impress her classmates with made up stories about the boarding school they would go to, where there would be lots of rich girls with beautiful clothes and plenty of money.

'But, Mammy,' Margaret went on, disillusioned, 'if we're not very rich, why aren't we?'

What was the answer to that, Teresa wondered. She tried to tell the girls that it wasn't important, that while not rich they were comfortable, that there were more important things than money. Margaret sulked a bit, and Philomena, noticing Margaret's mood, decided to sulk as well.

****

The Stauntons were a united family. They kept in touch with other family members. Catherine came regularly for weekends, and there was a promise that when the children were old enough they could go and spend weekends in her Galway home.

Two or three times in the course of the year they went to Murgintra, to visit Timothy and Ellen, who now had two sons.

And every summer they went to Dublin, where they stayed with Dominic and Una, whose daughters were now grown up. Included in their Dublin stay there was always the visit to the convent to see Anne. The rigid visiting rules had been relaxed, Anne was no longer confined to four visits a year, a fact of which she kept reminding them. She congratulated Hugh and Teresa on their fine family, and always remarked that while Dominic and Una had brought up three fine girls, wouldn't it be great if one of them had a vocation to enter the convent. Wouldn't Margaret and Philomena make grand nuns, she asked Teresa. And Kevin, he would be just a perfect priest. It was the duty of parents to foster vocations in their children, she added.

When time came for leaving, she vigorously reminded them that she could have more frequent visits, that they should come back soon, and that, indeed, the time was coming when nuns would be allowed to visit their relations at home.

****

In the summer of 1956, Margaret had completed her first year at boarding school. Philomena was to join her in the new term, and Kevin was in sixth class. Catherine had come to spend a few days, and one evening, the conversation turned to holidays.

'Would you believe,' said Teresa, 'that I haven't set foot in Scotland since before we were married?'

'True,' continued her husband. 'Many a time I think that it would be nice to go back. But time goes on, you think about doing things, and don't get round to it.'

'Well,' said Catherine, 'why not go this year? This summer? Next week? I could stay here and look after the children. The two of you could go off and enjoy yourselves. It would be a good break for you.'

'Go on Mammy! Please go!' shouted Margaret. 'We'd love to have Auntie Catherine minding us!'

'Yes!' added Philomena enthusiastically. 'Auntie Catherine always buys us presents!'

Catherine had been very good to the children over the years. A very generous person, she had kept in close touch with them, never forgetting birthdays, communions, confirmations and other family occasions. The children were very fond of her.

And so it was decided. Hugh and Teresa were going to take a holiday, their first holiday alone, together, for many years. As always, once the decision was made, the plans were as good as made. A week later, they took the cross channel ferry to Scotland.

The holiday was very relaxed. They visited Teresa's sister Patricia and her family. They called on many friends and ex-colleagues from the past. They went walking on Portobello beach, and hiked in the Pentlands, as they had done many years ago. They were strongly reminded of the summer they became engaged, when they danced, went to the cinema, and just wandered where the spirit led them. It was also reminiscent of the weeks in Kincade before their wedding, when they went off to Donegal for weekends.

Briefly, they rediscovered the euphoria of those past days. The holiday was like a second honeymoon.

Some time after their return home, Teresa said to Hugh, 'Guess what? I'm pregnant.'

She was in no doubt. She had had the symptoms three times before. The impossible had happened.

CHAPTER 13

The Christmas holidays came. Margaret and Philomena were home from boarding school. Kevin, in his last year at primary school, had just got his first pair of long trousers. He was very much on his dignity, and not at all amused when the girls teased him about his adult attire.

'Mammy, why are all our birthdays at Christmas?' suddenly demanded Margaret. 'It's Kevin's birthday on Christmas Eve, and mine on the twenty-seventh, and Philomena's on the thirtieth.'

'We don't choose our birthdays, Margaret,' said her mother. 'We just have to take the one we get.'

'It still is strange,' insisted Margaret. 'Nobody at school can believe it when I tell them that we have all our birthdays in one week. And it's not fair that all our birthdays are at Christmas. It means that we get only one set of presents a year.'

'Well, I've a surprise for you all this year,' said her mother. 'We're going to have a new baby in the family. And the birthday won't be at Christmas, it'll be at Easter.'

'A new baby!' shrieked Margaret and Philomena simultaneously.

'Will it be a boy or a girl?'

'What'll we call it?'

'I can't wait to tell the girls at school!'

Kevin maintained an aloof, disinterested silence. There were boys in his class who had infant brothers and sisters in their families. But it wasn't a thing boys would talk about. Only girls or cissies talked about babies.

'We don't know if it will be a boy or girl until it comes,' said Teresa. 'You know that. So we can't start thinking of names yet.'

'I hope it's a girl,' said Margaret. 'Though I suppose Kevin would prefer a boy. Would you prefer a boy, Kevin? To play football with?'

Teresa laughed.

'Even when the baby comes, and if it is a boy,' she said, 'he'll be much too small to play football for a long time. And, don't forget, I'll be expecting all of you to help me look after the baby.'

Margaret and Philomena, who were usually very reluctant to help with household chores, were very excited at the prospect. Kevin's face registered total disbelief. The idea of looking after a baby, when he was a grown up boy, in seventh class, was just out of the question.

'Maybe it'll be twins!' clamoured Margaret. 'A boy for Kevin to play with, and a girl for me and Philomena. Or even triplets! Two girls and a boy! I can't wait to tell my friends at school.'

The Christmas holidays passed, with all the birthdays. Cards and presents arrived in the post from all the aunts and uncles. In the card from Timothy and Ellen there was the news that they also were expecting a baby in the near future.

Catherine was spending Christmas at Murgintra. She divided her holiday time among the three families.

Dominic and Una enclosed a long letter, telling about the endless round of dances and parties that their grown-up daughters were invited to attend during the festive season. Margaret was green with envy. She said that she couldn't wait until she was old enough to go to dances.

There was a card from Anne, including a holy picture for each member of the family, and a note to let them know that she would be praying for them all.

On the last day of the holidays, Teresa stood at the front door, waving goodbye to the two girls, as Hugh drove them back to school. Kevin did not condescend to come out to say goodbye. Teresa thought wistfully of the coming months, and about how nice it would be to have a baby in the house again.

****

On the last day of term, Margaret and Philomena, with some of their classmates, paced around impatiently inside the front door of the school, waiting for their parents to arrive. For the last few days, holidays had been the only topic of conversation. Girls were exchanging confidences about how they were going to spend the ten days at home. Many of them presented a very enviable picture of the hectic social life in their own town or village, often slipping in a hopeful comment about some good looking young man who would be on the scene. They would shortly be on their way, where they would almost certainly spend the holiday at home, in the house, helping their parents and visiting relations. But the fantasy build up was all part of the excitement.

Every few minutes, someone would stand on tiptoe to see out the small high window at the side of the door. Then they would announce whose parent was arriving, or what kind of car was pulling in. The lucky girl would then gather her belongings and rush out the door with shouted goodbyes, impatient to get home to all the action without a second's delay.

'There's the Stauntons' car!' shouted someone. 'The big black one. Isn't that your car, Margaret?'

Margaret and Philomena hastily grabbed their cases and rushed out.

'I wish Daddy would get a new car,' Margaret whispered to Philomena as they ran down the drive. 'This one is so shabby. I always think they're all laughing at it.'

'I know,' said Philomena. 'Everyone else seems to get new cars, and we always have the same old one. It's not fair.'

Hugh welcomed the girls as they clambered in, and told them the news immediately.

'You've a baby sister,' he said. 'She was born last night. We'll be going to see your Mammy and the baby as soon as we get home.'

'Wait a minute, Daddy,' shouted Margaret. She leaped out of the car, ran back to the school door, and excitedly passed on the news to the girls who were still waiting in the hallway.

'The new baby's been born!' she shouted. 'It's a girl! I'll tell you all about it after the holidays.' And she turned and raced back to the car.

'She'll tell us about it,' muttered one of her classmates cynically. 'In fact, we'll hear nothing else for the next term.'

Back in the car, the girls bombarded Hugh with questions.

'What size is she?'

'What colour is her hair? Is it straight or curly?'

'What colour are her eyes?'

Hugh tried to answer the rapid fire questions.

'What's her name? What are we going to call her?' demanded Margaret urgently.

'Treasa Aideen,' replied Hugh. 'We talked about names this morning. And we decided on Treasa, after your mother, and Aideen for a second name.'

'What!' exclaimed Margaret. 'You can't call her Treasa Aideen! There's a girl in my class called Aideen, and she's absolutely horrible!'

'And Treasa!' protested Philomena. 'That's Irish! Nobody has Irish names nowadays. Roisin Moynihan in my class changed her name to Rosaleen. Everybody hates Irish names!'

'Can we call her a pretty name, Daddy?' clamoured Margaret. 'Like Caroline? Or Shirley?'

'Or Vanessa? Or Audrey? Or Angela?' added Philomena.

The rest of the journey was spent with the girls discussing all possible pretty and fashionable names.

****

Later that evening, in the hospital, the family visited Teresa and the baby. Kevin stood in the background, aloof, as Margaret and Philomena, awe-struck, admired their little sister, touched her, stroked her hair.

After a while they discussed the christening, which was to be held the following day. Their aunt Patricia in Scotland, and her husband, were to be godparents. But of course they couldn't come for the christening. So Margaret, being the eldest girl, was to stand in for the godmother. The stand in for the godfather was to be John Flynn, a young man from Kincade, a past pupil of Hugh's, who was working in the hospital.

Margaret was ecstatic. Wouldn't this be a story to tell! She was going to sponsor the baby, and in the company of a handsome young man. Well, he wasn't exactly handsome, he was rather small, but she wouldn't tell that to her classmates. And he must be at least twenty. She spent the rest of the evening at home, trying on her best clothes, then trying on Philomena's best clothes, and rehearsing in her mind all the time how she was going to tell the story back at school.

****

The next afternoon, Margaret carried baby Treasa Aideen, with John Flynn walking beside her, the short distance from the ward to the chapel. Philomena accompanied them. On the way, Margaret and Philomena talked non-stop about pretty names, forgetting entirely that the baby had already been named.

The priest was waiting for them at the chapel. When the ceremony started, Margaret and John Flynn recited the responses they had rehearsed the previous day. And when it came to the question of the name the baby was to be christened, Margaret replied unfalteringly, 'Angelina Audrey.'

So Treasa Aideen, who had left the hospital ward half an hour earlier, was, on her return, Angelina Audrey.

CHAPTER 14

'Mammy!' shouted Margaret. 'Angelina's done it again! She's put sticky fingers on my good skirt. She's always ruining my clothes!'

'Well, clean her fingers, can't you?' called Teresa from the kitchen.

'And yesterday she broke my bracelet,' moaned Philomena, taking her cue from Margaret as usual.

Teresa appeared in the doorway, drying her hands.

Kevin sat at the window, saying nothing, while he surreptitiously pushed away the lively three year old who was now trying to climb up the side of his chair.

'Now, look here, you lot,' she said, 'would you stop complaining about your little sister and do a bit to help. Just because you're college students, it doesn't mean that you can lounge about all day. If Angelina has jam on her fingers, would one of you clean it off. Can't you see I'm busy out here with the washing?'

Margaret and Philomena glared at each other, each one muttering that it was the turn of the other to do this unpleasant chore. Kevin sat in his armchair, wearing an expression of disapproval, making it clear that this had nothing to do with him.

The three teenagers, on holiday from boarding school, were bored. Margaret and Philomena missed the company and the conversations with their classmates. Their mother tried to keep them busy with household chores. But they did these so badly, and with such a bad grace that Teresa found it easier to do them herself.

****

Teresa tried to encourage them to go out a bit, rather than spend the days sitting in the house. She suggested that they should make contact with some of the girls they had known at primary school, and go out cycling or swimming as other young people seemed to do. Margaret was quite contemptuous of this suggestion. After spending term time with the daughters of wealthy parents, how could they now mix with girls who came from farming families? Philomena was, predictably, of the same opinion as Margaret. Kevin was just bored, but he was bored anyway, whether he was at home or at school.

During term time, Hugh and Teresa made a monthly visit to the three children at boarding school. Since Angelina was born, they had started going out together more. With the little girl in the back of the car, they took regular outings on Saturdays and Sundays. In good weather, they visited the local seaside resorts. They sometimes brought a picnic, and sometimes had lunch in a hotel. On one Sunday a month, they spent the afternoon visiting the seminary where Kevin went to school, and another day they would visit Margaret and Philomena in their convent boarding school.

Angelina was growing into a happy energetic child. She was petite and pretty, with a porcelain like complexion and bright blue eyes. Unlike the older children, she had inherited her mother's fair hair, which framed her face with a halo of golden curls. She had a happy sociable nature, and, as time went on, she enjoyed the weekly outings as much as her parents did.

One Sunday afternoon, in the sombre parlour of the boys' school, Hugh and Teresa sat talking to Kevin. Angelina was sitting on her mother's knee, but shortly became restless, and scrambled down to the floor. Conversation was stilted. Kevin never had much to say, and from time to time he glanced at his watch as if willing the visit to end soon.

Towards the end of the visit, Father McNamee, the school principal, looked in. While he chatted briefly with the parents, Angelina went over and tugged at his soutane. He looked down, smiling.

'That's Kevin,' said Angelina, pointing to her big brother.

'It is, indeed,' said Father McNamee, patting her head. 'Aren't you the grand little girl? What's your name?'

'Angelina,' she answered. 'And there's my Mammy and Daddy,' she added, pointing to her parents.

Hugh and Teresa laughed at her childish talk. Father McNamee laughed. Angelina, delighted with her success, laughed loudly. Kevin darted furious looks, first at Angelina, then at his parents.

Shortly afterwards, on the way out to the car, Kevin spoke to Hugh and Teresa.

'Don't bring that baby here again,' he ordered them. 'This school is no place for little girls.'

He turned and walked away without saying goodbye. As an afterthought, he turned round to remind them that he wanted jam and biscuits in his next food parcel.

From that day on, either Hugh or Teresa alone visited Kevin, bringing the required food parcel. They regretted that he was so self-conscious and pompous, but they supposed that it was teenage awkwardness, and that he would grow out of it.

****

The visits to the convent school were completely different. Margaret and Philomena greeted their parents enthusiastically, and spent the time telling them the news about their classmates, about their teachers and the nuns, and all the minutiae of day to day school life.

Then they would take Angelina, each of them holding a hand, and lead her down to the recreation hall to see their friends. The other girls would make a fuss of Angelina, talking to her, carrying her around, playing little games with her. Then Margaret and Philomena would bring their little sister back to the parlour, where they would inform Teresa of their needs for next month's parcel. When their parents were leaving, the two girls would follow them out to the door, from where they would wave at the departing car.

Back at home, Hugh and Teresa talked about the school visits. They were pleased that the children were doing well at school, and that there had never been any trouble with them. But both felt a certain unease about their children's attitudes. They often remarked that not one of the three seemed happy. All of them seemed to have an unnecessary preoccupation with their image, with the opinion of their peers, with their standing in the small communities of which they were members.

Hugh wondered about this. He asked himself whether all teenagers were like this. He tried, in vain, to remember how he had felt at their age. But he did not come up with any answers.

Teresa said that this was typical teenage behaviour. Teenagers, she said, had a lot of silly notions, which they would outgrow in time.

****

The summer holidays came, and Hugh went to the two schools to bring the children home. There was little conversation on the way. Out of school, the two girls had little to say to each other. Margaret was quite ebullient by nature, very forceful in her opinions. Philomena, who rarely had an opinion, mostly took her cues from Margaret. Kevin was just not interested in what either of them had to say, and often cast disdainful glances at his sisters when either of them spoke.

At home, they had little time for Angelina. When the girls wanted to show off their pretty little sister to their schoolfriends, that was fine. But at home the three year old was just a nuisance. She had to have her shoes tied, her hair brushed. She had to have stories read to her at bedtime. They strongly resented the chores that came with having a young child in the family.

Often, Teresa tried to reason with them. She reminded them that not so long ago they were small children themselves, having to depend on older people to look after them. She told them that in a family, all should be willing to help each other. Margaret was not convinced. She insisted that when she was three years old she could tie her own shoes and brush her own hair. She was certain of it, she could remember. Angelina was just spoilt, she insisted, it was time someone taught her to do things for herself.

****

It was a good summer, which meant that the turf had been cut, dried and brought home in good time. Hugh always built a turf stack at the back of the house and another behind the school for winter days. In some primary schools, children were asked in the winter to bring a sod of turf per child per week. Father O'Lorcan strongly opposed this practice. He said that it was too much to expect children from a large family, maybe a poor family, to bring along a supply of turf throughout the winter. Hugh and Miss Margan wholeheartedly agreed with him. Father O'Lorcan paid, from parish funds, for a local farmer who had a bit of bogland, to provide a supply of turf for the school. Hugh attended to the delivery of the turf, and stacked it when it arrived.

Last year the turf stack at the back of the school had gone down a lot more quickly than usual, even though they had had just the normal number of fires. Hugh was puzzled about this, and then he found out what had happened.

One afternoon, as the summer holidays approached, some of the sixth class boys were helping Hugh to tidy up the schoolyard. One of the boys, Michael Flannery, had a small brother in tow, a five year old called Patsy who was in the infants' class. The younger classes had gone home, but Patsy had to wait until his older brother was ready to go.

'Are you making another turf stack this year, Master?' asked Patsy, as they swept out the area which normally housed the turf for the winter.

'Yes, Patsy, I am,' answered Hugh.

'My granny says the master's turf is great,' Patsy went on gleefully. 'Doesn't she say that, Michael?'

Michael tried frantically to make the child stop talking.

'Would you shoosh, Patsy,' he ordered crossly, 'and let us get on with our work.'

'And how does your granny know,' asked Hugh, 'that the master's turf is great?'

'Because we had it on the fire all winter,' said Patsy. 'Granny brings it home in her shopping bag. And she says the master would never miss it because he's rich and he can buy more.'

'Don't mind him, Master,' said Michael, red faced and furious. 'He's only ravin'. And Patsy, you shut up and stop talkin' nonsense. I'll tell Mammy on you.'

When Hugh thought about it, he remembered several occasions during the past winter when he had seen Nellie Downes, Patsy's granny, at the back of the school. She had always said hello, and chatted a bit, explaining why she was there. Patsy had lost his pencil, she might say. He dropped it at playtime, and then he couldn't find it, so she came back to look for it. Or another day she might say that she had come to take Patsy home. She hadn't realised that the infants' class had already gone.

Hugh had taken little heed of these visitations. He had thought that Nellie was a bit confused. He now remembered that she always carried a large shopping bag. Maybe she wasn't so confused after all.

In August, Hugh was again stacking the turf at the back of his house. He had the school turf delivered with his own, and was building the two stacks side by side.

Nellie Downes came up the road. She normally went up and down the road three or four times a day. She was carrying her large shopping bag.

'That's a grand stack of turf you're building there, Master,' she called out.

'It is, Nellie,' he answered. 'It won't be so easy to get into the shopping bag from here.'

'True for you, Master,' she answered. 'It was grand and handy there at the back of the school.'

And she made her way up the road, carrying her bag, which Hugh noticed was tightly packed with something that looked like a bundle of hay.

****

'I'm going to be a nurse when I leave school,' announced Margaret, as they all sat round the table after tea one evening.

'That's good, Margaret,' said Hugh. 'It's a good job. I think you'd like it.'

'I didn't know you were interested in nursing, Margaret,' said Teresa. 'But I'm pleased to hear it. Many a time I thought I might have liked nursing myself. As your Dad says, it's a good job. I'm sure you'd find it very satisfying.'

'If you go to be a nurse in a hospital, you could marry a doctor,' Margaret went on, job satisfaction low on her list of priorities.

'Veronica Draine's sister was a nurse in the hospital, and when she was twenty she married a doctor. And Nancy Lunny's sister started nursing last year and she's engaged to a doctor already.'

'Margaret!' exclaimed Teresa. 'You're not seriously contemplating going into nursing just to marry a doctor?'

'Of course I am,' said Margaret smugly. 'Why not? That's where the money is these days. When I have a family of my own, they are not going to grow up in poverty the way we did.'

'Don't be ridiculous, Margaret,' said Hugh angrily. 'You didn't grow up in poverty. We certainly are not wealthy, but none of you has ever wanted for anything.'

'Well, why don't we have a decent car, then?' demanded Margaret. 'I'm ashamed when you come visiting in that battered old thing. All the other girls' parents have good cars. And their young sisters come to visit properly dressed, in coats with velvet collars. You brought Angelina to the school all winter in that tartan duffel coat. I'm sure everyone is talking about us.'

'I'm going to be a nurse as well,' said Philomena.

Hugh and Teresa tried, at length, to talk sense to the two girls. They did not need a new car, because the one they had was adequate for their needs. Angelina would of course have a new coat for next winter, but the tartan duffel coat had been all right. It was warm and practical. Velvet collared coats were quite impractical for young children.

'Anyway, we should have a maid,' said Margaret. 'We shouldn't have to wash dishes and make beds when we're at home. All the other girls in my class have a maid, except Marie Harbinson, and she's just a nobody.'

She flounced out of the room and went upstairs, where she spent the rest of the evening re-reading letters received from her classmates since the start of the holidays, and looking at school snapshots.

'Don't worry about her, Hugh,' said Teresa. 'It's just a phase. Lots of teenage girls have notions like that.'

Hugh nodded. 'I suppose so,' he said. 'She'll grow out of it.'

But both Hugh and Teresa felt saddened by Margaret's attitude, and both were slightly uneasy in case she wouldn't change.

Philomena dashed up the stairs to let Margaret know that she was going through a phase, and was expected to grow out of it.

CHAPTER 15

In 1962 Miss Margan retired. Her place in the infant classroom was filled by Josie O'Donoghue, a young teacher, just qualified.

Over the last ten years, the numbers on the school roll had nearly doubled. Both classrooms were crowded. The desks with bench seat attached, intended for seating two pupils, now had to take three. The long narrow benches along the side walls of the classroom were packed to overflowing.

Hugh had discussed this problem with Father O'Lorcan on a few occasions. One day he came into the school to see for himself.

'Yes, yes, Mr Staunton,' he said, 'you've too many pupils. I'll employ another teacher.'

'We have the numbers for another teacher, Father,' said Hugh, 'but where would you put another teacher? We need another room.'

'We'll see, we'll see,' said Father O'Lorcan, as he walked away.

Another new teacher was appointed a short time later. A young man called Tom Kenny, who had worked for a few years in Dublin, joined the staff. Hugh put him in charge of second, third and fourth classes. This meant that he worked sometimes in Hugh's room, sometimes in Miss O'Donoghue's room. It was not a successful arrangement.

Hugh called with Father O'Lorcan again, and outlined the difficulties of the new situation. Father O'Lorcan promised to look into it, and the next day he arrived again at the school.

'You need to see them at work to realise how impossible it is,' said Hugh, as he led Father O'Lorcan into the junior classroom. Miss O'Donoghue was practising spellings with her class, while Master O'Donoghue was explaining multiplication sums to second class.

'It can't be done,' explained Hugh, 'having two teachers working together in such a small space. The very idea of second class trying to concentrate on arithmetic, while first class are reciting spellings at the top of their voices, is, as you can see, a problem. And I know, when Mr Kenny is working in my room, the pupils sometimes become confused about which of us they are supposed to be listening to. The classwork is bound to suffer.'

Father O'Lorcan agreed that there was a problem, and accompanied Hugh back to his desk, where they discussed it at length.

'And it's not just a matter of building another room,' explained Hugh.

He pointed out, in detail, all the inadequacies of the present building, the outside toilets, the twelve hooks in the porch which were supposed to accomodate the coats of fifty children, the very small playground, where, due to increased numbers, minor accidents were becoming a day-to-day occurrence. He invited Father O'Lorcan to look through the roll books with him. It was in the three junior classes, lower infants, higher infants and first class that the numbers had dramatically increased. There were now over twenty in each of these classes, where the average intake used to be ten.

'And you know yourself, Father,' Hugh added, 'that there is at the moment a large number of young married couples in the area, new bungalows going up everywhere, and there are even people working in the towns who prefer to live out here. If this trend continues, within three or four years we'll have a hundred and sixty on the roll. It's not just another room we'll be looking for. We need a new building with five classrooms.'

'We'll see, we'll see,' said Father O'Lorcan, lifting his hat and walking stick as he rose to leave.

****

A few days later, Father O'Lorcan set off for Dublin. Hugh had advised him that their local TD was the best person to approach the Department of Education on the subject of an extended school building.

Father O'Lorcan had brushed aside the idea. We need this school building quickly, he had pointed out, so why waste time with TDs and their likes when you can just go straight to the Department yourself?

He climbed into his car, pushed his hat to the back of his head, and set off on the long drive. The next day he returned, well pleased with his venture.

Within a few weeks, Hugh had a visit from an inspector who examined the roll books and had a look at the classrooms. He had no hesitation in backing up Father O'Lorcan's case.

Shortly the plans for the new school were set in motion. A site was decided on, in a field adjacent to the school. The building was designed, the site was cleared.

On Sundays, Father O'Lorcan constantly harangued the congregation to support fund raising for the new school. Cake sales, bazaars, guest teas, sales of work were all being run to help finance the new venture.

Miss Margan, even though she was retired, was very pleased to help by organising concerts and plays.

Father O'Lorcan was continually in evidence, strolling round the site, watching the work in progress, asking questions, ensuring that everything was being done according to his specifications.

The overflow of pupils from the small school building was now transferred, on a temporary basis, to the parish hall.

Two years later, in the autumn of 1964, the new school was ready to open.

****

On a summer evening, shortly before the start of term, Hugh and Teresa walked round to the new building to have a look. Hugh thought with satisfaction about the coming term, when they would escape from the cramped conditions of the old school, and the classes which had been lodged in the hall would now have proper accomodation. Teresa also was very impressed with the new building.

Back home, as they sat having their supper, both were aware of a certain uneasiness.

'It's a fine new school,' said Hugh, 'and I'm pleased to see it finished. It marks a new era, the end of the old primary school. It's a change for the better.'

'It is, indeed,' said Teresa. 'It's good to see the children getting the chance to work in a fine new building. Time flies, and everything changes. And, you know, Hugh, I'm sometimes a bit anxious about the future.'

Teresa had voiced Hugh's unspoken anxiety. He was acutely aware that it was eight years until retiring age, that when he retired they would no longer have the school residence at their disposal. Money had never been plentiful, and with Margaret and Philomena both trainee nurses, and Kevin going to Maynooth in the autumn, things were not likely to improve. Angelina was still at primary school, so there would be her education to think about.

'I've been wondering about that,' he said. 'I mean, about where we'll live when I retire. Maybe we could go to Murgintra. We could build a bungalow in the small field up beside the quarry. That field was never any use for growing anything.'

As he spoke, a number of confused thoughts flashed across his mind. Murgintra. Timothy. Teresa. He looked across at his wife, at this placid,

94

loving woman with whom he had shared so many years. He rarely thought nowadays of the Murgintra interlude, over twenty years back. But the thought of going back to live there, of having a home built in the small field beside the quarry, filled him with conflicting emotions. He wished he had not made the suggestion.

'I'd really prefer to stay here,' said Teresa. 'I know we haven't much money, but we could start looking out for a small site, or a small house in this area.'

'I think you're right,' he said, relieved.

'We've been here a long time,' continued Teresa. 'We've put down roots. We have a good life, and we've made friends here. I feel that I belong here more than I could belong anywhere else.'

****

Margaret, now in her second year nursing, came home one weekend with her boyfriend. He was Peadar Gillen, a young doctor from the hospital where she was working. He was a very pleasant young man, and got on very well with the family. Predictably, he caused quite a stir in Kincade, as he and Margaret had arrived in a brand new car. And predictably, Margaret made sure that the information slipped out that Peadar was a doctor.

CHAPTER 16

'And so both Margaret and Philomena have gone into nursing,' remarked Anne, as they sat in the car on the way from Wicklow to Kincade. 'And Kevin's going to Maynooth. What a blessing! Though I don't mind telling you that I've had all the nuns praying for a vocation in the family. They'll be delighted to hear their prayers have been answered.'

Hugh and Teresa, with Angelina, had been spending a few days in Dublin. They had called with Anne, who was now permitted to leave her convent on family visits. This was her first time outside the convent since before she had entered, forty-three years earlier. They were now on their way home to Kincade, where Anne was going to spend a week, before going to Catherine's home in Galway. She would have liked to visit also to their home place in Murgintra, she had said, but she had to be back in her convent at the end of the second week, so she couldn't possibly fit it in.

'So it's great that we've one vocation in the family anyway,' continued Anne. 'I always thought that one of Dominic's girls might have entered. But they were running to dances from no age. And what about Angelina?'

She put her arm round the shoulder of the young girl sitting beside her in the back of the car.

'You'd make a grand little nun, Angelina,' she said. 'What age are you now?'

'Seven,' answered Angelina.

'Now, don't forget,' said Anne, 'when you're seventeen or eighteen, you can be a nun.

'And I hear that Margaret has a boyfriend,' she added.

'Yes,' said Teresa. 'He's called Peadar Gillen. He's a very nice fellow. He comes home with Margaret sometimes at the weekend.'

'And he's a doctor, I hear,' went on Anne. 'I always knew Margaret would choose well. A sensible girl she was always.

'But don't you go getting a boyfriend,' she said to Angelina, laughing and hugging her playfully. 'Remember, you're going to be a little nun!'

Later, at home, Angelina asked her mother, 'Mammy, do I really have to be a nun?'

'Not at all, dear,' said Teresa, giving a despairing look towards the ceiling, while Anne was unpacking in the room above.

An hour later, Teresa sent Angelina to tell her father and Auntie Anne, who were chatting in the living room, that dinner was ready. In honour of their guest, Teresa had set the table with a linen tablecloth and the best china. As Anne entered, Teresa directed her to a chair beside the window, where she sat until Teresa had served the meal.

'Do you not have a dining room?' asked Anne, looking enquiringly around.

'No, we don't,' said Hugh. 'We always eat in the kitchen. But we don't need a dining room. There's plenty of space here, and with the range it's always warm in the winter.'

'All the other nuns who go home have their meals in the dining room,' Anne pointed out. 'Even if their families usually eat in the kitchen themselves, they would use the dining room when a nun or priest is visiting. Out of respect, you know.'

'Well, I suppose while you're here, we could have our meals at the living room table, if you'd prefer that,' said Teresa.

'Yes, I think that would be more suitable,' said Anne.

A minute later, when they had started their meal, Anne, her knife and fork still unlifted, was looking puzzled, irritated.

'I thought we were going to eat in the living room?' she said enquiringly.

Patiently, Hugh, Teresa and Angelina lifted the dishes, cutlery and tablecloth, and moved everything across the hall, into the living room, where they set the table. Anne sat, her hands folded in her lap, until all was ready. Then they all had a rather cool dinner.

Somehow, Anne had the knack of making them feel in the wrong, making them feel that she, as a nun, was entitled to a degree of respect that they were not showing.

It was going to be a very long week.

****

'Can we go to visit your parish priest today?' Anne asked. 'It's my second last day here.'

'Father O'Lorcan? Why?' asked Hugh.

'When nuns go to visit their families it is customary to take them to visit the parish priest,' Anne answered. 'The parish priest, and some pious families of the parish. Five days I've been here, and you haven't

97

introduced me to anybody, except that woman Miss Margan, that retired teacher who called the other day, the one with the red dress and earrings. I can't imagine what type she is, dressing up like that at her age.'

Hugh and Teresa exchanged covert glances. They would, later, be able to laugh at those ridiculous remarks. But now, it was anything for a quiet life.

'All right,' said Hugh. 'We'll go and see Father O'Lorcan.'

On the way round to the parochial house, they were greeted by some of the local people. Anne smiled graciously in return. She remarked to Hugh that it was such a fine thing that the people of Ireland had such respect for nuns, and she was not entirely convinced when Hugh told her that they always spoke to him, or Teresa, or the children, when they met them out walking.

As they arrived, they met Father O'Lorcan at the door, carrying his hat and walking stick, obviously on the point of going out.

'Ah, good morning, Mr Staunton,' he said. 'Would you believe it, I was just going round to see you.'

'Good morning, Father,' said Hugh. 'This is my sister, Sister Assumpta from Wicklow. She's on holiday with us for a week.'

'Pleased to meet you, Sister,' said the old man. 'Sadie!' he called to the housekeeper. 'Would you take Sister Assumpta into the parlour and give her a cup of tea? Mr Staunton and I have things to talk about.'

Sadie led Anne into the parlour, and Father O'Lorcan and Hugh strolled to the gate.

'We're going over to see to a few things in the old school,' said Father O'Lorcan.

When they reached the school building they went in, and discussed at length what classroom furniture was worth keeping and transferring to the new building. All the desks could be kept, they decided, even though they were an old style, they were still solid and serviceable. The benches were wobbly, had been repaired several times, and were on the point of disintegrating altogether. They could be discarded. The cupboards were in good condition, a coat of paint would freshen them up. The teacher's desk would be quite out of place, they both agreed. Hugh's office in the new school was already equipped with a modern desk, a flat-topped table with drawers down the side.

'I'd like to keep the old desk myself,' said Hugh. 'I've always wanted a writing desk in the house.'

He sat down at the desk, and glanced, a shade nostalgically, round the empty classroom.

'Surely, that's a good idea,' said Father O'Lorcan, as he put down his walking stick and sat on top of the front desk, facing Hugh.

'A long time you've been here, Mr Staunton,' he continued. 'It seems like only last week you arrived here, straight from Scotland.'

'It's twenty-seven years now since I came,' answered Hugh. 'A long time. And a lot of changes have taken place.'

'Time flies,' remarked Father O'Lorcan. 'Tempus fugit. And everything changes, no matter how much you want to keep it the same. Tell me, Mr Staunton, what do you intend to do when you retire? Will you go back to the farm?'

'I don't think so,' said Hugh. 'I've been too long away from Murgintra now. There's nothing there for me now, and Teresa would be lost in a place like that. We've been here a long time, and it's here we'd like to stay. I suppose we should be thinking of a small house, or a bungalow in this area.'

'You see this school?' said Father O'Lorcan, glancing round the empty building. 'There are buildings like this all over the country. A new school is built, the old school is left to go derelict. When I was in Donegal last summer, I saw no less than three buildings like this, stone walls, fine slate roof, just standing empty.

'What I'm saying to you, Mr Staunton, is that you could have this old school, get it converted into a bungalow, and you'd have a home for your retirement. We could decide on a suitable price. What do you think?'

Hugh didn't take long to think.

'The idea appeals to me a lot, Father,' he said. 'I'd have to discuss it with Teresa, but I know she'd be interested. I'll get back to you in a few days.'

****

'Father O'Lorcan seems to be a very nice man,' said Anne, as she and Hugh made their way back to the house. 'He seems a bit quiet, though.'

Hugh did not answer, he was preoccupied with his thoughts.

Anne was thinking of her return to the convent, where she would be able to tell how she had met the parish priest, how she had had tea in the parochial house. But she wouldn't say that when she arrived he just went out and didn't come back for an hour. No, she'd leave out that bit. She would just say that he was a very quiet man who didn't have much to say.

At the end of the week, Hugh drove Anne to Catherine's home in Galway. As he left, he wished Catherine well. Back home, he and Teresa recalled at length and laughed at the ludicrous style of life Anne had imposed on them for a week. Even Angelina joined in the laughter, happy now in the knowledge that she did not really have to be a nun.

And they discussed Father O'Lorcan's suggestion about the conversion of the old school into a bungalow. Both were very well pleased with the prospect.

CHAPTER 17

Towards the end of the summer Margaret was engaged to Peadar Gillen. They were to get married the following year, and were making preparations to buy a house in Sligo, where Peadar was now a partner in a local practice.

Margaret and Peadar came to Kincade for a few days, accompanied by Philomena. Margaret made a point of letting everyone know of her engagement. She left Peadar in the house, chatting with her parents, while she strolled round in a smart new suit, with her engagement ring very much in evidence. She talked at length, to people she had barely condescended to acknowledge in the past. She told all and sundry about her wedding plans, about Peadar's job, about the fine house they intended to buy in Sligo.

Back in the house, she seriously advised Philomena about how to catch a suitable husband. She mentioned a few young doctors of their acquaintance who would be eligible, and told Philomena about which dances and social functions they were likely to frequent.

Philomena, always in agreement with Margaret, and envious of her good fortune, promised that she would do as advised.

****

Hugh and Teresa, after the minimum of discussion, decided to accept Father O'Lorcan's offer to sell the old school house. He sold it to them for a reasonable sum, and insisted on having receipts and documents properly in order.

'I'm getting on in years,' he explained to them. 'When I've passed on, a new fellow might come who wouldn't be entirely in favour of selling parish property. I want to see that everything's in order.'

Together they looked over the old building, measured it, and drew a scale plan of how it could be converted. The senior classroom would become a living room, with a smaller room leading off towards the back which could be a small sitting room or a bedroom. A wide area of the junior classroom around the chimney breast, could be made into a kitchen, and a passage could be built down the side of the kitchen, leading to a bedroom and bathroom. The porch could be converted into a fine spacious hallway. Father O'Lorcan pointed out that the roof was pitched high enough to have a staircase and attic space.

There was a big heavy door which had not been opened for years, at the back of the junior room. It would have opened out into the playground, but Miss Margan had always said there was a draught, and had insisted that it should be bolted and barred and insulated. It had even been painted over, the last few times the walls had been done, in the unchanging shade of dark green, and now merged, almost invisible, with the surrounding wall.

They looked at the door, and decided that it would be a good idea to remove it, and have a new door fitted, leading out to the back.

'Silly bat,' muttered Father O'Lorcan, as he usually did when anything reminiscent of Miss Margan's teaching days was mentioned.

The schoolyard, too small and totally inadequate for the games and recreation of the pupils, would be ideal for a garden, with a lawn at the front, and maybe a vegetable garden at the back.

Hugh and Teresa were both very pleased with the plans. There was no hurry with the conversion, as they had several years to have it completed. There would be no shortage of labour. Hugh had many past pupils in the locality who were experts in the various areas of building, and who would be only too pleased to get a bit of extra work.

Margaret, preoccupied with strolling round the village arm in arm with Peadar, showed no interest in the plans for the new home. Philomena, also preoccupied with Margaret's engagement and wedding plans, was no more interested. Kevin sat in the living room of the school house, a gauche eighteen year old in clerical black, who had no interest in either wedding plans or house plans.

'Margaret, can I be your bridesmaid?' asked Angelina one evening, when they had been talking about the wedding.

'Don't be silly, Angelina!' snapped Margaret. 'Philomena's the bridesmaid. You're far too young. And you wouldn't know how to behave yourself.'

Seeing Angelina's look of complete disappointment, Peadar intervened.

'Angelina could be flower girl, couldn't she?' he asked.

'Oh, I suppose so,' said Margaret. She hadn't thought of having a flower girl, but now it seemed quite a good idea.

Later, Peadar pointed out to Margaret that Angelina had seemed very unhappy when Margaret had told her quite brusquely that she couldn't be a bridesmaid.

'Not at all,' said Margaret. 'She's only seven. What would she know about weddings?'

'A seven year old girl still has feelings,' explained Peadar. 'A wedding is a big family event, and a child of seven naturally wants to feel part of it.'

'I suppose you're right,' said Margaret, who didn't suppose anything of the sort. She just wanted to get on with the more pressing business of who was to be included on the guest list.

Since the initial excitement of Angelina's birth and christening, Margaret had shown little interest in her little sister.

****

A few months of frantic preparation followed. There was the wedding dress, the bridesmaid's dress, the flower girl's dress, to be designed and made. There was the mother of the bride's outfit. Margaret took a very emphatic interest in the choice of this item. It was most important to impress the Gillens, she explained.

Having put down a deposit on their new house, Margaret and Peadar were busy with furnishings and decoration.

And, as the day drew closer, there was much fuss about the cake, the bouquets, the taxis, and many, many other items.

On the morning of the wedding, Angelina was sternly warned by her two sisters to behave herself, and not to make a show of herself in front of the Gillens.

Philomena, elegant in her bridesmaid's dress of pale pink, was warned by Margaret about the best man, Peadar's brother Cathal.

'Don't get too friendly with him,' she instructed. 'He's a very nice fellow, but he's only a teacher.'

Philomena, much to Margaret's annoyance, had not so far managed to establish a relationship with a doctor in the hospital.

Teresa, on the wedding day, felt strangely sentimental. Her mind went back to her own wedding, and to all that had happened since. In one way it seemed a long, long time, an eternity away. In another way, it felt like yesterday.

Hugh, in his role as father of the bride, was his usual sociable self. He was always hospitable, welcoming, tending to be quite flamboyant in company. He was very popular, and, Margaret noticed with some satisfaction, got on very well with the Gillens.

Kevin, home from the seminary, in clerical black, was bored.

CHAPTER 18

Miss Margan, in her retirement, kept up her keen interest in drama. She was a well known figure in local drama festivals, and a very popular actress. In fact, Mags Margan had become a household name, and her participation usually ensured a good attendance at plays in parish halls throughout the area.

Her last performance was in the role of Bessie Burgess, in 'The Plough and the Stars', which was running for four evenings in Sligo. The first three evenings had been very successful, and on the final night the hall was packed to capacity.

Miss Margan gave a truly splendid performance. She really surpassed herself that night. She was humorous where possible, irreverent where possible, sympathetic when necessary.

Towards the end of the last scene, Bessie Burgess died most dramatically, after remonstrating with the poor demented Nora who had unwittingly caused her death.

And it was only, a few minutes later, when the curtain went down, and the cast assembled to make their final bow, that they realised that Miss Margan had made her final bow. She had died with Bessie Burgess.

****

As time went on, Margaret and Peadar had three children. Irish names, which, a decade or two back, had been considered unfashionable, were now very much in style. Margaret drove regularly over to Kincade, with Feargal, Sinead and Oisin in the back of the car. She often left the children with their grandparents for the day on Saturday, and sometimes overnight, while she went golfing or socialising.

Angelina was now at secondary school. As there was an improved bus service, she did not have to board, but set off on the early bus every morning. Sometimes Hugh would drive in to meet her in the afternoon, and on the way home, on some of these journeys, he taught her to drive.

'You never know when you might need to be able to drive,' he said.

When Margaret left her children in her mother's care, she left strict instructions about what they could eat, where they could play, and, specifically, she insisted that they were not to be left in Angelina's care.

Angelina was too flighty, she said, she might neglect to keep a careful eye on them.

Angelina was far from flighty. She was a lively, extrovert girl, very fond of children. She would not have let them out of her sight for an instant. In fact, she couldn't wait for Margaret to go on her messages, so that she could sit on the floor and play with them undisturbed.

Philomena was still nursing in the hospital, and much to Margaret's concern, had failed so far to make a suitable match.

'You'll need to get your skates on,' insisted Margaret. 'You're twenty-six this year, and not one day further on than when you started nursing.'

Philomena was apologetic.

'I don't know what it is, Margaret,' she complained, 'but as soon as an eligible man comes on the scene, he seems to disappear with someone else.'

'You're just not trying hard enough,' said Margaret sharply. 'Get your act together. We're having a bit of a party in our house next weekend. Have a hair-do, and get dressed up and come along. We'll see if we can fix something for you.'

Margaret's weekend soirées became regular events, but another year passed with Philomena still unattached.

****

In 1972, Hugh retired. There was a presentation party in the parish hall. Tom Kenny, who was to take over the post of principal in the primary school, made a speech in praise of Hugh's great work in the school over the years. Father O'Lorcan, now in his eighty-eighth year, also spoke in glowing terms about Mr Staunton's contribution to the life of the community. He was presented with a writing desk from the parish, and book tokens from the pupils of the school. There was a concert to follow, which was quite enjoyable, but which everyone agreed was not of the same calibre as the concerts in Miss Margan's time.

The next day, Hugh, Teresa and Angelina moved across the road to their new home. The old school building had been converted, at a leisurely pace, over the last few years, into a very attractive home.

Tom Kenny and his wife Josie, the young teacher who had started in Kincade at the same time, now moved into the school residence.

Hugh did not have much difficulty adjusting to retirement. He had his golf, his books, his garden. He enjoyed driving to Sligo, and Teresa sometimes accompanied him. Sometimes they would call with Margaret and her family, sometimes they would meet Philomena in town. And they could always lift Angelina from school, and maybe give her a driving lesson on the way home.

Kevin, now a curate in a County Longford parish, came to visit occasionally.

Angelina sometimes did baby-sitting for Tom and Josie Kenny. It was like home from home, baby-sitting in the house where she had spent her childhood. More and more she found that she enjoyed working with children, and dreamed of the day when she would have a career, maybe as a children's nurse, or an infants' teacher.

But that was away in the future, and, when the baby-sitting was over, she turned her attention to the more immediate issues of friends, socialising, dances and cinemas.

CHAPTER 19

In 1974, Angelina's last year at secondary school, she failed her Leaving Cert. After the initial disappointment, there was the problem of deciding what to do next. Teresa and Hugh were both of the opinion that she should train for something, but Angelina had, so far, shown no interest in any career, except, vaguely, working with children.

The Kennys' home help was leaving, she was getting married and going to live in Ballina. Angelina had done baby-sitting for the Kennys, on Friday evenings, and at weekends, for the last two years. She had stayed overnight on a few occasions when the parents were away. The daytime job was now available. The Kennys would have been happy, Angelina would have been happy, Hugh would have been happy, if she was willing to take it. Teresa had misgivings. It might be all right for a year, she thought, but in the long run Angelina should do a course in something that would be useful for further employment.

During this discussion Margaret breezed in. She was about to deposit her children while she went golfing.

'Well, I'm not surprised she failed,' she started. 'The way she was skiting about all year, what else could you expect? Running to dances and films all the time, with that scruffy crowd she knocks about with.'

Margaret, as usual, did not speak directly to Angelina, but referred to her in the third person, while addressing other members of the family.

Angelina felt upset and miserable. Of course she knew that she should have studied more for her exam. But Margaret was being unduly hard on her.

'So what's she going to do now?' pursued Margaret. 'Not going back to school, I hope, with the other dumdums who failed?'

'We thought she might work with the Kennys for a year,' said Teresa. 'It would give her time to think what she wants to do eventually, and then she could maybe enrol for a course this time next year ....'

'She'll do nothing of the sort!' snapped Margaret. 'You know, Mum, I really don't understand you. Skivvying for the Kennys, and her the headmaster's daughter. What would the Gillens say, or what could I tell them at all? You're out of your mind to even think about it.'

'Well, what would you suggest?' asked Teresa.

'Send her to France. Get her an au pair job for a year. Wasn't she good enough at French at school? At least, it's one of the subjects she didn't fail. After that, we could decide what to do next.'

'Am I right in thinking,' asked Hugh, 'that au pair work is child minding and housework, just the same as she'd be doing in Kennys'?'

'It is, of course,' answered Margaret. 'But nobody here would know that. You just tell everyone that Angelina's in France, and that's it.'

Hugh and Teresa, both having grown up in families where it was a struggle to make ends meet, and where education had been achieved by dint of substantial sacrifices, had not reached the stage where they could be relaxed about the situation. They knew Angelina was bitterly disappointed. They would both have liked to keep her at home for a while, working for the Kennys, and then see her happier in herself before she moved on. She was now seventeen, and Hugh remembered that every member of his own family, except Timothy, had left home at that age. Dominic had been at university at the age of seventeen, Anne had been a novice in the convent. Both he and Catherine had been at teacher training colleges.

Margaret was rattling on.

'Jean Morris, that's Doctor Morris's wife, was telling me about her daughters. They are both students at UCG, and every summer they go to Paris. There's a convent there of Irish nuns who fix girls up with au pair jobs. I'll see Jean this evening, and we'll see what we can do.'

****

A few weeks later, Hugh and Teresa made the journey to Rosslare by car to take Angelina to the overnight ferry to France. Jean Morris had made the contact, and, as it happened, the nuns knew of a family who wanted an au pair immediately, for a year.

Angelina was excited, but bewildered. It had all happened so suddenly. One minute she was comfortably at home, in the security and comfort she had known throughout her childhood. Now she was catapulted into the unknown, to a foreign country where she would know nobody. It was all quite frightening, and when she said goodbye to her parents at the boat, she was close to tears.

'Don't worry, love,' her mother reassured her. 'We'll write to you every week, and don't you forget to write back! And you'll be home again next summer.'

'It's a great chance,' Hugh tried to persuade her. 'You'll see a foreign country, and get to know what life is like abroad. I wish there had been chances like this when I was young.'

Angelina was not convinced that there was any good reason, at that moment, for being on this journey. She had been the envy of her friends at home when she told them she was going to spend a year in France. To be out of a backwater like Kincade, to be living abroad, away from parental restrictions for a year, was, to them, incredibly good luck. But as Angelina started her journey, she would have given anything to be back home.

The night on the boat seemed very, very long. The cabin was stuffy, and Angelina was sharing with a middle-aged woman who kept talking about an operation she had had the previous year. Every time she dozed off during the night, she woke up a few minutes later. When morning came, she was totally worn out. She tried to eat some breakfast, but had no appetite. And it was a long, tedious spell until the boat docked at last, in early afternoon, in Le Havre.

Next was the train journey to Paris. Jean Morris had asked her daughter, who had made this journey several times, to explain the itinerary to Angelina. They had recommended that when she reached Paris she was to take a taxi to the convent, where the nuns would tell her where to go next.

Uneasily, Angelina remembered the warnings her two sisters had given before she had left home.

'Have you warned her about not talking to strangers?' Margaret had asked her mother, as they were all discussing the travel plans. 'They're all over the place in France, trying to pick up young girls. And it's the stupid ones like her would get picked up.'

Philomena had agreed with this. Some of the nurses she knew had been on holiday in France last year.

'The French men are lechers,' she informed them. 'Oversexed they are. It's something to do with the climate, or maybe the food. They're out there all the time, with just the one thing in their minds.'

When Angelina got off the train at Paris, she looked around, wondering where to find a taxi. What was the French for taxi, she asked herself. She remembered a word, 'fiacre' she thought it was, from some French book at school. As she looked around anxiously, she saw a man approaching her. He was walking straight in her direction, he was smiling. Help! she thought to herself, here's one of those French lechers Margaret and Philomena were talking about. What will I do?

While she panicked over the next move, the man spoke.

'Hello,' he said. 'Aren't you Angelina? Kevin Staunton's sister? I saw you at the ordination. I was ordained the same day as Kevin.'

Torn between relief at finding that this was not a lecherous Frenchman lying in wait for her arrival, and bemusement that someone from Ireland had actually recognised her, Angelina managed to answer.

The man continued.

'I'm Joe Fagan,' he said. 'I don't suppose you remember me. Well, there were a lot of us ordained that day, weren't there? I'm on holiday here for a fortnight, in fact I'm doing a course at the Alliance Francaise. Don't be alarmed that I'm not dressed as a priest, when you're out of Ireland nobody bothers.'

'Joe,' said Angelina, 'oh, sorry, I mean Father, can you tell me the French for taxi? Is it fiacre?'

'Joe will do all right,' he answered. 'The word for taxi is the same, just taxi.' He pointed towards an exit, where there was a line of taxis, with the familiar word on top of each vehicle. 'A fiacre was a horse drawn cab, centuries ago. It seems this sort of transport was introduced by Saint Fiachra. An Irishman, of course.' Noticing Angelina's anxiety, he said, 'How about a coffee? You must be tired after the journey. And then I'll get you a taxi, or a fiacre, whichever you prefer!'

Angelina was only too pleased to be able to sit down in the coffee bar, and collect her thoughts.

Over a cup of coffee, they talked about Angelina's plans for the coming year, about the convent she was going to, about the nuns who had found her a job. Joe advised her about taking a taxi, about having the right change ready, about tipping the driver. They went to a bureau de change, where Joe, speaking in fluent French, changed one of her notes into suitable combinations of small change. He then found her a taxi, and wished her well as she set off for her destination.

'Vingt-huit, Rue de Lubeck,' she said to the taxi driver, who looked quite puzzled and impatient. It seemed that her Sligo French was not intelligible to the Parisians. She showed him a slip of paper with the address written on it, and he set off at a frantic speed, depositing her very shortly at the door of the convent.

She stood, bewildered, on the pavement. She was faced with a high, blank door. She rang the doorbell, and heard a buzzing sound. In a moment of panic, she hoped no one would answer. She felt very small and frightened, in a strange country, arriving at a convent of strange nuns, going to work with a strange family.

She rang again. After some minutes, the door opened, and a young nun stood in the doorway.

'Hello,' said the nun. 'Would you be the girl from Sligo? Angelina Staunton?'

Angelina put her cases down in the hallway, and dissolved into tears.

CHAPTER 20

'Now, the first thing you need,' said Sister Aine, 'is a cup of tea. After that, you'll have a rest. And then we'll see what to do next.'

While Angelina drank her tea, sitting in the reception area of the convent, she heard Sister Aine on the phone, conversing in French with someone. She was saying that the Irish girl had arrived, and would be ready to start work on Monday. This was Friday, Angelina thought. She was quite relieved to hear that she would have two days before starting work. She did not feel ready to cope with anything at the moment.

Shortly afterwards, Sister Aine took her to a small bedroom, where she closed the curtains, telling Angelina to sleep as long as she wanted.

It seemed like a long time afterwards that she woke up, from a sleep riddled with dreams, dreams about a woman in a boat cabin who had had an operation, about a priest in plain clothes who had got change of a five hundred franc note, about a Paris taxi driver speeding through the town centre in Sligo, about a tall terrace building with an inscrutable front door, about a French woman with five or six very large and very unruly children who had come to live in the Kennys' house in Kincade.

Exhausted, but relaxed, Angelina woke up, to see Sister Aine at her side, carrying a tray with pancakes, tea and jam.

Sister Aine sat down, and chatted while Angelina had her tea. She had hoped to find a room for Angelina for the weekend, she said. The hostel was full, but they would work something out. The room where she was at the moment was Sister Aine's own room. Of course she could stay there if necessary, but they'd see what would turn up. There would shortly be a meal for the students in the dining room. Would Angelina like to join them? There were a few Irish girls who were very nice, and would help her to settle in.

After dinner with the students that evening, Angelina felt quite at home. She had got to know Mary Conlon from Waterford and June McConomy from Clare. Later, she saw Sister Aine, who seemed very pleased about something.

'I knew something would turn up,' she said triumphantly. 'Susan Gilroy has just phoned in to say she's staying with friends in Fontainebleau for the weekend. So you can have her bed. She shares room seven, on the first landing, with another Irish girl and an American girl. So you'll be all right until Monday.'

'Staying with friends in Fontainebleau? What friends?' demanded a sharp-faced middle-aged nun who was looking round the doorway.

'I don't know what friends. She never said what friends,' answered Sister Aine.

'And you didn't ask her? And what am I going to say if Susan Gilroy's uncle Father Corr from Mullingar rings tonight? Am I to say she's away in Fontainebleau, and I don't know with whom, or why? What, in heaven's name, am I going to tell him?'

'Tell him to take a running jump to himself,' said Sister Aine, audibly enough to make Angelina giggle, but keeping carefully out of earshot of the older nun.

****

Over the weekend, Sister Aine took Angelina out and showed her around the area. They walked to the street where Madame Thibault, her future employer, lived. They strolled around the markets and the shops. On Saturday they walked up to Chaillot to look at the Eiffel Tower.

By Sunday, Angelina had reached the conclusion that Paris was not such a bad place after all. That evening, in the bedroom, she wrote a letter to her parents. She let them know that that Paris was all right, that the nuns were very good to her, that she had met quite a few Irish girls in the hostel. She gave them the address of her new employer, and promised to write again soon.

When Angelina was leaving to go to her work on Monday, Sister Aine invited her to come back any time, on her day off, or whenever she had time. There would always be someone at the convent, if she was feeling lonely.

****

Life in the Thibault household was, from the start, very pleasant. Madame Thibault was very welcoming, and quite unconcerned about Angelina's faltering French, telling her that this would improve in time. Monsieur Thibault was rarely seen, leaving early every morning, arriving back late in the evening. The two children, Georges, aged four and Louise, aged two, were good-natured and sociable. The work was not unduly demanding, as there was also a home help who saw to all the

113

heavy housework. Madame Thibault told Angelina that when she wasn't working she was free to go out and explore the district.

Within a short time, Angelina had settled into her new way of life. When the parents were out working, she was in charge of the children. When the parents came home, she was free to go out, and, at first, not knowing anywhere else to go, she walked round to the convent, where she always found company. Sister Aine was always there, and she got to know the other students, girls from Ireland, America, Mexico and other countries.

She wrote regularly to her parents, letting them know that the work was all right, and that she was happy, and enjoying living in Paris.

****

Back in Kincade, Philomena brought Martin Murray home to meet her parents. Martin Murray was a vet. Margaret had given her approval. Well, a vet made a good living, she had said, and that was what it was all about. Hugh and Teresa welcomed the newcomer to the family.

Margaret and Peadar had a new baby boy in the winter. Philomena and Martin talked about getting engaged in the summer.

****

One day as Easter approached, Angelina strolled into the Alliance Francaise. She had got into the habit of going into this centre for coffee, and meeting some of her friends from the convent who were doing courses there.

She bought her coffee and sat down at a table near the door, hoping to meet some of her friends. Nobody turned up that day, but she sat there, happily enough, drinking coffee and watching the students coming and going.

Suddenly she noticed that she was not alone. A man, balancing a cup of coffee and a plate, politely asked if he could share her table. She nodded agreement, wary as ever. During her short stay in France, she had been repeatedly warned never to get involved in conversation with a stranger.

The man sat down.

'Vous etes anglaise?' he asked.

'Irlandaise,' she answered.

'En vacances?' he continued.

'Non, je travaille ici,' she explained.

He was smallish, she noticed. He was not young, maybe mid-thirties. He was dark haired, dark eyed, a shade unkempt.

In broken English, he addressed her.

'Do you mind if we speak English?' he asked. 'I am learning English. It is for my work. Can we speak English, and you tell me if it is right?'

Angelina hesitated before answering, and, sensing her discomfort, the man continued.

'It is no problem. We sit here. You tell me English words. At what time you return to work?'

Angelina explained that she had an hour to spare, but would have to return to her work immediately after that.

They sat for an hour, and they talked a lot. Angelina told him the English for many everyday words and phrases. He was quick and eager. He repeated the words and phrases. He made notes on a creased envelope which he pulled from his pocket. When the envelope was covered with writing, he found a paper serviette to continue his notes. He asked questions, and concentrated seriously on the answers.

At the end of the hour, as Angelina rose to go, he introduced himself. He was Bernard Lemoine. He asked her name, and then said that Angelina was a very beautiful name. He asked if he might meet her next week, at the same time, in the same place, to continue his instruction in the English language.

Angelina, while she had enjoyed the conversation, had misgivings. But Bernard Lemoine seemed to dispel her anxiety.

'You do not know me,' he said. 'Naturally, you are not sure. But, next week, we shall sit here, at the cafe, like today, and I can learn English. What could be more simple?'

Angelina felt reassured, and agreed.

CHAPTER 21

Angelina did some detailed preparation for her next lesson with Bernard Lemoine. She tried to think back to her French textbooks at school, and to reproduce something similar for a foreigner learning English. She was quite pleased when she had completed several pages, including lists of vocabulary, verbs and practice drills.

Bernard joined her at the students' coffee bar as arranged. He greeted her, and glanced at the pages she had prepared. Rather impatiently, he flicked them aside, and said, 'It is not to write English I need, I have to speak English.'

Noticing Angelina's look of disappointment, he relented.

'Thank you for all this work you did for me,' he said. 'We can use it another time. Today we will walk. And you will tell me how to say the English for everything we see.'

They strolled the length of Boulevard Raspail, while Angelina described things along the way. They stood for ten minutes outside a tall terrace building, at the end of which Bernard knew the English words for everything from basement to attic. He could count the windows, he could tell the colours of the stonework, the doors, the window frames. He was an enthusiastic learner, and once he learned a word he always remembered it.

They walked through the Jardin de Luxembourg, where they talked about the trees and the flowers, and Angelina was embarrassed as she realised that she did not know the names of trees and flowers. They talked about the dog owners and dogs they met out walking. Everyone had to be described. Their height, girth, hair colour, attire were all part of the lesson.

Angelina found herself thinking that if the French of her schooldays had been taught in such a manner, she might have been more proficient when she left home some months ago.

At the end of the lesson, they sat down at a pavement cafe for a drink. Still insatiable for knowledge, Bernard read through the menu and wanted everything translated.

When he was leaving, he gave her a hundred franc note, and arranged for the same time next week. Angelina was hesitant about the money. It was too much, she told him. She knew other girls who were teaching English to French people for only half that amount.

He was insistent. 'You teach me so well,' he said. 'It is worth not one centime less.'

****

'Listen to this, Hugh,' said Teresa, as she read Angelina's letter. 'Angelina's teaching English to a French man. He needs to know English for his work. She takes him for an hour's lesson once a week.'

'Very good,' said Hugh. 'That's interesting. What does he work at, that he needs to learn English?'

'I don't know, she doesn't say,' answered Teresa. 'But she says that he pays her well, and he's learning fast. Here, read it yourself.' She handed Hugh the letter.

Later, Margaret called in. She wanted to check that Teresa would be free to baby-sit that evening. She lifted the letter from the mantel piece and read it.

'What's this?' she demanded. 'Angelina teaching English to a French man? Where did she find him anyway?'

'In France, probably,' said Hugh.

'I know that, but what sort of a French man is he? I mean, does Angelina think she can get mixed up with just anybody while she's over there?'

'Let there be no worry,' said Hugh. 'Doesn't she say that other Irish girls do this kind of work? It will be good experience for her.'

Margaret thought that it was a thoroughly unsatisfactory arrangement, and let her parents know this in no uncertain terms.

Teresa started writing her weekly letter to Angelina, giving her the home news, including Philomena's engagement to Martin Murray, which was to take place in the near future.

****

The summer holidays were approaching. Angelina's weekly lessons with Bernard Lemoine continued. His English was improving rapidly.

Madame Thibault asked Angelina when she intended to return to Ireland. If she did not have to go immediately, she would be very welcome to accompany the family on their annual holiday to the Pyrenees.

In the middle of July, Bernard told Angelina that he was going to America for a fortnight. It was to do with his work, and with all the help Angelina had given him with his English, he would do very well at the project he had to work on. He thanked her courteously, kissed her goodbye, and hoped she would still be there when he would return.

Angelina went on holiday with the Thibault family. In the course of the holiday, Madame Thibault told her that she would be very happy if Angelina could stay on for another year. Georges was at the ecole maternelle, where Louise would go in another year. The children had grown used to Angelina, and were very fond of her. If she could only stay until next summer, they would be most appreciative.

Angelina had no difficulty in deciding. She would have liked to take a fortnight at home first. Madame Thibault suggested she should have a break at home. But when she checked the price of the boat fare, she found that she could not possibly afford it. She had used her savings to buy clothes for the holiday, and for the coming autumn. She had been quite taken aback at the price of clothes in France. Madame tactfully suggested that she could help with the fare, but Angelina would have been too embarrassed to consider this.

She also knew that she would only have to mention to her parents that she wanted to come home for a while, and they would have willingly bought her ticket. But always, she felt that she had let them down by not passing her Leaving cert, and felt that she should learn to be independent and not make any demands on them.

And, deep down, in the back of her mind, something else was looming. Bernard. Since he had gone to America, she missed the weekly lessons. She thought of him a lot, of his generosity, his gracious manner, of the way he always made her feel good. And then she told herself that it was silly to think like this. After all, he was quite old, over thirty. But she still found herself looking forward to seeing him again.

She wrote home, telling her parents that she was very happy in her job, and would like to stay another year.

Hugh and Teresa both felt a shade regretful when they read the letter.

'I really was looking forward to her coming home,' said Teresa. 'The house is very lonely with them all away.'

'True,' said Hugh. 'But she'll be home next year. And isn't it great that she's enjoying it where she is?'

'I suppose so,' said Teresa. 'And I know that we've to let go sometime, and accept that our children have grown up. Every one of them, when you think of it, had gone their own way at seventeen or eighteen.'

'What's this?' said Margaret on her next visit, as she lifted the envelope and read Angelina's letter. 'So she's staying on in France? Well, I suppose that's the problem on the shelf for another year.'

****

Angelina and the Thibault family arrived back in Paris in the middle of August. Bernard Lemoine had also returned from America. He phoned her shortly after he arrived.

Was she going home to Ireland, he wanted to know. If not, he wanted more help with his English. The lessons so far had been very helpful, and his work, as a result, had been very successful. If she could help him a bit more, he would be very grateful.

She readily agreed.

As autumn came in, the language lessons took on a new aspect. Instead of walkabouts and discussions, they often went to expensive restaurants. He told her she was beautiful, and that he was in love with her. And Angelina found this a tremendously exciting experience.

In the springtime, Bernard proposed, one evening as they walked hand in hand along the bank of the Seine. Angelina hesitated. She did want to marry him, of course. She had never felt as loved and cherished before. In her schooldays there had been boyfriends, gauche, inept, devoid of charm and courtesy. In contrast, Bernard always made her feel so good.

She told Bernard that she would marry him. But, as they walked on, she explained that she would need to go home first, to talk it over with her parents. She was only nineteen, they might want her to wait a while.

Bernard was most persuasive. They were going to get married anyway, so why not sooner rather than later? They could go on honeymoon to Ireland, and meet Angelina's family. It all seemed to make sense.

****

'You know, Hugh, I think Angelina has a boyfriend,' remarked Teresa, as she read Angelina's most recent letter. 'She keeps referring to Bernard. I think that's the fellow she was teaching English to.'

'Well I hope he's OK,' said Hugh. 'She has always been full of praise for him in her letters. Though, from something she said once, I got the impression that he was a good bit older than her.'

****

Bernard was more than fifteen years older than Angelina. He had told her that he was thirty. He was, in fact, thirty-five. She did not really know what work he did. He was employed by a pharmaceutical company, he had told her. She thought that maybe he was a sales rep, travelling round the country. The trip to America had been a bonus, indicating that he was doing well, and on the way to certain promotion. When she asked any questions about his work, he never said anything definite.

Also, since her engagement, she never knew when she was going to see Bernard next. He might call for her on four or five consecutive days, then, without explanation, she wouldn't see or hear from him for over a week. He would say vaguely that he had been called away on something to do with work.

Angelina talked to Sister Aine about Bernard, about the English lessons, about his job, about his marriage proposal. Sister Aine, more worldly wise, warned her to be careful, and begged her not to set a date for the wedding, not for a while yet. Had she met any of Bernard's family, she asked. There was no hurry, she said. There were too many unanswered questions. Angelina was very young. Don't make any definite arrangements, insisted Sister Aine, wait a few months and think about it.

Angelina agreed with everything Sister Aine said. In the cold light of day, it all made sense. Especially if she had not seen Bernard for a few days, she realised that she wanted some time to think. Deep down, she knew that she wanted to go home, to see her parents, to see her friends, to relax in the easygoing life of Kincade. And after every conversation with Sister Aine, that was her firm intention.

And then Bernard would call for her and take her out for the evening. He would bring her a gift, he would take her to an expensive restaurant, he would pay her extravagant compliments. He would talk about their wedding as if it was settled, arranged, and immediate. And Angelina found him irresistible.

****

In June that year, Angelina wrote home again.

120

'Oh no! I don't believe it!' said Teresa. 'Angelina's talking about getting married, to that Bernard person.'

'You're not serious?' said Hugh. 'When's she coming home? Isn't it time enough to think of marriage for a while yet?'

'That's the whole point, Hugh. 'She's not coming home. She's talking about getting married now, in a couple of weeks, and coming to Ireland on honeymoon.'

Margaret arrived later, talking excitedly about a bridge party she was going to attend later. Could Teresa come over now, she asked, to mind the children, and maybe stay overnight if they were late?

Teresa told her Angelina's news.

'What's that you're saying? The brat! The wee bitch! With Philomena getting married in August, how could she do this sort of thing? Nineteen years old, and trying to upstage Philomena.'

'It's not like that, Margaret,' interposed Teresa. 'She's not trying to upstage Philomena. She's just too young. Your Dad and I want to be sure she knows what she's doing.'

'Here, give me her address,' said Margaret, grabbing the letter. 'I'll fairly let her know what she can or can't do! What could I tell the Gillens, if she got married like this, out of the blue?'

Philomena, in the midst of her wedding preparations, was no less exasperated.

'I thought she would be home,' she said petulantly, 'to be my bridesmaid. After all, it is rather silly to have Margaret as matron of honour, and her with four children, and with all the weight she's put on recently.'

Margaret was, predictably, enraged at this point of view.

****

A few days later, Angelina received three letters.

'Dear Angelina,' wrote her father, 'We were so happy to have your letter. So you're thinking of getting married? We'll be very pleased to welcome Bernard here. Come soon, I suppose he has some holidays coming up. And why not get married in Ireland? We'll talk about it when you come home ....'

'Dear Angelina,' wrote her mother, 'We got your letter. We had heard so much about Bernard, but we didn't know it had become serious! We hope to see you both during the summer holidays, and we'll talk about the wedding ....'

121

'Dear Angelina,' Margaret wrote, 'Haven't you the right nerve? As you well know, Philomena has been engaged since last summer, and is getting married in August. Now don't you dare come out with any talk about getting married first! Philomena is twelve years older than you, and don't you try to upstage her. And you know how it would look, what would people say? It would be a great embarrassment for me to have to explain it to the Gillens ....'

****

Angelina read all the letters. She showed them to Bernard.

'Your parents are good loving people,' he said. 'So why not get married and go to Ireland to visit them?'

'Your sister is cold,' he added. 'She is too concerned about images. And anyway, what does it matter if you get married before or after Philomena?'

Angelina showed all the letters to Sister Aine.

'Your parents are right,' said Sister Aine. 'You do not, at this moment, have a date fixed. Go home, bring Bernard over, think about setting a wedding date at home.'

She made no comment on Margaret's letter. She felt that it might do more harm than good.

And, strangely, it was Margaret's letter that was the deciding factor.

'Why should Margaret tell you what to do?' asked Bernard. 'Wasn't she married young, well, nearly as young as you? And if she writes a hurtful letter to you, why listen to her?'

****

Bernard and Angelina were married in Paris in July. It was a small wedding, attended only by Kate Diver, a friend of Angelina's from the hostel, and a man called Robert, an acquaintance of Bernard's. Angelina had hoped this would be an occasion to meet Bernard's family. He had told her previously that his parents were dead, and that he had two older brothers who lived with their families, one in Normandy and one in Lyons. She was disappointed when Bernard had told her, without giving any reason, that they would not be able to come.

Bernard and Angelina did not go to Ireland on their honeymoon, or attend Philomena's wedding in August. They were let know by Margaret, in no uncertain terms, that they would not be welcome.

122

After the wedding, they set off to spend a week in the seaside town of Royan on the west coast. Bernard told Angelina that he had found them a small apartment where they would live on their return to Paris. He owned a luxury apartment on the Front de Seine, he had told her a few months ago. But he did not live there, because his work involved a lot of travelling around. So he had let it to a tenant for a year. When he was in Paris, he stayed in small hotels, or with friends. By next year, he said, the tenant's lease would have expired, and they would move into his flat.

On the third day of their honeymoon, Bernard left Angelina sitting in the hotel lounge while he went to make a phone call. On his return, he seemed preoccupied and uneasy. Shortly he explained to her that the phone call was to do with work, that he had been told that he would have to return to Paris immediately as there was some urgent business to be completed.

Angelina hid her disappointment, and they soon packed up and prepared for the return journey.

CHAPTER 22

'It's in here,' Bernard told Angelina. 'It is not a very good apartment, but it is cheap, and it will do for a while.'

Angelina's heart sank when she saw the building they were entering. It was incredibly drab and forbidding. They went into a narrow hallway, where a large untidy woman, with tousled hair and wearing a shabby black and red caftan spoke to them. At a small reception desk in the corner she produced the forms, and showed Angelina where she was to sign.

'Your maiden name,' whispered Bernard, as Angelina dithered about signing her newly acquired married surname.

'You write Staunton, your maiden name, here,' explained Bernard. 'That's the way they do it here.'

Unquestioning, Angelina did as Bernard said. From a wallet bulging with notes, he then paid two months advance rent. The woman told them there was a phone in the apartment. The last tenant had had it installed. It would cost extra if they wanted to keep it. Bernard said that they did want to keep it. A phone would be quite necessary for his work. He paid her the required deposit, and she handed him the keys. Bernard led the way upstairs.

The apartment was on the fifth floor. There was no lift, and the grey stairs were dark and dusty. The walls were drab, with the paint of many years flaking in places.

The flat was small and dark. It consisted of a narrow living space and a small bedroom. The living area contained a rusty gas cooker, an old-fashioned sink with one tap, a formica topped table and three chairs. On the wall was a small cupboard with one door hanging loose on its hinge. To walk in this space, it was necessary to move sideways, moving the chairs in order to get past. There was a small grimy window, where a piece of newspaper stuck with adhesive tape covered a broken pane. In the bedroom there was a bed and a cupboard, and those two items took up most of the floor space. The bathroom was across the landing, shared by the occupants of three similar flats.

Angelina opened the kitchen cupboard, as if hoping to find something pleasing in this dingy place. There was nothing inside but three or four cracked coffee cups. In a newspaper-lined drawer in the formica table, she found several items of greasy looking cutlery. Almost in desperation, she walked over to the window and looked out, as if hoping for, at least, a pleasing outlook. A few feet away, she was faced with the high grey wall and the dusty windows of another apartment block. She was close to tears.

Everything about Bernard had so far been stylish, gracious, elegant. This just did not make sense.

'Don't be unhappy, my princess,' he said, embracing her. 'I know that it is not a good apartment, but it's only for a short time. We will next year move into my flat, and it is beautiful. And in the meantime we will go to Ireland on holiday, and when I have work in America you will come with me. So it's not really so bad, is it?'

He reached for his wallet, and pulled out several large notes.

'When I am at work tomorrow,' he continued, 'you could go out and buy things to make better the flat a little, some good cups and plates, some flowers, whatever you think. And now we shall go out to dinner. I have in mind a very good restaurant which you have not yet seen ......'

Angelina managed to smile. Bernard was always able to make her happy. Of course she could put up with this awful place for a short time. She would do her best to make it nice. And the main thing was that they were together.

****

A few weeks later, Angelina was very miserable. Bernard worked at all sorts of odd hours. Sometimes it was quite late before he returned home in the evenings. The flat was a most depressing place to spend time alone. She had tried to make it more attractive, with little ornaments and flower arrangements. She had cleaned the windows and bought white lace curtains. But there was so much basic decoration needed, her home improvements showed little result. She missed her work, and her only break was when she took a walk to the convent. She had many friends there, but regretted that she could not invite them to her home. There wasn't even adequate seating space for anyone who might call.

She decided that she would look for a part time job.

'Why would you want to work, my dear?' asked Bernard anxiously. 'We are not short of money. And, the way my work is going, we are going to be very well off soon.'

'I'm bored, Bernard,' Angelina explained. 'When you're not here, and I've nobody to talk to all day, it's very lonely. I'd like a little job, just to give me an interest.'

During the next few days she went out and walked around the area. In a small supermarket, she noticed a hand-written card in the window, advertising for a checkout assistant. She went in, and asked to see the owner. After a short conversation, during which she told him about her previous job, he agreed to employ her, and asked if she could start the following Monday. Angelina was very pleased, and looked forward to having something to fill her days.

****

The autumn went on, and Angelina enjoyed her work. She had to operate the old cash register, and help the customers to pack up their purchases in plastic bags. Her employer, Monsieur Blanchard, was very nice, and regretted that he could not pay her a higher wage, but times were bad, he explained, the bigger supermarkets had taken away a lot of his customers.

At home, life was not so pleasant. Bernard's working hours were increasingly erratic. He was often very late home in the evenings. Sometimes, after their evening meal, the phone would ring, and he would have long muttered conversations with someone, after which he would go out, maybe for several hours. He always told Angelina that it was an important client he had to see urgently.

Occasionally, men arrived at their door. Bernard said that they were colleagues, coming to discuss some business matter. They never came in, but stood on the landing, one, two or three of them, and talked in hushed voices.

Sometimes Bernard would come home in high spirits, a well stuffed wallet in his pocket. On those occasions they would dine out, and he would make a great fuss of Angelina. He would bring flowers, and have a little gift for her. They would have a happy relaxed evening together.

Other times he seemed to have no money, and was moody and irritable. Angelina would then have to use her supermarket wages to purchase the essential groceries.

It was on one of his bad days that Angelina had her pregnancy confirmed. She waited excitedly for Bernard to come home, so that she could tell him. When she saw the mood he was in, she felt certain that her news would cheer him up.

He barely noticed what she was saying. Shortly, he made a phone call which lasted about half an hour. Then he went out, and did not return until after midnight.

****

Christmas was another disappointment. Angelina had gone to a lot of trouble to purchase a good present for Bernard. She eventually decided on a watch, which cost most of her savings. She told Bernard that she would do an Irish style Christmas dinner. Some weeks before Christmas, she wrote to her mother to ask for advice about the cooking of turkey, ham, puddings and other Christmas fare. Teresa responded immediately, with a long letter full of useful ideas.

Angelina put a lot of effort into shopping and preparation. On Christmas morning, she wrapped Bernard's present, and started early in the morning to organise the dinner.

Bernard unwrapped his present, thanked her effusively, embraced her and told her that it was beautiful. Then, without trying it on, he set it down on the window ledge. During dinner, he was silent and distracted. He showed little appreciation of the meal that had been so carefully and lovingly prepared. He kept looking at the time, on his old watch. After dinner, without a word, he went out. He returned a few hours later.

'I have a present for you, my love,' he said affectionately. 'But, unfortunately, I do not have it now. Last week by mistake I left it in the apartment of a friend, in a briefcase of documents I was carrying. I went to look for it there now, but there was nobody in. I shall get it for you tomorrow.'

'That's all right, Bernard,' said Angelina, relieved almost to the point of tears that he had not forgotten, or neglected to get her a present, and that he had actually gone out on Christmas day to try to get in to her in time. 'It'll be lovely, when you do manage to get it. What is it?'

'I will not tell you now, my dear,' he answered. 'It must be a surprise. But I know you will like it, it is a very beautiful present.'

A few days later, Bernard took Angelina out to dinner. They went to one of their favourite restaurants, where they had a leisurely meal, in pleasant surroundings, with soft music in the background. As they drank their coffee, Bernard produced a gift wrapped package. Angelina opened it, and found a magnificent pearl necklace with matching earrings. She was overjoyed. And Bernard was so happy this evening. He was attractive and loving, and he made her feel so good.

The next day, Angelina lifted a crumpled piece of paper from the floor. It was a receipt for the necklace and earrings, purchased the previous day.

****

At Easter Angelina was six months pregnant. She was still working six days a week in the supermarket. Bernard's movements and moods were still changeable. Sometimes she was very weary.

Monsieur Blanchard, the owner of the supermarket, was having problems. Business was not good, he could not compete with the larger stores in the area. He had got an offer from a man who wanted to buy his business and modernise it. Monsieur Blanchard was giving the idea serious consideration. The man who wanted to buy it, Monsieur Meunier, was offering a very good price.

Monsieur Blanchard confided in Angelina that that he felt he was getting too old to compete in the modern market. If he accepted Monsieur's offer, he could afford to retire. But he did not want to see Angelina left without a job. He would recommend that the new owner would keep her employed in her present work, at which she was very competent.

A few days later, Monsieur Meunier came into the shop, a sharp-faced man with an impatient manner. He spent some time with Monsieur Blanchard, looking at the fittings and stock, and, while Angelina sat at the till, she overheard them discussing her position.

Monsieur Blanchard exhorted Monsieur Meunier to keep Madame Lemoine in employment. She was competent, honest, and a quick efficient worker. She was always in time, and was pleasant to the customers. She did not mind staying late if there was extra work to be done.

Monsieur Meunier glanced contemptuously in Angelina's direction. His daughter-in-law, he explained, would be doing the checkout. They would have to get a new modern machine. Madame Lemoine would not be required to continue. In her condition, and in a shop with a new image, he did not want her.

Monsieur Blanchard was almost as disappointed as Angelina.

Three weeks later, the shop was sold. Monsieur Blanchard was most apologetic to Angelina about the loss of her job. With her final wage packet, he paid her a generous bonus. He wrote her a very good reference for future employment.

Bernard was most reassuring.

'You do not need to work, my angel,' he said. 'Soon I will have the big promotion, and soon after, we go to live in my flat on Front de Seine. And you should be resting, you should not be working, with the baby so soon.'

As always, when Bernard said everything was all right, Angelina smiled and hoped that everything would be all right.

But, of late, she had had a few misgivings.

When it was one of Bernard's good days, he was very attentive, very anxious that she should rest, that she must eat well, that she must not be tired. But, while he seemed concerned about Angelina herself, he seemed to steer the conversation away from the baby. Angelina, as she felt the new life growing inside her, would have loved to talk about it. Would it be a boy or girl? Which would Bernard prefer? What names would they consider? Would the baby be dark, like Bernard, or fair like herself? Sometimes she was worried about the coming months, and wanted to talk about her fears. But as soon as she spoke at all on the topic of the baby, Bernard always seemed to have something to do or somewhere to go immediately.

Sometimes, in the flat, on a long lonely evening, she wondered about the future, and couldn't avoid a premonition that Bernard might never see the baby. And then she told herself that she was thinking nonsense.

Maybe men were like this, she told herself. When the baby arrived, he would surely show more interest. But she dearly wished that she could talk to someone about it. In those moments, she sometimes felt very homesick, for Ireland, for her parents. Her mother would have been so reassuring at a time like this.

Angelina did not tell Bernard about the bonus that Monsieur Blanchard had given her. She lodged it immediately in her bank account, deciding to save it for a rainy day.

She had no idea how quickly the rainy day was to follow.

****

A few days later, Bernard arrived home in a state of agitation. He hastily moved round the apartment, putting some papers into a briefcase.

'I must go away for a few days, my love,' he said distractedly.

'But where are you going? And for how long?' asked Angelina, dismayed.

'For a few days, maybe a week, maybe two weeks,' he answered. 'There is a very good promotion at work, which I should get. But there is another firm trying to get the contract I am working on. My promotion depends on getting this contract. So I must be there first. And when this contract succeeds, my sweetheart, we shall be rich, very rich.'

'Where do you have to go?' asked Angelina, nearly in tears.

'Do not be sad, love,' pleaded Bernard. 'I will phone you every evening. And you must rest, and look after yourself. When I return, I will take you on a holiday. And then there will be the baby, and everything will be perfect.'

'But where are you going?' asked Angelina, again.

'America,' he said, on his way out the door. He hurried down the stairs without a backward glance.

CHAPTER 23

For hours Angelina lay on the bed and wept. Towards morning she fell asleep, and it was late in the day before she woke up. She wandered round the flat, from bedroom to living area and back again, dazed and miserable. Then, since there seemed to be nothing else to do, she crept back into bed.

That evening, Bernard phoned. He had just arrived in America. He missed her terribly, he was full of endearments and comforting talk. He would be starting his project in the morning, and if all went well he would be back in about a week.

Angelina brightened up as she talked to him. When he rang off, she felt a bit better. She realised that she had eaten nothing all day, and she looked in the cupboard to see what was there. There was not much, and she had some coffee and stale biscuits. Tomorrow, she told herself, she would go out and do some shopping.

The next day she did not go out. She stayed at home, telling herself that she did not want to miss Bernard's phone call. She dined again on coffee and stale biscuits.

Bernard phoned again that evening, and was very reassuring and loving.

On the following day, she eventually made the effort, took her shopping basket and purse, and went down the stairs.

Madame Castel accosted her in the hallway. Was Monsieur at home, she wanted to know. She had wished to see him for some time, but had always missed him. There was a matter of two months rent owing. She could not understand why it had not been paid. She had thought of going up to their apartment, but there were so many stairs, and her legs were bad.

She showed Angelina the rent book, which had no entries for the past two months. Angelina promised that she would settle the account, and Madame added that she would like a further two months advance rent, as it was easier to manage that way.

Angelina went to the bank, and withdrew her precious nest egg, with which she paid the four months rent. As Madame was making the entry, Angelina noticed that the rent book was not in Bernard's name, but in her own maiden name. She remembered the day they arrived, when she had signed some forms in her maiden name, but she was puzzled about why it was her name only in the book. Then it occurred to her that it might be to do with tax, or something in the business world that she did not understand. She would ask Bernard about it later.

Before starting the long ascent of the stairs, Angelina checked her mail box. There was a letter there from her mother.

Dear Angelina, she read as she climbed the stairs, we have been missing your letters lately. We hope all is going well with you. No doubt you are very busy with preparations for the baby, but be sure and look after yourself ....

Teresa went on to tell the family news, about what Margaret's children were doing, about Philomena who was also expecting a baby in the summer, about a visit they had from Kevin last weekend. Her father was well, he was very busy in the garden at this time of year. She herself was knitting baby clothes for the two grandchildren who were due in the summer.

Finally she reminded Angelina to write soon, as they always loved getting her letters.

Back in the flat, Angelina decided that she must write home. But there was no news, nothing to write about. She searched around for a notepad, opened it and wrote her address at the top. Dear Mum and Dad, she started. After thinking for a few minutes, and not having come up with any news to send home, she abandoned the idea and dropped the notepad and pen at the side of the bed.

She spent most of her time in bed those days. There was not a comfortable chair in the flat, and there was so little space that the bed seemed the only place to be. And in spite of spending so much time in bed, she always felt tired.

I should eat something, she thought, and then realised that with the distraction of the unpaid rent she had completely forgotten to buy her groceries. Even though it was early in the day, the journey down the stairs and round to the shops seemed impossible. She boiled some water, made a cup of coffee which she drank black, as the milk had gone sour. She found a tin of beans in the cupboard, which she ate with a spoon, cold, straight from the can.

Bernard phoned that evening, and every evening the following week. He was always loving and concerned, telling her enthusiastically how the work was going, about how he thought about her all the time and missed her so much, and looked forward to returning home. He always enquired whether anyone had called to see him.

Then, one evening, he did not phone. Angelina was distraught. Could he have had an accident, she wondered. She was in a state of complete confusion when the next day, and a few more days passed without hearing from him. When he rang at last, she was almost hysterical with relief.

He regretted so much that he had not called her, he said. But last week's work had involved a lot of travel. He was on the road all the time. It was not easy to make phone calls when you were moving around all the time. But the work was going brilliantly. They were going to be rich, very rich. America was a fantastic place. He would take her there some day.

As he said goodbye and rang off, Angelina was aware of two things. Bernard had not enquired about how she was, and whether she was resting and looking after herself. And he had made no mention of his return date.

Later that evening, she heard a knock at the door. This was strange, she thought. Nobody ever called, except the men who used to sometimes stand on the landing talking to Bernard.

Nervously, she opened the door a couple of inches, to see two policemen standing there.

'Bonsoir, madame,' said one, raising his hat in salute.

The other policeman produced a photograph and showed it to Angelina, asking, 'Vous connaissez cet homme, madame?'

The photograph was unmistakably Bernard. It was a small, passport size shot, and she noticed that the policeman was holding another picture of Bernard in profile.

She answered that the photo was of her husband, and the policeman directed an enquiring look over her shoulder into the flat, then asked if Monsieur was at home. Angelina explained that her husband was not at home, he had, in fact been away for over two weeks, and she did not know when to expect him back.

The other man asked where Bernard had gone, and they both looked distinctly taken aback when Angelina said that he had gone to America. They made their departure, muttering agitatedly to each other.

Angelina closed the door and sat down, in a state of shock. What was going on, she asked herself over and over again, but she could not come up with an answer. The visit from the police had unnerved her. She sat upright on her chair, tensely listening for every sound on the staircase outside her door.

Why did the police have photographs of Bernard? Why was the flat leased in her name? Why had she never seen his flat on Front de Seine that he had told her about? She remembered once asking him the address, and he had said something about the block being renamed, and then had immediately changed the subject. Why, if he was in regular employment, did he sometimes have lots of money, and sometimes nothing at all? Who were the men who came and talked to him on the landing? Were the police looking for them as well? She started as she heard footsteps on the stairs, and then heard a door closing across the landing, as one of the other tenants arrived home. What were the muttered phone calls about? Why did he leave the rent unpaid? Why, when she met him first, did he have to learn English in such a hurry?

She sat there until dawn, in a state of terror and panic. She would have given anything to have someone to talk to. If only she could phone someone, maybe one of her friends at the convent. But in the middle of the night this was out of the question.

When, with the first grey light of dawn, her fears abated slightly, her thoughts turned to home. She longed to talk to her mother, who she knew would always have practical advice. And she knew, as surely as if her mother was there, saying the words, the advice she would give. She would tell Angelina that she must look after herself, and think of the baby.

She thought of the baby, due in seven weeks. She was scared. What if something went wrong? What if she didn't get to the hospital in time? If only she could be sure that Bernard would be back .... But if he was back, and if the police were looking for him ....

She stumbled to the bed, fell into it, and dozed fitfully for several hours.

When she woke up, she walked around in a daze, made a cup of coffee, and then went out. She was not sure where she was going, but thought she would have a walk and try to work things out.

Outside the front door, she started as she heard her name called from across the street. Looking in the direction of the voice, she saw Kate Diver, her friend from Donegal who was doing a course at the Sorbonne, and who had been her bridesmaid. She answered, and waited until Kate crossed over the road to meet her.

'Hello, Angelina! You're a stranger! You haven't come to see us for ages. Sister Aine was asking about you just the other day.'

As Kate spoke, Angelina noticed her expression change. She knew why. Her clothes were crumpled, as she had not bothered washing or ironing anything for weeks. Her shoulder length fair hair, normally freshly shampooed and glossy, was lank and greasy, pulled back in an elastic band. She was not eating proper meals, and she knew that she looked a fright.

She did not feel up to having a conversation. Trying to appear cheerful, she said hastily, 'Oh, I've been so busy, Kate, with the baby due soon and all that. But I'll call round soon. I'm sorry, I've to rush now, I've an appointment .... with the doctor,' she improvised as she hurried off.

Kate watched Angelina disappear round the corner, and then she went back and took a long look at the building she had come out of. She made a mental note of the number and street name, and then went on to her lectures.

****

Angelina, after walking for about an hour, returned to the flat. She had intended to buy bread and milk and eggs, but hadn't bothered. Once again, she lay down on the bed, feeling close to desperation.

After about half an hour, the phone rang. It was Bernard.

'Hello, Bernard, oh, I'm so happy you phoned .... I'm in such a dilemma .... I don't know what to do .... the police were here .... I don't know why, they were asking .... what will I do if they come back? I'm so nervous .... but when will you be back? Bernard? Are you still there? Bernard? Bernard ....'

The line had gone dead. Angelina returned to the bed, where she sat, dazed, confused, for a long time.

About seven o'clock there was a knock at the door. She jumped with fright. Bernard had told her not to answer the door. But, as the knocking continued, after some deliberation, she opened it.

Kate Diver and Sister Aine were standing on the landing. Angelina was torn between relief and embarrassment.

They walked in. One glance around the flat told them everything.

An hour later, they were still sitting round the table, as Angelina, in floods of tears, told them the whole story.

'Now,' said Sister Aine, as brisk and business like as ever, 'we have to think what to do next. And for a start, you'll come back with us now to the convent.'

'I can't,' sobbed Angelina. 'I couldn't afford a room at the convent. I've no work. And I have to be here when Bernard gets back.'

'When did you last hear from him?' asked Sister Aine.

135

'This afternoon. I told him about the police, and he says it's nothing to worry about, but I'm not to answer the door or the phone until he gets back. And then I don't know what happened, we got cut off. And there seemed to be another man there, I heard another voice in the background.'

'Angelina,' said Sister Aine firmly, 'get a few things together and come back with us now. You can't stay here, scared out of your mind about who's going to call or phone. And if you're worried about how you can afford a room, I've got just the thing for you.'

She went on to explain that Sister Brigid, who did the convent secretarial work, was away on a course. Sister Isabel was trying to cope with letters and bills and so on, but was completely bewildered, and had reduced the whole thing to chaos. Reverend Mother had been saying that she would willingly employ a girl to work two or three hours a day, to stand in until Sister Brigid's return. Angelina could have the job, and her pay would easily cover her lodging expenses.

While Sister Aine talked, Kate was packing a bag for Angelina. They left shortly, after Angelina had told Madame Castel that she was going to stay with friends until the baby was born. Would she give Madame Castel the address and phone number of the convent, she wondered. Sister Aine said no, she could call back occasionally for mail or messages. She suggested that Angelina should leave a note on her own table, for Bernard if he should return. She did not say what she felt, that this young, rather naive and vulnerable girl must be kept clear of calls from the police, or unknown men on the landing, and possibly from her husband.

Angelina spent the next seven weeks at the convent, where she soon regained her strength and good humour. She quickly introduced order into the mound of mail to be dealt with. She was happy to be back among friends.

She called back to her flat several times, to see if there were any messages. Her note to Bernard was always there, untouched, as she had left it, on the table.

On the first of July, Claire was born.

CHAPTER 24

'I'm taking Claire home to Kincade for the month of August,' Angelina told Sister Aine, as she proudly showed her three week old baby to her friends at the convent.

'That's great,' said Sister Aine. 'You could do with a holiday, after all you've been through.'

Sister Aine had found a part time job for Angelina, to start in September. It was with a family who wanted a child minder from the end of the school day until about seven in the evening. The pay would not be much, as it was for only three hours a day, but it would do to go on with, and the house where Angelina would be working was only five minutes walk from her own place. She could bring her baby with her, so it was a satisfactory arrangement.

When Angelina came out of hospital, Kate Diver was there to help her. They went back to the flat, where Angelina was horrified when she realised the state she had let it get into. Between them they cleaned and polished the whole place, and bought the necessary groceries. Claire slept happily in her cot most of the time.

When Kate had gone, Angelina took out her bank book and studied her account. The rent was due again. She would pay two months, which would take her until September, when her part time job would start. She would have just about enough left to keep herself and Claire for the coming weeks.

Then it occurred to her that if her remaining cash would cover the fare by train and boat to Ireland, she would go home.

Hastily she did her calculations again. After a couple of phone calls, she was happy to find that the fare was just within her scope. She wrote immediately to her parents, letting them know of her plans.

There was still no word, either letter or phone call, from Bernard. On her return from the hospital, the note that she had left, two months ago, was still on the table. Angelina had stopped waiting and hoping. Now she had to get on with looking after herself and the baby.

****

At the beginning of August, Angelina set off to make the long journey, first by train to Le Havre, then by overnight boat to Rosslare. Fortunately Claire was a placid contented baby who slept most of the time. As the boat drew into Rosslare, Angelina thought wistfully of the day, nearly three years ago, when her parents had driven her here for her journey to France. So much had happened since. Would they be there to meet her, she wondered, anxiously looking out as the boat prepared to dock. But there was nobody there.

She took the train to Dublin, and then got a bus connection to Kincade. It was quite late at night when she arrived.

Angelina arrived at her home, and opened the front door, which, as always, was on the snib. Her parents, sitting in the living room, were amazed and delighted to see her. The letter had not arrived, so they had no idea that she was coming. They welcomed her joyfully, as Teresa took the baby in her arms, and Angelina, exhausted, collapsed into an armchair.

They talked late into the night, all happy to be together again. Angelina told them all about Paris, about her work, about her friends at the convent. Teresa told her all about her nieces and nephews, and about Philomena's baby Natalie, who was born a few days before Claire.

Teresa asked about Bernard, and Angelina answered that he was doing some work in America, so she had decided to come home herself. He would probably be back in Paris before her, she added.

Teresa made the bed in Angelina's room, and made up the carry cot with clean sheets and covers. She always had a supply of these, as Margaret's children had often stayed overnight when their mother was engaged in her social activities. Then they bathed the baby in a plastic basin, and settled her for the night. Shortly afterwards, Angelina, tired out from the journey, also went to bed.

'There's something wrong, Hugh,' said Teresa. 'Did you think so?'

'I did,' he answered. 'She didn't have much to say about Bernard. I wonder if everything is all right. Now, there's this bit about him going off to do some work in America. Do you think he's really in America?'

'I have no idea where he is,' said Teresa, 'and I'm afraid that neither has she. But let's not ask questions, she'll tell us when she's good and ready. Isn't the baby a real pet?'

'She is, God bless her. A lovely wee girl,' answered Hugh.

'She's exactly like Angelina at that age,' said Teresa. 'Do you remember? So tiny, with little squiggles of blond hair.'

The next day, Margaret and Philomena arrived. They both had appointments with their hairdresser, and Philomena wanted to leave baby Natalie in the care of her grandmother. That way they could relax a bit, maybe meet some friends in town have a coffee, not have to hurry back.

'I've a surprise for you,' said Teresa. 'There's a little cousin here for Natalie. Angelina arrived late last night with baby Claire. Come and see.'

'What?' demanded Margaret. 'Angelina? When did she come? Did you know she was coming?'

'No, we didn't know,' said Teresa. 'She wrote to us, it seems, but we didn't get the letter. If we had known she was coming, we'd have gone to meet her at the boat. The poor girl, she arrived exhausted, after travelling the whole way from France with the baby.'

Angelina, hearing her sisters arriving, came out to welcome them with Claire in her arms.

'Hello, Margaret. Hello, Philomena,' she greeted them.

She was totally unaware that both of them were still   disapproving of her actions in getting married just before Philomena. She was puzzled at their frosty reception.

'So how long are you staying?' asked Margaret.

'We'll be here for the month,' said Angelina. 'I've a new job starting in September, so I thought I'd come home for a while first.'

'And your husband, where is he?' asked Philomena.

'In America. It's to do with his work. He'll be back in Paris by the time I get back.'

'Well, aren't you the right modern madam,' snapped Margaret, 'going off on separate holidays. In the twelve years Peadar and I have been married, we've always gone on holiday together. If you ask me, there's something fishy about this.'

'Don't annoy her, Margaret,' said her mother. 'There's nothing fishy about it. Some people do have to travel abroad for their work.'

'Oh, no, don't annoy her!' said Margaret. 'No word of course about all the annoyance she's caused us. And would you tell me how she intends to spend the month here? She doesn't have any notion of going out and about with that child, does she?'

'Why shouldn't she go out with her baby?' asked Teresa, quite shocked.

'As you well know, Mother, the Gillens don't know that she was married before Philomena. I could never have told them that, goodness knows what they would have thought. And I covered up for her. I told them she was engaged last summer, and married at Christmas. And now she comes home with a baby. I'm telling you, she'll disgrace us if any of this gets out.'

'Now, wasn't that a silly thing to tell the Gillens?' said her mother. 'Not that there was any need to tell them anything. After all, we're not asking questions about what the Gillens are doing. So why should they be so concerned about us? Now, this is really nonsensical.'

She put her arm round Angelina's shoulder, and patted the baby's face. 'It's lovely to see her home again for a while. Don't make her unhappy, now that she's here.'

'And what about making me unhappy?' demanded Margaret. 'I'm telling you, it will be a terrible embarrassment if this gets out. It's well I didn't bring the children, they'd have spilt the beans back home.'

Margaret flounced off for her hair appointment, followed by Philomena, who had decided not to leave Natalie after all.

Teresa felt very sorry for Angelina, who was visibly upset by the lack of welcome from her sisters.

During the following days, Hugh and Teresa, wanting to give Angelina a good holiday, organised several family outings. But, anxious not to upset Margaret, they got into the car at the side of the house, in the shelter of the high hedge. Then they would drive off, sometimes to the seaside, sometimes to Donegal. When the sun shone, they would find a beach where they could have a relaxed walk, and maybe a picnic.

It was a happy time for all of them. Angelina wished nostalgically that she could stay. But she thought this would be impossible, as she had no work prospects at home, and a child to support. And she knew that any such plan would meet with strong opposition from her sisters. She still told nobody that Bernard had disappeared from her life. But her parents were aware of the fact that she never mentioned him.

On a sunny evening towards the middle of August, Father Kevin Staunton strode purposefully into his parents' house.

'I believe Angelina's here,' he said to his mother. 'Where is she?'

'Out there at the back,' replied Teresa.

Angelina had left Claire sleeping in the bedroom, and had gone out to sit on the doorstep in the evening sun.

Kevin opened the back door, and, without a word of greeting, started asking questions.

'Margaret tells me you're home without your husband,' he said accusingly. 'Why?'

'Bernard has work to do in America,' she answered. 'I just took a holiday on my own, with Claire. It's ages since I've been home.'

'When were you married?' demanded Kevin. Last year, when the news came of her wedding, he had not been interested.

'Last summer, the tenth of July,' she answered.

'And when was that child born?'

'Just six weeks ago. The first of July.'

'Hmm .... Were you married in church?'

'Of course I was. And in the registry office as well. That's the way they do it in France, they have two ceremonies.'

'What? Now I'm warning you, don't mention the registry office bit round here, in case anyone would get the wrong idea. It would not do if word of this got to my parish. You've been a real embarrassment to all of us, and I'd advise you to lie low as long as you're here. When do you go back?'

'The twenty-ninth of August,' she answered, feeling completely miserable.

With a disgusted look, he turned on his heel and went back into the kitchen, where Teresa was making tea at the range. She offered him a cup.

'No. I haven't time. I'm on my way to Margaret's and then I have to get back home tonight.'

He was away without another word. Nobody spoke, but they were all aware that he had not seen, nor asked to see his little niece.

At the end of the month, Angelina prepared for the return journey. Her parents drove her to Rosslare, and, as they left her at the boat, Teresa reminded her to write often, to keep in touch, and to come back again soon.

'I certainly will, Mum,' she answered. 'I'll come next summer. Just imagine, Claire will be a year old.'

After she had gone, Hugh and Teresa both remarked that Angelina had said 'I'll come next summer,' and not 'we'll come.'

'I get an impression that this Bernard fellow has deserted her,' said Hugh.

'I wish she'd come home to stay,' said Teresa. 'And I wish the others wouldn't be so hostile to her.'

'Totally unreasonable, I thought,' said Hugh. 'During the month we didn't see Margaret or Philomena, except on that first day, when they told Angelina that she wasn't to be seen out. Any other time, they'd be in regularly. And the day Kevin came, he was so disagreeable.'

'I would like them to be more understanding,' said Teresa. 'I must try to reason with them before Angelina comes again.'

But, deep down, Teresa knew that her three older children were firmly entrenched in their way of thinking. She and Hugh had been determined that their children should have every possible chance in life. She was very disappointed that, while they had each followed a chosen career, they seemed to lack any kindness or consideration. In this modern world, where so much seemed to depend on keeping up appearances, and on the opinion of others, Margaret, Philomena and Kevin had each ruthlessly carved a niche where nobody or nothing was going to intrude.

She was also aware that Margaret was obsessed with keeping up a life style that would impress the Gillens. A young sister in a foreign country, with an unknown husband and a child, did not fit into Margaret's cosy little circle. Margaret was a very domineering person, and Philomena and Kevin always followed her lead.

As for Angelina, she had always been in awe of the older members of her family. They were all years older than her, and because of this, she seemed to accept everything they said. When they were obviously displeased with her, she felt that it must be through some fault on her part. During the month she was home, she was aware of their disapproval, but was at a loss about how she could manage to get on better with them.

****

The next year, Angelina came home again in August, with Claire. By this time she had let her mother know, bit by bit, in her letters home, that Bernard was no longer with her.

Teresa tried in vain to persuade Margaret and Philomena to be more friendly, to let Claire get to know her cousins. But Margaret had made up the story, for her circle of friends and in-laws, that Claire was six months old. So she couldn't let anyone know about the year old child who was her niece from France. And, of course, she could not let it be known that Angelina's husband was no longer on the scene.

****

And so it went on, for the next nine years. Angelina and Claire came over every summer, and had a good holiday with the old couple. Over the years, Angelina had different jobs in Paris, most of them child minding, and had also part time jobs in cafes and small shops. On holidays in Ireland, Claire got to know other children of her age, and had an opportunity to play in the open air, a luxury rarely to be enjoyed in Paris.

In the summer of 1986, Teresa spoke briefly to Angelina on her last day at home.

'Your father and I are getting on in years,' she said. 'Time comes when you need to think of the future. Now, just suppose I die before your Dad, you might think of coming home to stay? He really lives for your visits, you know.'

Angelina was taken aback to hear her mother talking about death. She was in her seventies, but she was lively, healthy, and energetic as ever. Angelina had never known her to be any other way.

'I'd love to come home to stay,' she said. 'And Claire would love it too. But, Mum, you're not going to die, not for ages and ages. Look at you, you're the picture of health.'

'I wish we could all be so sure,' said Teresa thoughtfully. 'But do think about it. It would be lovely if you could stay.'

'I'd stay, and never go back,' said Angelina, 'if I thought I could get work. And you know that Margaret and Philomena wouldn't be pleased, or Kevin either. I think they still look on me as a kind of black sheep.'

'Don't mind them,' said Teresa. 'They all went their own way, nobody told them what they could or couldn't do. Let it be the same with you.'

Angelina affectionately hugged her mother, and promised her that she would think about what they had said.

CHAPTER 25

Teresa died in the winter of 1986. On a November morning, she made a pot of tea, poured a cup for Hugh, and sat down with him in the living room. Hugh was reading his paper and listening to the radio. Some time later, he spoke to Teresa, without looking up from his paper, telling her about something he had just read. On getting no answer, he looked up, puzzled. Teresa was sitting there, her teacup in her hand, looking very strange.

'Teresa,' he said gently. 'Teresa.' There was no response. Startled, he took the cup from her hand and rushed to the front door. Mrs Monks, a woman who lived near, was walking past.

'Mrs Monks!' he called. 'Mrs Monks, could you come in a minute?'

Mrs Monks followed him in. 'My God!' she exclaimed when she saw Teresa. 'I'll phone the doctor.'

She rushed back to the porch, where there was a list of phone numbers on a card sellotaped beside the phone. She phoned the doctor, though she knew, and Hugh knew, that there was nothing any doctor could do. Then she phoned the priest and the district nurse, both of whom were at the door within a few minutes.

When Mrs Monks had shown them in, she closed the living room door and returned to the phone. Then she dialled Margaret's number. When Margaret answered, she introduced herself.

'Hello, Mrs Gillen. I'm Cassie Monks, I live near your parents. I'm afraid I've bad news. Your mother's very ill.'

'What's wrong with her? How long has she been ill?' demanded Margaret.

'Just there now,' answered Mrs Monks. 'I don't know what's wrong, but it seems to be serious.'

'Where's my father? Get him to the phone.'

'He's inside there, with the priest.'

'With the priest? Is it that bad?'

'It is, Mrs Gillen. It seems to be very serious. I think it would be a good idea if you'd come at once. Wait a minute, I'll get the nurse to speak to you.'

'No need for that. I'll try to get over soon,' said Margaret.

Then Mrs Monks phoned Philomena. She was not at home, but Mrs Monks left word that her mother was ill, and to contact her parents' home at once.

The next call was to Kevin. Should she tell Father Staunton, she wondered, that his mother was dead? Being a priest, he should maybe be told at once. She had given the others time to get over the initial shock.

Father Staunton was not in. In a way, this solved her dilemma. She spoke to the parish priest, telling him that Father Staunton's mother had died suddenly, and left it to him to break the news.

Now there's the other girl, she thought, the young one. She's in France or somewhere. She comes home every summer with her wee daughter. She looked through the list of names on the card.

There it was, the name, Angelina Lemoine, complete with phone number and the Paris code. Mrs Monks dialled and waited. When she heard Angelina answering, she spoke.

'Hello. Is that Mrs Lemoine?'

'Yes.'

'This is Cassie Monks from Kincade. I don't know if you remember me.'

'Of course I remember you, Mrs Monks. Wasn't I talking to you in the summer when I was home?'

Why is Mrs Monks phoning me, Angelina asked herself.

'Oh no!' she said out loud. 'It's bad news, isn't it, Mrs Monks?'

'I'm afraid so, love. It's your mother. She had a bad turn this morning.'

'How bad, Mrs Monks?'

'Very bad. I've phoned the others.'

'Mrs Monks, tell me the worst. She's dead, isn't she?'

'She is, love. I'm so sorry.'

'Mrs Monks, thank you for telling me. I'll get a flight booked immediately. How's my father keeping?'

'All right, so far. I'll stay here and keep an eye on things until you all arrive. Look after yourself. Bye.'

At this point, Mrs Monks found herself nearly in tears.

Angelina rang off, and sat down under the phone and wept. She remembered the conversation during her last visit home. Did her mother have a premonition? Or did she have a health problem that she had kept secret?

She glanced at the clock, and sprang into action. She phoned a travel agent and booked a flight to Dublin, which was to leave in a few hours.

She packed an overnight bag, and, as always in times of crisis, she hurried round to the convent.

Sister Aine, as usual, came to the rescue. Angelina was not to think of taking Claire with her. Claire was only ten years old, she had a lovely memory of her grandmother. Let her keep that memory, Sister Aine said. She herself would meet Claire from school, and bring her back to the convent, where she would stay until Angelina's return. Well, they were full up, but they would find a camp bed somewhere, and Angelina could phone and talk to Claire as soon as she reached home.

****

Hugh appeared beside Mrs Monks in the hallway.

'I've phoned all the family, Mr Staunton,' she said. 'Mrs Gillen and Mrs Murray and Mrs Lemoine and Father Staunton. They're all on their way. Now, is there anything else you'd like me to do?'

'Thanks, Mrs Monks, thanks,' Hugh said distractedly.

Mrs Monks decided that she would just stay around, he would certainly need help as the day went on.

****

Later that day, Mrs Monks was alone in the house. The family had arrived, the doctor had come, an ambulance had been sent for, all had gone to the hospital. There was talk about a post mortem being arranged. Margaret had told her father to stay at home, but he insisted on going. Mrs Monks was in the kitchen, making buns and sandwiches and setting out rows of cups and saucers. By the time evening came, there would be many callers.

The phone rang in the porch. In the silence of the empty house, Mrs Monks started. Then she left her work and went to answer it.

It was Angelina at the Paris airport, about to check in for her flight. She wanted to speak to her father, and Mrs Monks explained where everyone was. Angelina said that her flight would arrive in Dublin at eight o'clock. Mrs Monks assured her that she would let the family know, and someone would be there to meet her.

About an hour later, the family arrived back. Hugh was weary and perplexed, and sat distractedly at the fire while Mrs Monks poured tea for everyone. Shortly, neighbours started arriving, everyone still shocked by the morning's happenings.

When Mrs Monks had passed tea to everybody, she spoke quietly to Margaret.

'There was a phone call from your sister in Paris, Mrs Gillen,' she said. 'She was about to get on the plane. She'll be arriving in Dublin .....'

'Oh, will she?' said Margaret, and turned to talk to someone who had just come in.

Slightly taken aback, Mrs Monks approached Philomena.

'Your sister Mrs Lemoine is on the way home, Mrs Murray,' she said. 'She phoned from the airport while you were all out. She'll be arriving in Dublin at eight.'

Philomena looked quizzically at Mrs Monks, as if wondering what this had to do with her.

'I was just wondering,' said Mrs Monks, 'how she would get down from Dublin?'

'How would she get here? By bus, I suppose. She comes every summer. She knows the way.'

Mrs Monks moved on to Father Kevin Staunton.

'Excuse me, Father,' she started, 'your sister Mrs Lemoine is on her way home. She'll be arriving in Dublin ....'

'All right, all right,' said Father Staunton, as he reached for another sandwich.

'Holy Jesus!' muttered Mrs Monks, silently to herself, rushing out the door. She hurried to her own house, just down the road. Her son John was sitting watching television.

'John, I can't believe it,' she exclaimed. 'That poor girl, the youngest of the Stauntons, is arriving off a plane this evening, after getting news of her mother's death. And not one of the others would go to meet her. I can't take it in. And on a bitter winter evening, hasn't she enough to cope with as it is? She can get a bus, Mrs Murray says.

'Look, son, you could go to the airport, couldn't you? Between you and me, I think it's a disgrace that not one of them would meet her, just for a bit of support at a time like this.'

'Surely, Mother, I'll go,' said John, getting up. 'What time is the plane? I'd need to be on the road right away.'

Mrs Monks returned to the Staunton household, to see to the callers.

About eleven that night, Angelina arrived in with John Monks. She spoke to her sisters and brother, who barely acknowledged her. She spoke to the neighbours, all of whom she knew by name. Sitting on the arm of her father's armchair, she comforted him, as he related to her the events of the day. Mrs Monks made supper for her, and she gratefully thanked Mrs Monks for her help and support.

The next two days passed in a daze. In a spell of bitterly cold frosty weather, there was the journey from morgue to house, then to chapel, followed in the morning by the funeral mass and burial. Throughout the proceedings, Angelina stayed by her father's side.

After the funeral there was a meal arranged in a Sligo hotel. As people left the cemetery, Hugh graciously thanked them for coming, and invited anyone who had travelled a distance to join them at the hotel.

Margaret was immediately at his side, warning him not to invite too many people.

'Don't forget we've the hotel booked for fifty,' she said urgently. 'You mustn't ask too many more.'

'They did say that it didn't matter if it was over fifty,' said Hugh. 'And anyone who has come a long journey has to be invited. Anyway, I don't think we're anywhere near the fifty yet.'

'Of course we're near the fifty, if not over it. By the time you count the Dublin ones, and the Murgintra ones, and the Gillens and the Murrays, and I invited five or six from the bridge group, there are at least forty. So don't you go inviting every Tom Dick and Harry. You didn't invite that Mrs Monks, did you?'

'Yes, I did, and her son John. But they wouldn't come. They said it was a family occasion, and they wouldn't want to intrude.'

'Well, thank goodness for that.'

'Who are the people from the bridge group?' said Hugh. 'I don't remember meeting any of them. Where are they?'

'Oh, they didn't come to the funeral. You couldn't expect them to travel down in this weather. But I phoned them and told them to come to the hotel. You didn't invite that Nicholas Healy, did you?'

'I did, and he's coming. He's a very good friend. Why not?'

'Oh Dad, I wish I had warned you in time. The Gillens don't like Nicholas Healy.'

'Well, I'd have invited him anyway. I've known him since I came here, nearly fifty years ago. It would be totally uncivil not to ask him.'

Nicholas Healy was a solicitor, whom Hugh had first met when he arrived, as a young teacher, in Kincade. They had played golf together over the years, and had become very good friends. The Gillens did not like him, because, on an occasion many years back, he had defended someone against whom the Gillens were making a claim.

During dinner, Angelina told her father that she would have to go back to her work, and to see to Claire. But she would come again soon, and spend some time with him in the summer. He told her he would be very happy for her to come.

Later, back in the house, when all except the family had left, Angelina went to her room for a rest, and Hugh sat in his armchair at the fire. Margaret, Philomena and Kevin, with significant beckoning gestures, moved out to the porch, closing the door behind them.

'He can't stay here on his own,' Margaret was saying urgently. 'He's over eighty. He'll have to move into a home.'

'How could he go into a home?' asked Philomena. 'Those places cost money, you know. And I've enough on my hands with the children, without taking on anything else.'

'He could use his pension, of course,' said Margaret. 'Hasn't he his teaching pension and his state pension? That would keep anyone in a home, except the luxury type places.'

'You're right, Margaret,' added Kevin. 'He can't stay here. It just isn't suitable. Will you find out about homes?'

'I will, indeed,' said Margaret. 'And then this house could be sold, and we could have our share now.'

'Just what I was thinking,' said Kevin. 'So you'll see to it, Margaret, and we'll get things fixed up as soon as possible.'

'Sh ......!' warned Margaret. 'Don't let him know yet that he'll be moving. Just in case he raises any objections.'

Sitting alone in the living room, Hugh, who had heard every word of the conversation, silently said to himself that he would not be moving. Still grief stricken and dazed, he was not prepared to get into any conversation about it at the moment. But soon ....

Margaret, Philomena and Kevin then looked in round the door to say goodbye. Angelina got up for a while, and sat, silently, with her father, before they both retired for the night.

Early the next morning, John Monks drove Angelina to the Rosslare boat. She chose to travel by boat as it was cheaper than the plane. It was a long, long journey back. On the way, she thought of the coming summer.

She would have to get some extra work, to save up as much as possible for the holiday. She would try to give her father a good time. She would hire a car. He had not been driving for a few years now, not since he had been involved in a slight accident on the Sligo road. He had not been at fault, but he was acutely aware that traffic was now much heavier than in his early driving days.

Paris in the winter, on Angelina's arrival back, looked incredibly drab.

CHAPTER 26

It was Christmas Day 1986. In Paris, Angelina and Claire went, as usual, for Christmas dinner in the convent. Angelina, although she was saving for the summer holiday, decided to bring the nuns a good present. She baked a Christmas cake in her little gas oven, using a recipe she had learned as a teenager from her mother. She also bought a big box of chocolates, and, in the watery winter sunshine, she and Claire walked round to the convent.

The nuns had dinner in the convent dining room, and Angelina and Claire joined the students who had not gone home and other guests in the students' dining room. Sister Agnes from Mayo, who was in charge of the kitchen, always made a traditional Irish Christmas dinner with all the trimmings. After dinner, everyone came together in the front reception lounge, where they played cards or scrabble, or watched the television. If the weather was mild, some of them might go for a walk on the nearby streets, deserted except for a scattering of solitary individuals, who, for one reason or another, seemed not to be involved in the season's festivities.

****

In the Gillen household in Sligo, the family sat around, opening their presents. The older children, aged twenty, eighteen and seventeen, were bored at the prospect of a whole day at home, a day when nobody went anywhere. The two younger children were excited with their presents, and were trying out their new toys and games. Margaret was in a bad temper, scolding about all that had to be done, and about how nobody was doing enough to help, and about how Christmas had become too commercialised anyway and there was too much fuss. Peadar sat in a corner reading, hoping the day would go over without too much fuss.

****

In the Murray household, the children, aged ten, seven and two, opened their presents. Natalie, the eldest, was helping the other two to set up the games they had got in their packages. Martin Murray was hoping that some farmer would send for him on a job before the day was out. Christmas Day was such a drag. Philomena fussed as she prepared the dinner, saying that she wondered whether Christmas was really worth all the bother.

****

Father Kevin Staunton, after saying early morning Mass, went to the parochial house. Later there would be Christmas dinner with the parish priest. For the afternoon, he had been invited to join Father Pius Padden, a contemporary of his from seminary days, on a visit to his family. It was a good day, he thought. It was quite a long journey, about fifty miles, to Father Padden's home. But he might as well go as he didn't have anything else to do, and it would pass the time.

****

Hugh Staunton walked slowly home after Christmas morning Mass in Kincade. Neighbours wished him good morning, but in view of his recent bereavement did not wish him a happy Christmas. He went into his house, started cooking a bacon and egg breakfast, and turned on the radio.

He heard a tap at the door, and went out to see Mrs Monks standing on the doorstep. She had brought him a box of Christmas fare, a cake, some chocolate biscuits, some fruit, ham and cheese.

'How are you keeping, Mr Staunton?' she asked, knowing that for him it would be a day laden with memories.

'All right, thank you, Mrs Monks,' he answered. 'And thanks for the parcel. It was very kind of you.'

'Not at all, it was nothing. Well, I suppose the family will be coming? Or are you going to them?'

'Neither, by the looks of things,' answered Hugh.

Hiding her disbelief and dismay, Mrs Monks asked Hugh to come over and join herself and John for Christmas dinner. There were just the two of them, she said, they would enjoy the company if he would come.

He accepted readily.

****

Later that evening, when Hugh returned home, he had a phone call from Nicholas Healy. He enquired how Hugh was keeping, and suggested that they should get together in the New Year. Hugh agreed enthusiastically, adding that he had a bit of business about which he would appreciate some legal advice from Nicholas.

A bitterly cold spell of weather followed. Hugh did not go out much those days, except for the five minute walk to the shop to get his Irish Times. If Mrs Monks did not see him out by ten o'clock, she would go and get his paper and leave it in with him. She dropped in frequently, to do a bit of housework, and to see if he wanted anything. Within a short time they made it a firm arrangement, she would do a half day's housework a week, for which he would pay her.

At the start of February, Hugh started to venture out a bit more. He went for walks, and started to look at what would need to be done in the garden in the spring. He took an occasional walk to the pub in the afternoon, where he enjoyed the company of neighbours and acquaintances. He was getting used to living and coping alone. Sometimes it crossed his mind that he must contact Nicholas Healy, and he always told himself that he would do it soon.

****

On the tenth of March it was Hugh's birthday. He was eighty-one. He had forgotten that it was his birthday, one day was so much the same as another these times. It was only when he glanced down at his Irish Times, noticing the date, that he remembered.

At that moment he heard a car pulling in at the front door. Looking out, he saw Margaret, Philomena and Kevin coming towards the house. Margaret was carrying a box which she was balancing carefully.

They crowded in, wishing him a happy birthday. Philomena gave him a scarf, wrapped in crumpled Christmas paper. Margaret gave him a bottle of aftershave.

Hugh offered to make tea.

'Not at all, I'll make the tea,' said Margaret, bustling out to the kitchen. 'And I'll put on the dinner. I've got a casserole here for you. I'll just pop it in the oven. Now, Dad, you just sit down and rest.'

A minute later she was back.

'This casserole needs to be done at a medium heat,' she said. 'Dad, what's a medium heat in your oven?'

'I don't know, Margaret,' he said. 'I never use the oven.'

He noticed the significant glances she exchanged with the other two.

'Well, I'll try it at a hundred and eighty,' she said. 'Only I hope it won't be spoiled. I spent ages putting it together yesterday evening.'

There was an awkward silence, as Philomena and Kevin sat with Hugh, waiting for Margaret to bring in the tea. It did not improve much when she returned with the tray, so Hugh tried to initiate some conversation. He enquired about each of his grandchildren in turn, and Margaret and Philomena, as always, became quite voluble on the subject of their sons and daughters, what they were doing, where they were going on holidays, how they were progressing at school.

Later, when Margaret served the casserole, she brought up the subject that had brought them all to visit Hugh.

'We've been thinking about you, Dad,' she started. 'It must be lonely for you here by yourself since Mum died. Would you not think of going into a home?'

'That's right, Dad,' said Philomena. 'At your age, you really shouldn't be alone. Suppose you took ill or anything. If you were in a home you'd be well looked after, and you'd have your meals cooked for you, and you'd have company.'

'Margaret was looking at some homes that might be suitable,' added Kevin. 'You could easily afford it on your pension. And you'd even have some pocket money left over.'

Hugh, silently enraged at this gross insensitivity, looked at each one of them as they spoke. Then, after a long pause, he gave them his answer.

'Your mother and I,' he said, 'lived here for a long, long time. We built a life here together. And it's here I'm going to stay.'

He could have said a lot more. There was a lot more to be said. But now was not the time. He had just managed to adjust to living alone. He would need to keep everything on an even keel. He refused to be drawn into any further conversation on the topic.

Enraged, his three visitors left the table and went out into the porch, where he heard angry whispers. At one point he heard Philomena, he voice slightly raised in irritation, asking how much the house would be worth.

Margaret replied that houses were fetching a good price at the moment, and now would be a good time to sell.

The voices dropped again, but Hugh was only too aware of the trend of conversation.

Shortly they reappeared and told Hugh they would have to leave, as it was getting late, and there was frost forecast for the evening. They went out the front door, and talked angrily among themselves for another few minutes before departing.

As soon as they had gone, Hugh went to the phone. He called Nicholas Healy, and asked him if he could call soon. Nicholas answered that he would come tomorrow. He would be able to get a lift down with his son in the morning.

CHAPTER 27

The next morning, Mrs Monks arrived early with the Irish Times.

'Hello, Mr Staunton,' she greeted him. 'Here's your paper. And are there any messages you want today?'

'Thanks, Mrs Monks,' said Hugh. 'Yes, I'd like you to get me two steaks when the butcher's van comes. I'm having a friend coming for lunch today.'

'Surely, Mr Staunton. I'll leave them in with you,' said Mrs Monks, as Hugh handed her the money.

Hugh then lit the turf fire in the living room, but unlike other days, he did not sit down and read his paper, or listen to the radio. He paced around, his mind crowded with thoughts. Several times he walked out the front door, down to the gate, and looked down the road. He chatted briefly with the milkman, and with two women who were walking past.

'A grand man he is, for his age,' said one of the women.

'He is, indeed,' answered her companion. 'Wasn't it tragic about his wife? And a fine healthy looking woman she was. Who'd have thought she'd have gone before him?'

They walked on, changing the subject to the activities in their everyday lives.

About twelve o'clock, Hugh heard the car stopping at the gate. He went out to greet Nicholas, and the two shook hands cordially. Nicholas was now joined by his son Bart who had dropped him off.

'How long will you be staying, Dad?' he asked. 'When do you want me to come back for you?'

Hugh answered for Nicholas.

'A long time, Bart,' he said. 'Can you make it about nine o'clock? All right, Nicholas?'

'Nine o'clock, all right,' said Bart, as he got back into his car and drove off.

Nicholas and Hugh went into the house. Hugh threw another few sods of turf on the fire. He took out the whiskey bottle and two glasses, and they sat down.

Mrs Monks arrived shortly, bringing the two steaks, and a freshly made apple tart. She greeted the two men, put the steak and the tart in the kitchen, and left.

Back in her house, she said to John, 'You know, he's a remarkable man. He's so independent. I'd have made lunch for himself and his friend, if I had thought it necessary. But I know he'd rather do it himself.'

At the fireside, Hugh and Nicholas had a whiskey, as they exchanged civilities, enquiries about each other's families, news about mutual acquaintances.

After about half an hour, it was time to talk seriously.

'Shall we get down to business?' said Nicholas.

'It was twenty-five years ago,' started Hugh, that I made my will. 'It was quite straightforward. I left everything to Teresa, supposing that I would be the first to go. And now that things have turned out differently, I'll need to do some rearranging.'

'You're thinking of revoking the old will and making a new one?'

'No.'

'No?'

'No. I'm eighty one now. If I made another will now, there are those who would not agree with the terms, and might contest it. And worse, they might succeed.

'Now, here's what I have in mind. Apart from Angelina, the others in the family are well set up. Margaret and Philomena both have well off husbands, and have a life of comparative luxury. Both of them have fine homes, grand houses, with cloakrooms, patios, spare bathrooms, sun porches, conservatories, what have you. Kevin is also comfortable. He has his own house, his own car. His future is secure, whether he stays in his present parish or moves somewhere else.

'So my concern is for Angelina. She has no place of her own. She lives in a tiny flat at the top of a high building in Paris. It costs half her wages to pay the rent. She has done a variety of jobs, mostly part time, and I know that she finds it difficult to make ends meet.

'Now, I was thinking that I would like her to have this house, so that if she ever comes back to live in Ireland, at least she'll have a roof over her head.'

'You said, Hugh, that you don't want to make a new will, in case the others would contest it. Why would they do that? As you say, they are well set up. Why should they concern themselves about Angelina having this house, which, as you know yourself, isn't in the same bracket as their own homes?'

'Not only do I think they would contest a new will, I know they would. They would say I was over eighty, and therefore senile and incapable of making a correct decision. They are well off, certainly, but such a mercenary crowd you cannot imagine.

'Do you know, they were here yesterday, trying to persuade me to go into an old people's home, so that they could sell my house and divide the money. And, I'll add, it was the first time they set foot in this house since the day of Teresa's funeral. Not a word, not a phone call, nothing more than a card at Christmas. And as long as Teresa was alive, Margaret and Philomena were in here every week, leaving the children to be looked after, or wanting baking done for a party, or wanting her to go and baby-sit while they went out socialising.'

'You're sure that they want you to sell the house?'

'I'm certain. I don't know whether they think I'm deaf, or just plain stupid, but they stand around whispering, and I can hear what it's all about.'

'And in their reckoning, where does Angelina come in? Will they offer her a home when she comes home on holiday? If the house were sold, would they give Angelina her share?'

'No, and no. Angelina doesn't count at all, as they see it. She is, to quote them, flying her kite in a foreign country. They aren't even civil to her when she comes home.

'I'm telling you, Nicholas, and I know them well enough, all they want is to get me moved into a home so that they can get their hands on the price of this house.

'Now, as I see the situation, I am not going to make another will. They would be certain to contest it, and I'd be afraid they would succeed. They are all very persuasive and persistent people.'

'You're right, Hugh. I can see the problem. And I know the set that Margaret and Philomena are in with in Sligo. There are a few legal people there whom I would not trust. Ruthless and cunning they are, and would be prepared to go to court over a five pound note. I agree entirely that you should not make a new will.'

'What I hope to do, Nicholas, with your help, is to sign over to Angelina the house, its contents, and my savings. That way it would be her property from now, and nobody could question it later.'

'Now, wait a minute. That seems to be a good idea. But what about Angelina's husband? You told me some years ago that she was married to some chancer who disappeared.'

'Oh, that's past history now. It's eleven years since she married this fellow, and within months he just faded out. He said he was going to America on some business for the firm he worked with, and she never saw him again. He never even saw the baby.'

'There could be a problem here, Hugh. If you sign the house over to Angelina, part of its value could be legally her husband's property. And she still is legally married, even though she hasn't seen him for ten years. And suppose he showed up?'

'I see what you mean. Though it's unlikely that he'll show up now, or, if he did, that Angelina would have anything to do with him.'

'Tell me more about him. Did he leave any message when he left? Did she know anything about his family, his friends?'

'There's very little I know really, Nicholas. She told us nothing at the time. I think she was hoping he'd come back. Later she told Teresa bits and pieces. It seems that he rented a small flat for them immediately after the wedding. For some reason he insisted on having the lease signed in her maiden name. She didn't know any of his friends or family. Sometimes men came to visit, but they never came in. They just stood talking outside the door. He told her that he owned a luxury flat somewhere that he rented to a tenant, but he would never tell her where it was.'

'How did she meet him in the first place?'

'I'm not sure. She was teaching him English. It seems there was some urgency about this, as he had to learn English for his work.'

'And his work?'

'Again, there's a question mark over that. He told her vaguely that he worked for a pharmaceutical company, but never said where he was based, or what he actually did. Sometimes he had a great deal of cash. Angelina could be a bit naive, you know. It didn't occur to her that it was a bit strange that he came in sometimes with large wads of notes. When he went away, he told her that he had been sent by his firm on an important contract in America. At first he phoned every day, and then the calls became less and less frequent, and eventually stopped altogether. And then the police came looking for him one evening.'

'Those men who came to visit. Did she know anything about them?'

'No. She rarely saw them. They would arrive in the evening, tap on the door, and he would go out and stand talking to them on the landing, often for a long time. He never invited them in.'

'There's something unsavoury about this fellow, Hugh. I would say even criminal. Maybe drugs. Maybe prostitution. All the secrecy and unanswered questions could indicate criminal connections. And if the police were looking for him, no doubt they had their reasons.

'I thought at first that he might have gone off with another woman, or that he might have been married already. But there's this bit about learning English as a matter of urgency. If it was all above board, and I gather he was a man of mature years, why didn't he go to classes, or do a

160

course? And having the flat in Angelina's name shows that for some reason he wanted to cover his tracks.

'The point I want to make, Hugh, is that a guy like this can dock up again, and if he does it's bad business. If Angelina owns a house, he could claim part ownership. There are people who have an amazing capacity for sniffing out property, or anything that can be turned into money, even ten years later, or in a different country, even a different continent.'

'What would you suggest?'

'Can Angelina get an annulment? It should be possible to prove that this fellow never intended to stay with her. I'd like to have a talk with her next time she's home. On second thoughts, I'd like to talk to her as soon as possible, if you'll give me her phone number. After that, we'll arrange everything about the house.'

'So far, so good,' said Hugh. 'We've reached some conclusions about the first part of the business. We'll have some lunch.'

He went out to the kitchen, where he put on some potatoes and carrots, and fried the steaks in the pan. He opened a bottle of wine, and they had a leisurely lunch at the kitchen table. Then they sampled Mrs Monks's apple tart with mugs of tea.

About an hour later they returned to the living room.

****

'Another problem, and a big problem, as I see it,' started Hugh, 'could come from the other three, from Margaret, Philomena and Kevin. They are very serious about getting me into a home, not out of any concern for me, but for how it would benefit them. Now, in the near future, we'll have the house business settled. But I know them well, and they won't let it rest. They would take legal advice, and they would put pressure on Angelina. And I'd be afraid that she might be innocent enough to give in to them.'

'I know, Hugh, too well I know. I haven't come through a lifetime in the legal profession without knowing exactly what you're talking about. I don't underestimate in the least the trouble they could make.'

'It never ceases to amaze me, Nicholas, how children turn out. When you look back on it, you can sometimes understand it better. But they were brought up without any of those pretensions or mercenary notions. Teresa was very down to earth. She would never allow them to think that they were superior to their peers. But, in primary school days, they were

161

warmly dressed, properly fed, never went barefoot. This unwittingly put them on a plane above many of the other children. And, of course, there was the added prestige of being the master's children. So in a way it was inevitable that in primary school days they got an idea that they were a cut above the average.

'Then, at secondary school, it was a bit of a leveller. They were now mixing with children of families who were very well off, and they resented the fact their classmates no longer looked up to them. At this stage Margaret developed some very foolishly pretentious notions, and, as always, Philomena copied her. And Kevin the same.

'Teresa and I thought, and hoped, that they would outgrow those notions. But time went on, and they were so firmly entrenched in their way of thinking that there was no moving them.

'I wouldn't care if they had set their minds on getting on in life and doing well, if they would be kind, caring individuals. But not one of the three has ever shown a scrap of consideration, either for their mother or me. And the way they treat Angelina is disgraceful. I'm convinced that she and Claire would have come home to stay years ago, if they hadn't been so hostile.'

'I know what you're saying, Hugh, and I understand your fears about their reaction when they would find out that Angelina was the owner of the house. At best they can be a nuisance, at worst they could pester you and wear you down. What they won't do, I'd be fairly sure, is let the matter drop. At our time of life, we can do without that sort of hassle.'

'True, true. Nicholas, I have an idea about how to deal with them, but I'll need your advice. We're going to get the house business settled for Angelina. We know that they will create an almighty fuss. And yet, there is a story I could tell, a story that goes back fifty years, that would take the wind out of their sails. It's a true story, and I am the only living human being who knows it. But if I told them, firstly, they would not believe it, and secondly they would have me certified insane.

'Nicholas, Angelina is my only legitimate child.'

'How so?'

'Well, it's a long story, though, come to think of it, not so long. My older brother Timothy was the father of the other three. When we were a few years married, I was told by a doctor that I could not father children, for medical reasons.

'You remember Father O'Lorcan? He was having hysterics in case the master and his wife did not have a family, you know, bad example in the parish, contraceptives, that sort of thing. So it was he who engineered the arrangement with Timothy. It was by mutual agreement, and all parties concerned were sworn to secrecy.'

'And Angelina?'

'As I said, Angelina is my only child. The medical reasons must have disappeared by then.'

'Well, surrogate parenthood seems to be quite widespread nowadays, and I suppose that in the past it was not entirely unknown.'

'Now, Hugh, the thing is that you could handle this lot better if you had the information on hand, ready to produce, but only to be used as a last resort? Your trump card, so to speak?'

'Precisely.'

'The first thing we want is a sworn statement, signed by yourself, Teresa, Timothy and Father O'Lorcan. I'll see to the wording, you find what signatures you can.'

'You mean ....?'

'I mean that I never forge a signature unless it's absolutely necessary. I suppose you'll have something in your desk dating back to Father O'Lorcan's time? Teresa's signature should be no bother. Timothy's might be a bit more difficult, but there's nothing like a bit of well judged improvisation. Now, I'll put together the document, you know, all that stuff about the greater good and so on. You go and find something with Father O'Lorcan's signature on it.'

While Hugh rummaged through old papers in his desk drawer, Nicholas wrote, rewrote, and was finally satisfied with his work. Looking at the papers Hugh showed him, he expertly signed the three names, using an old fountain pen and blue black ink that had been in the back of the desk for many years. Finally, Hugh added his own signature to the document, and Nicholas said he would take it away, photocopy it, return one copy to Hugh and keep one himself. He crumpled up the rough copies of his work, and threw them into the back of the fire.

'It's a fine day out there,' said Hugh. 'Shall we take a walk? We need to rest the brains after all that.'

They set off, and walked slowly along the road in the spring sunshine. They went past the teacher's residence where Hugh had lived a long time, and then turned into the road where the new school stood. They went past the chapel and the parochial house, and stood for a moment looking over at the now disused railway station. The track was completely overgrown, and the platform was completely covered with moss and weeds. And in the middle of all this, strangely undamaged by weather and neglect, was the bench where passengers used to sit waiting for a train. Nicholas and Hugh walked over to the bench and sat down.

'I'm worried, Nicholas,' said Hugh after a few moments. 'About the document. Margaret and Philomena and Kevin are very persistent, as you know, and they are very likely to make trouble. Now, if they suspected that the document was forged, you've no idea the lengths they'd go to. There's the question of falsified birth certificates, for a start.'

'You've no need to worry. Think of the contents of the document. Would Margaret or Philomena take the slightest risk of this becoming public? Would they even tell their nearest and dearest? And Kevin, at the time he went to the seminary, he just would not have been considered for the priesthood. So you can rest assured that you'll have no trouble on that score.'

'True, now that you say so, none of them would dare question it. When and if I have to use it, it'll be safe.'

The disused railway track, in the shade of the trees and away from the main road, had become a popular walking place. Sometimes mothers took their toddlers to play there, sometimes couples strolled along.

As Hugh and Nicholas sat there, three teenage girls came by. One was telling about how, during the previous week, some of their classmates had been sitting in a cafe up the town during afternoon class time, had seen a teacher's car stopping outside, and had run out the back door of the cafe. To their horror, they had found an alsatian in the yard and had spent twenty minutes hiding in a doorway, uncertain about whether to face the teacher or the dog. The other two girls were greatly amused at the story, and were laughing uncontrollably.

As the girls came level with the two octogenarians, they became silent, and walked on past. When they were out of earshot, one of them spoke.

'You know, I'm really sorry for old people,' she said. 'They can have nothing to talk about.'

Hugh and Nicholas shortly got up and walked back to the house. Their business completed, they remembered that the whiskey bottle was in there, neglected, on the fireside table.

CHAPTER 29

Once again, it was the tenth of March, Hugh's birthday, 1993. The years had drifted past, he was in good health, and most of the time life was good. He spent his days reading, gardening, walking. He strolled over to the pub in the afternoons, where he had many enjoyable conversations. He was a well known, well respected figure in the village. Mrs Monks looked after his house, her son John saw to odd jobs and messages. Angelina and Claire came every year for the month of August. Life was good, he had no complaints.

The only irritation was the annual birthday visit from his family. Philomena and Kevin rarely bothered him for the rest of the year. He had regular visits from Margaret, visits which inevitably ended up in arguments as she continued to pressurise him to to give up his independence.

He sometimes wondered why the three of them made this a birthday ritual. Perhaps they thought that if they tried first to make it a festive occasion, they might meet with more success in persuading him to go into a home. Or perhaps they thought that the arrival of each birthday should remind him of his increasing age, and therefore imminent helplessness.

Two years ago he had overheard Margaret saying that his health was bound to deteriorate soon, and this would render him more manageable. This, of course, made him more determined to remain well and strong.

Last year he had, on the spur of the moment, decided to go out for the day. He had taken the morning bus into Sligo, and had spent some time sauntering around the town. Then he had lunch in the hotel, and took a bus home in the middle of the afternoon, only to find that his visitors were still at the house. They were very irate that he had not been there. They had demanded explanations. Did he not know they were coming? Did he not know they always came on his birthday? What did he mean by going out on his own like that without telling anybody? They had been on the point of notifying the Guards. And, inevitably, they exchanged significant looks, looks that said he was not safe to be left alone.

He had decided that it was more trouble than it was worth. Anyway, he asked himself, why should he have to go out of his own home, to avoid anybody. And here he was again, on the tenth of March, thinking of the hours ahead with no enthusiasm.

They would be here shortly, he thought. He put on the kettle to have a quiet cup of tea before they arrived.

Hugh sat down in his armchair, and placed the mug of tea on the table beside him. He glanced at the clock. Half past nine. He would savour the half hour of peace before the invasion. He lifted from the bookcase beside his chair a Sunday newspaper. It was a few weeks old, and he had set it aside, intending to re-read an article that had left him feeling a bit concerned. He opened it, folded it over, and read through a full page article about committal of patients to psychiatric hospitals.

It seems, he read, that there were many people throughout the country in these hospitals who should not have been there, but had been committed on some whim of their near relatives. And the alarming thing was that this could happen. If your relatives deemed it necessary, they could take steps to have you taken away, kept under sedation, kept for long periods of observation, refused any rights.

Hugh folded up the paper and put it down. He sat upright, feeling, at first, a vague sense of disquiet, which developed into serious unease, and within a short time he was actually aware of a feeling of fear.

And for the second time in his long memory, Hugh Staunton felt vulnerable.

The first time had been fifty years ago. It had been the day when he had arrived home on the train after his visit to the Dublin clinic, in the early years of his marriage. But there was no time now to dwell on things long past. He had to adjust immediately to what was happening now.

Any minute they would arrive, these people who affected an interest in his health, in his well being. They would give a rather unconvincing display of concern, after three hundred and sixty four days of minimal contact. They would treat him like an idiot, darting significant glances in his direction. They would watch like hawks, waiting for him to make one slip, to say or do something that would justify them in claiming that he was senile, incompetent, unfit to be living alone. They would use anything they could to further their own ends.

Five years ago, he and his good friend Nicholas Healy had discussed at length how he could ward off their troublesome attentions. He had in his possession a document, locked in his desk drawer, which he kept carefully in reserve as a last weapon. But this was not foolproof. If he produced this document, or if they found it, they would certainly destroy it. There was another copy which Nicholas had filed away somewhere. But

166

Nicholas had died during the winter. The original document could be very hard to find. He hoped that Nicholas had passed the document on to his son Bart, also a solicitor, who now ran the business. But he had no way of being sure.

Hugh felt confused and unsteady as he stood up and went out to the phone. Uneasily, he lifted the receiver and dialled Mrs Monks's number. He heard the double tone of the phone ringing, and then Mrs Monks answered.

'Hello ..... Hello .....'

'Hello ..... Mrs Monks .....' he began.

'Hello ..... Mr Staunton? Hello? Are you all right, Mr Staunton?'

'Yes, of course .....' Hugh didn't know what to say next.

After a few moments silence, Mrs Monks spoke. 'Listen, I'll be over in a couple of minutes.'

He put down the phone and went out the front door. He walked to the gate, and, as he expected, he saw Mrs Monks scurrying out her door, fifty yards down the road.

'Mr Staunton, is there anything you'd like me to do?' she asked breathlessly as she came level with him.

'No, no, it's all right ....' he answered. She waited, knowing that in his own time he would say what was on his mind. He looked clearly distracted. It was better not to rush him.

After a few moments he asked, 'Mrs Monks, do you think that I'm senile?'

'Good heavens, no, where would I get that idea?' said Mrs Monks. 'You're just great. In fact, you're far less senile than a lot of people half your age,' she added, laughing.

He remained solemn, preoccupied. Then he asked, 'Mrs Monks, do you think I should go into an old people's home?'

Mrs Monks was taken aback.

'I certainly do not, Mr Staunton,' she sharply replied. 'Why would you go and do a thing like that? You're in the best of health, and you enjoy life as it is. Why would you think of doing anything else?'

As she looked at him, comprehension dawned.

'Is it the family?' she asked. 'Do they think you should go into a home?'

He did not answer, and she knew that she must be discreet, mustn't ask too many questions.

'I'll tell you about old people's homes,' she said. 'They are grand for some people. My aunt Minnie was in one for years. I used to go and visit her. She loved it. She loved chatting with the other old ladies, and they had bingo and things in the evenings. And they had all sorts of knitting and crochet and craft things organised. She had bad arthritis, and she would have had bother getting round without help. Some people love living in a home. But it's not your scene, Mr Staunton. You're too independent.'

'But I'm also eighty six,' he said, looking at her questioningly.

'So what?' she said sharply. 'Haven't you me down the road, and John, and we'll always keep an eye out for you. Don't let them talk you into anything.'

She realised again that she mustn't make any criticism of the visitors. But she had observed them before, and thought they were a bit snooty. They wouldn't give her the time of day, and, apart from Mr Staunton's birthday, they rarely bothered visiting him. And she remembered the time of Mrs Staunton's funeral, when none of them would go to meet Angelina at the airport.

'Would you like me to drop in?' she asked gently. 'I could always be cleaning the porch or something.'

'No, no, it's all right, thanks,' he replied.

'OK then. But, if you want me to do any housework or anything, just dial the phone, the way you did there now. You needn't say anything, I'll just come if I hear from you.'

He smiled, and agreed. They understood each other. He had an ally.

'Have a good birthday. And don't let anything annoy you. And don't forget, I'll be there if you want me.'

As she scuttled away, Father Kevin Staunton's car turned in to the gateway.

CHAPTER 30

Hugh waited while Kevin drove up to the door, got out of his car and locked it. Together they walked into the house and sat down in the living room.

'Well, Kevin, how's it going?' asked Hugh. 'I suppose you could do with a cup of tea?'

'No, no,' said Kevin hastily. He didn't intend to waste time over tea, he wanted to say his piece and have things settled before his sisters would arrive. 'Here's your birthday present.' He took from his pocket the crumpled package containing two pairs of socks.

'Thanks, Kevin, thanks,' said the old man. 'What sort of a run down did you have?'

'Oh, all right, all right ....' answered Kevin.

'You're a long time on the road,' said Hugh. 'You must have had an early start. I'll make you a sandwich, or toast or something.'

'Ah, no, no, I'm all right, don't bother,' said Kevin. He was frantically chasing the words to broach the subject he had been rehearsing in his mind during the journey.

'Well then,' said Hugh, 'hasn't it been a grand spell of weather? The front hedge has come on well during the spring. I'll have to get it cut back one of these days.'

'Cut back? Who'll do that for you?' demanded Kevin.

'John Monks,' answered Hugh. 'He mows the lawn, and does a few outdoor jobs from time to time. I pay him, of course.'

This was just the opening Kevin needed. Why should his father be paying money to have work done round the house? Money spent like this was money lost. Margaret was right. She was always going on about how the money their father spent on unnecessary things could go towards keeping him in a home. Kevin fidgeted, moving his hands restlessly.

'Don't you think ....' he began.

'I'll make tea,' said Hugh, getting up from his armchair. 'I'm having a cup anyway, so you may as well join me.'

Kevin was further disconcerted. He really was very ill at ease in this house. In his experience, women made tea. In childhood, his mother and sisters had made tea. During seminary days, tea came from the kitchen, maker unknown. In the parochial house, the housekeeper made tea. When he visited Margaret or Philomena, it was they who made the tea. There was something inappropriate about this aged man going out to the kitchen to make tea.

'Dad ....' he called towards the retreating back of the man who was already on the way to the kitchen.

He would have to put a stop to this. He began to feel masterful. What were the points he had rehearsed in the car? The possibility of a heart attack. The possibility of a fall. The danger of fire. The lack of security in the bungalow.

Hugh reappeared carrying a tray on which were two mugs of tea and a packet of biscuits.

'Dad ....' Kevin began, but Hugh was already talking.

'Do you ever see Michael O'Carroll these days?' he asked.

'I do not,' said Kevin petulantly. 'He's left, you know.'

'Left?' enquired Hugh.

'Yes, left the priesthood. He went off with a woman. Everyone knows about it, he didn't even make any attempt to keep it quiet. Though it was to be expected, when you think of it. That fellow had no background, no background at all. He should never have been accepted in the first place.'

'Why not? What was wrong with him?' asked Hugh.

'Don't you know? I'd have thought everyone knew. It was a shotgun affair.'

'Shotgun?' queried Hugh, deliberately obtuse.

'You know what I mean,' said Kevin peevishly. 'He wasn't illegitimate, strictly speaking, because his parents were married when he was born. But he was born five months after the wedding. Somehow or other they managed to cover it up, and he was accepted for the priesthood.'

'And,' pursued Hugh, 'did this vagary on his parents' part make him less eligible?'

'Of course it did,' answered Kevin. 'You have to have a top calibre of person for the priesthood. It was better in the old days, when anyone with a question mark over his parentage would just not have been considered. And rightly so. Nowadays you never know what sort of characters are just accepted, no questions asked.'

'And are you suggesting that a young man whose parents are not married should never be a priest?'

'Certainly. That's the way it used to be, and that's the way it should still be. We can do without the Michael O'Carrolls of this world.'

Hugh, at this point, gave a loud laugh, which he hastily turned into a cough.

'Well, to take that argument a step further,' he continued, 'who's to know who's legitimate and who's not, even within marriage? You must be well aware that there are offspring in marriage as the result of an affair? Would a fellow, born in wedlock, but with a question mark over his parentage, not be a suitable candidate?'

'Strictly speaking, no,' said Kevin. 'But there are two points of view in that sort of case. A man like that would obviously have some character defects, considering his parentage. But on the other hand, so long as it wasn't common knowledge, and there would be no scandal, allowance could be made.'

'You mean that it would be all right if nobody knew?'

'Quite so. The fellow might even have some very good qualities. He could possibly be a very good priest.'

'Too true, too true,' said Hugh. 'What the eye doesn't see, the heart doesn't grieve over. Have another biscuit.'

'Dad, there's something we have to talk about,' said Kevin, quite insistently.

As if I didn't know, thought Hugh. This time, he had decided how to respond. He was going to put a stop to the talk before it got properly started.

'Do you not think,' Kevin started, 'that you're spending too much money on things that aren't really necessary? There's that woman who comes in to clean, for example, and that man who cut the hedge. Money spent like this is money wasted.'

'Why so?' asked Hugh. 'Don't you pay a full time housekeeper? Doesn't Margaret have a daily home help, and Philomena as well? Don't you all pay someone to do gardening and odd jobs?'

'Yes, but that's different,' said Kevin. 'At your age you shouldn't have strangers in the house. Some people are only too quick to take advantage, if there was money or anything valuable around, you know what I mean. You know that it isn't at all suitable for you to continue living here alone. You might have a heart attack. You might fall and break a leg. The house might go on fire. You could be burgled. Now, Margaret was telling me on the phone the other day about this great place she had found ....'

'That'll do, Kevin,' said Hugh authoritatively, gesturing to Kevin to be quiet. 'All right, I'm eighty six. I might drop dead in ten minutes. Or on ten days. Or in ten years. But this is my home, and here is where I'm going to stay. I can cope well on my own. If a time ever comes when I cannot cope, I'll reconsider the situation then. And for the rest of today, I'll request you lot not to do that odious whispering round corners, thinking I can't hear. I can hear, and I've always heard your comments.

'And now, since you've come to visit me for my birthday, why not try to make it a pleasant day?'

Kevin sat, speechless, taken aback, as they heard Margaret's car turn in the gateway.

CHAPTER 31

'Yoo-hoo!' called Margaret as she struggled in the front door, carefully balancing the cardboard box containing the casserole. 'Hello, Kevin. Happy birthday, Dad. You'll never believe this, but Philomena isn't coming. She phoned me last night, to say she was going to have a perm. And I just told her it was a disgrace that she arranged to have her perm today, of all days. Anyway, I'll put the lunch on, and then we can all have a chat.'

She bustled out to the kitchen, calling over her shoulder, 'What's a medium heat in your oven, Dad?'

'A hundred and eighty,' he called after her.

'Are you sure?' she shouted. 'That seems rather low. I think I'll put it at two hundred.'

'You might as well do that, Margaret. Just put it at two hundred,' said Hugh, who hadn't the remotest idea about the workings of an oven.

'Now, I see you have tea. I'll just put on the kettle and top it up. I could do with a cup myself. It was an early start this morning, and you know I have bother with my varicose veins and my gallstones. None of us are getting any younger. Oh, before I forget, Dad, here's your present.'

She stood smiling indulgently as he opened the package and took out the two pairs of socks.

'And here's Philomena's present. By the feel of it, it seems to be more socks. Still, you can't have too many socks.'

'Quite so, you can't have too many socks,' said Hugh, as he set the four pairs of socks down beside the ones Kevin had already brought.

Margaret returned to the kitchen, and in a moment came fussing in again, holding the brown paper package she had found on the kitchen table.

'What's this?' she demanded.

'A half bottle of whiskey, I would think by the shape,' answered Hugh. 'A present from Mrs Monks.'

'Whiskey!' yapped Margaret incredulously. 'Has that woman no sense at all, giving you a bottle of whiskey? You could have a bad fall after drinking whiskey. And anyway, why is she giving you a present? She just wants to keep in with you, so that she can get more money out of you.'

Hugh watched as Margaret turned away from him and faced Kevin.

'We can't leave it here,' she mouthed at him, still holding the half bottle of whiskey.

'You can leave it here, and you will,' he said firmly.

'Margaret's right,' said Kevin. 'You shouldn't have whiskey in the house at your age. You might think it safe enough to have a drink, and then it could hit you before you know it. It's a health hazard, you know.'

'It's about as serious a health hazard as all those pairs of socks,' said Hugh. 'Now, will you please put it in the cupboard.'

Margaret was so completely taken aback that she did as requested, but still aimed glances in Kevin's direction, indicating that she did not intend to let the matter drop.

They sat, the three of them, in the living room, making fragmented attempts at conversation for an incredibly long ten minutes. Then Margaret went back to the kitchen, and returned with the information that the casserole was coming along nicely.

'I'll just prepare some potatoes,' she said briskly. 'And I'll set the table. Everything will be ready in an hour. Dad, wouldn't you like to go for a nap? Kevin could read the paper while you're sleeping.'

'No, no,' said Hugh. 'I'm not tired. Though I wouldn't mind a stroll in the sunshine. Do you want to come, Kevin?'

'Ah, no, no. I'll just read the paper. Don't go too far, you don't want to tire yourself too much.'

'And don't drop in anywhere, or stop to talk to anyone,' added Margaret. 'Remember, dinner will be ready at one.'

Hugh lifted his walking stick and hat from the hallstand, and sauntered out into the spring sunshine.

CHAPTER 32

He stood at the gate and looked up and down the road. The village street
was quiet and deserted. Parked cars on either side of the street caught the
bright sunlight. Hugh thought of the time when he first came to live in
Kincade, when there would not have been more than two or three cars on
the street.

It was fifty six years ago when he had first come here. And yet, apart
from the influx of cars, and new facades on some of the shops, the main
street was very much the same now as it had been then.

Hugh strolled out the gateway and turned right. He walked past the old
school residence which had been his home for many years, now renovated
and occupied by Tom Kenny, the school principal who had taken over
from Hugh twenty one years ago. It was a sign of the changing times,
Hugh thought, the way Tom Kenny was known to all, informally, by his
first name. In Hugh's time, the principal was always known as the
master, and addressed as Master. In fact, to this day, many of the older
people still called him Master.

He crossed the road, and turned into the side road that led past the
parish hall, the new school with its five classrooms, and the parochial
house. This was the same route he had taken on the day Nicholas Healy
had visited him five years ago, to help him sort out his problems. He
thought regretfully of his good friend, who had passed away a few months
ago. And as he thought, he took the turning towards the old railway
station, now deserted and overgrown. A grass covered track showed where
the railway had been, running out of sight into a tunnel under the road.
The platform had tufts of grass growing through the cracked concrete.

As on the day they had walked there together five years ago, Hugh
went over to the old bench and sat down.

He sat there for a long time, he had no idea how long. His thoughts
strayed back to the first time he had got out of a train on this platform.
He remembered the impatient figure of Father O'Lorcan pacing up and
down the platform. As if in a slow motion film, the events of the last
fifty six years seemed to play back again in front of his eyes, in bright
vivid technicolour.

Finally, he thought again about Nicholas, and about the help and
support he had received from him. He remembered the article he had read,

about two hours ago, in an old Sunday newspaper. He reminded himself that he must be very wary, must play it quietly until it would be time for his visitors to go. He must not let himself get irritated about anything. But he was aware of feeling alone, very much alone.

Then he told himself to take charge, as he always had done before. He would return home, he would humour his guests, but would enter into no conversation with them about what he should or shouldn't do.

He blinked in the bright sunlight, and unsteadily stood up. He pulled out his pocket watch. Margaret would have the dinner ready. She would be fussing if he wasn't there in time.

As he stood up, he felt the first stab of pain in his chest.

CHAPTER 33

Angelina sat with Sister Aine in the back garden of the convent. Over a cup of tea, they were talking about a rather disturbing phone call Angelina had received from Ireland just before coming out.

Mrs Monks had phoned from Kincade, her home village. Mrs Monks, Angelina explained, was a neighbour who did a bit of housework for her father. She had phoned about an hour ago, apologising for taking the liberty of calling. Angelina's father was not ill, she had said, but at the moment he was just not himself. She hoped she wasn't intruding, but she thought that Mr Staunton was under pressure from the others in the family. They wanted him to go into a home. Now, she had been calling with Mr Staunton for years. She knew his ways and his needs. He would never settle in a home. He was too independent. And the others didn't seem to understand this. And they were putting the pressure on.

'He's a man who can't cope with pressure, Mrs Lemoine,' Mrs Monks had added. 'Don't ask me how I know, but I just know. He can cope with anything else, but not pressure. And you know, Mrs Lemoine, he always enjoys your visits in the summer, with wee Claire. But the others, I don't want to speak ill of them, and I'm sure they mean well, but Mr Staunton just isn't himself today.'

Angelina had thanked Mrs Monks, taken her number and promised to call back later. But, as she told Sister Aine, she was completely taken aback. The idea of her father in a home was ludicrous. All right, he was eighty-six, but Angelina always saw him as lively, capable, irreverent, humorous and completely indestructible. And so, an hour later, she was telling the whole story to Sister Aine.

'Your father lives alone?' asked Sister Aine.

'Yes,' answered Angelina, 'but he's happy that way. Mrs Monks calls every day with the paper, and she does housework for him. She keeps an eye out for him, in case he ever needs help.'

'And the others in the family,' went on Sister Aine. 'Do they call often?'

'Not really,' said Angelina. 'They seem to be always very busy with this and that. They always come on his birthday. I think they see it as a sort of occasion for a family party. I can't think why they would want him to move into a home.'

'They wouldn't be wanting him to sell the house?' queried Sister Aine, who was a canny judge of character, even of people she had never met. 'Sometimes people think it's too much responsibility for an aged person to run a house.'

'No, not at all,' said Angelina. 'It couldn't be that. They couldn't be thinking of selling. You see, the house is mine.'

'The house is yours?' said Sister Aine, surprised.

'Yes,' said Angelina. 'Dad signed it over to me few years ago. He showed me the documents, and gave me the name of the solicitor. He said that Margaret and Kevin and Philomena all had their own homes, and I should have the bungalow so that I'd have somewhere to live if I ever came back home to stay.'

'Angelina!' exclaimed Sister Aine, 'you are not seriously telling me that you own a house in Ireland, that you have a father who obviously idolises you and would love to have you home, and you continue to live in a poky garret in Paris?'

'Well, it's not just as easy as that. Many a time I've thought of going home. It would be very good for Claire, and I'd love to go back home to stay. But suppose I go home. I'm not qualified to do anything, and the employment situation in Ireland is grim at the moment. Owning a house does not put bread and butter on the table.'

'Now look here,' said Sister Aine, 'you're a well experienced child minder. There are more and more working mothers in Ireland these days, so there's more demand for child minders. And you have experience of shop work. Don't forget that you're fluent in French, and I'm sure there's many a student would want tuition for exams. There's a good chance that you'd get work in your area. Even if you got something part time, you'd still be better off than you are here. Look how much you're paying for rent, for a start.'

Angelina found herself very quickly convinced by the sense of this argument. Maybe she could go home. Claire would love it. Her father would love it. She would love it. She had found and coped with various jobs in Paris. Surely she could do the same at home.

'Well, maybe when the summer holidays come ....' she started.

'Never mind the summer holidays. There's no time like the present,' said Sister Aine. 'Just think about it. It's today Mrs Monks phoned, and she didn't phone without good reason. Suppose you don't do anything until the summer, you never know what might happen. You might regret it if you don't do something now.'

Angelina then told Sister Aine about Madame Lambert, with whom she was working until July. She also mentioned Madame Lambert's plan to keep her on part time for half her present wage.

'I'll take care of Madame Lambert,' said Sister Aine. 'I know her well. In fact, didn't I put you in touch with her in the first place? There's a girl staying here, Joanna Craig, from Longford. She's up in the top back room, and she's eating her nails off because she's been here a fortnight and we haven't got her any work yet. I'll take her round to see Madame Lambert this evening. In fact, Angelina, there's no reason why you shouldn't make plans to go as soon as possible.'

It took Angelina only a few minutes to adjust. The more she thought about it, the more she realised that Sister Aine was right. They had another pot of tea, and went over the plans in detail.

An hour later, they had phoned a travel agent and booked a flight to Dublin, for Angelina and Claire, for the following afternoon. Sister Aine had spoken to Madame Lambert, who had been angry and blustering at first, but had soon got used to the idea that she would immediately have a new girl to look after little Jean Louis.

And so, on a day that had started like any other day, Angelina found herself standing in the hallway of the convent with Sister Aine and Joanna Craig. She had to go to the bank, after which she would return to the flat, see the concierge to give immediate notice, phone her daughter's school, and then she'd be ready to start packing. Sister Aine and Joanna Craig were about to go round to Madame Lambert's.

'I can't thank you enough, Sister,' said Angelina. 'I doubt if I would have ever made this move if you hadn't pushed me in the right direction.'

'I'm so happy you're going home,' said Sister Aine. 'You won't regret it. And now, there are two things you have to remember. First, you must come back to us on holiday. And secondly, next time I'm home in Ireland, I'll be coming to see you, and your father and Claire. So be warned!'

The two women embraced each other, and promised to keep in touch. Angelina set off to withdraw some cash from the bank, and then hurried back to her apartment. As she turned her key in the lock, she heard the phone ringing.

CHAPTER 34

'Take your time,' said Hugh to himself, as he stood up shakily. 'Walk slowly. Breathe gently. Wait for the pain to go away. As he felt the pain fading, he steadied himself, and moved carefully along the road. As he passed the school the pain returned, and again he concentrated on gentle movement, willing it to go away. Leaning on his walking stick, he carefully made his way homewards. It was about one o'clock, he thought. Kevin and Margaret usually went off about five. He must cope with this pain without letting them suspect anything. As soon as they had gone, he would call Mrs Monks.

With some difficulty, he arrived back at the house, to find the table set and Margaret anxiously asking what had kept him. They sat down to eat, and Hugh realised that he was quite hungry, and enjoyed the meal. The pain came and went. When it came it was sharp and excruciating, but lasted only a few seconds. When it went away, he felt an amazing sense of exhilaration and well being. He also felt light hearted, almost to the point of frivolity. But he kept reminding himself to be careful.

As they sat, at the end of the meal, with a cup of tea, Margaret started the inevitable line of talk.

'I saw Maureen Cullen last week,' she said. 'Do you remember Maureen? She was in my class at school. Well, she was on the way to visit her father. He's in a lovely new home, St Cecilia's in Knockore. I went with her, just for the company, you know. You should see the home, Dad, it's just beautiful. The rooms are lovely, all with their own wash basin. And there's a nice garden, with seats and tables. And there's a trained nurse on the staff.'

Hugh at that moment felt a severe jab of pain, and made no attempt to comment.

Margaret continued. 'Would you not think about it, Dad? It costs a hundred and eighty pounds a week, so your pension would cover it. You give in your pension book when you move in, and they look after the banking and so on. You'd have no worries about money, or about the upkeep of the house ....'

The pain had gone. Hugh was feeling well, exuberant, even bloody minded.

'I've no money worries as I am,' he said. 'And about the upkeep of the house, well, I'd be worried about the house if I wasn't here to see to it.'

'Oh, but Dad, we'd --- you'd sell the house. And Kevin and Philomena and I would look after the money for you. We'd bank it, and we'd see to it that you'd have anything you'd need.'

'Yes,' said Kevin. 'You know that it's a good idea, Dad. This house must be worth about thirty thousand pounds. It could be gathering interest in your bank account.'

Or in your bank account, thought Hugh. Or Margaret's.

'I can't sell this house,' he said. 'It isn't mine to sell.'

Margaret and Kevin looked at each other, aghast.

'What do you mean, it isn't yours to sell?' she demanded fiercely.

Hugh toyed with the idea of telling them about his arrangement with the house, but another jab of pain sharply reminded him that now was not the time.

'This is serious,' whispered Margaret to Kevin. 'His mind is wandering. He thinks he is still living in the old school house.'

She leaned over and spoke earnestly.

'Of course it's your house, Dad. Do you not remember? It was the old school. You had it converted into a bungalow when you retired.'

Hugh remained silent, while Margaret continued to extol the good points of St Cecilia's.

'And another thing you'll like about St Cecilia's, they have a great social life. Just think of it, no more lonely evenings sitting here on your own. There is something on for residents on four evenings every week. They have bingo, and sing songs, and quizzes. That's what you'd love, the quizzes, all that general knowledge and things you'd be so good at. In fact,' she turned and winked at Kevin, 'within a month you'd be the quiz champion of St Cecilia's. And they have a brilliant craft shop. They have all the old people working on some craft.'

'That sounds interesting, Margaret,' said Kevin. 'I always say that old people would have fewer problems if they were kept busy. What sort of crafts do they have?'

'Well, it's mostly knitting and crochet for the ladies. But on Thursday morning they have a basket day, and most of the men are making baskets. Maureen's father has become really keen on making baskets. And if you are really interested in it, you don't have to wait till Thursday, you can take your basket and continue it in your own room.'

Hugh was now free of pain.

'I have got through the last eighty six years,' he said, 'without ever making a basket. I do not intend to ever make a basket, on a Thursday or any other day.'

He found himself trying to recollect a story from long ago, something about a hermit who spent all his spare time making baskets. This story seemed to come from the very distant past, from his childhood, when an old teacher in primary school used to read tales from the lives of the saints on Friday afternoons. He concentrated hard, as he tried to remember the details.

The hermit, it appeared, when he was not engaged in prayer or spiritual exercises, would go out into the wilderness and cut willows, which he brought back to his hut and made into baskets. Satan, he had been warned before he embarked on the life of a hermit, would find work for idle hands. He must therefore keep busy. So he spent his days making baskets for which he had no conceivable use. At the end of each year, he piled up the baskets in an enormous heap and burned them. He would then start immediately to make the next year's supply of baskets.

Hugh marvelled at the thought that it was possibly eighty years since he had heard this story of the hermit, on a long past Friday afternoon in infant school. At this moment, he was strongly aware of the futility of a basket making life.

No, he thought, they can make all the baskets they want in St Cecilia's in Knockore. But they'll have to make them without me.

Margaret and Kevin had left the table, and were standing over at Hugh's desk. They were whispering urgently. This time Hugh, assailed again by pain, did not hear what they were saying.

'What's this?' demanded Margaret, lifting a page from the desk. 'Your phone bill! You haven't paid it!'

'It came only yesterday,' said Hugh. 'I don't suppose Telecom Eireann will have to close down if I don't send it for a day or two.'

'And there's no calls charge. Just the rental,' she went on, staring accusingly at him as if this showed some negligence on his part.

'I haven't made any calls for months,' he said. 'So it's just as well they didn't charge me for any.'

He heard the two of them, in incredulous tones, asking what was wrong with a man who paid rental for a phone he never used.

'And look at this!' said Margaret, in a tone of disbelief. 'Look what he threw in the bin!'

From the waste basket under the desk she lifted a gaudily coloured envelope, unopened, bearing the message: Open quickly to discover this

182

fantastic prize that could be waiting for you. You have been chosen as one of the lucky entrants in a draw for the first £5,000 to be paid off your new holiday residence in the sun ......

'Why did you throw this in the bin, Dad?' she squealed. 'It could be worth five thousand pounds!'

'Bullshit!' said Hugh, and got up and walked out of the room, hearing the frantic mutters behind him.

Out in the hallway, he went straight to the phone. He lifted the receiver, and from the card on the wall he carefully dialled the code for Paris, followed by Angelina's number. He heard the phone ring at the other end, seeming to go on for a long time. Then he heard Angelina's voice answering.

'Angelina ....' he said hesitantly.

'Oh Dad, I was going to ring you later. Guess what? I'm coming home tomorrow, with Claire. We'll be on an early flight, and we'll be with you in the afternoon. And we're going to stay, I'm going to look for a job at home ....'

'Dear girl,' said Hugh. 'Thank God ....' And he replaced the receiver.

'What on earth are you doing?' demanded Kevin, who had just appeared as he put down the phone.

'Frying eggs!' snapped Hugh. 'What do you think I'm doing?'

'Dad, were you making a phone call? Who were you phoning?' said Margaret.

'I was phoning Angelina,' he answered. 'She's coming home tomorrow.'

Margaret, suddenly solicitous, took him by the arm and led him back into the living room and over to his armchair.

'Sit down, Dad,' she persuaded. 'You'll be all right. Don't worry. Kevin and I will look after everything.'

She left him and went back to the hall.

Hugh sat back in his armchair. He felt relaxed, though the pain niggled from time to time. He thought about Angelina. He wondered briefly about her unexpected decision to come home. He felt happy and reassured that she was coming. Then he heard Margaret's agitated tones as she spoke to Philomena on the phone.

'Hello, Philomena ..... well, you chose the right day to stay away ..... you've no idea the trouble Kevin and I have had today ..... Dad will have to be moved as soon as possible ..... and not to a home ..... he needs hospital care ..... he's totally confused ..... he's talking nonsense.

He was standing at the phone thinking he was talking to Angelina ..... he doesn't know where he is, he thinks he is in the old school residence. We'll have to see a doctor about this ..... you and I will go and talk to Dr Morris tomorrow ..... no, of course his own doctor won't do, we'll need to get someone who will listen to our point of view ..... do you know, he thinks that Angelina phoned and said she was coming tomorrow ..... we need to have a doctor's report stating that he's not safe to be left alone ..... once we get him committed we can see to the house ..... you know, this might be a blessing in disguise ..... as usual, there was no talking to him ..... and he had thrown in the bin a voucher which had a chance of winning five thousand pounds ..... and he said that socks were a health hazard ..... you've no idea the way he's rambling ..... and it seems he's drinking a lot, that woman Mrs Monks brings in bottles of whiskey wrapped in brown paper ..... so now we're leaving shortly ..... would you phone Dr Morris and make an appointment for us to see him tomorrow ..... yes, you are coming with me, you left me with enough on my hands today, what with making the casserole and then the worry of finding him in such poor shape ..... so get you on the phone right away and make that appointment and I'll see you later this evening. We'll be coming back her in a couple of days, so don't go arranging anything else.'

Hugh opened his eyes to see Margaret and Kevin standing beside him.

'We're going now, Dad,' she said. 'But don't worry. You'll be all right.' She patted him on the arm. 'And we'll be back soon.'

'You're going early,' Hugh pointed out. 'It's only three o'clock. Normally you don't go until five.'

'I know, but we want to avoid the rush hour traffic. And we have to see Philomena this evening about something. And, Dad, we'll be back in a few days. We'll be bringing a doctor, just to give you a wee check up. You can't be too careful, you know, at your age.'

'True, true, you can't be too careful,' said Hugh. Dear God, he prayed, keep this pain away until they've gone.

As they opened the front door, without a backward glance, Hugh felt suddenly, irrepressibly, mischievous.

'Margaret!' he called. She looked round, impatiently. 'Did you know that ants move colony when the queen gets too old to lay eggs?' he asked.

He felt tempted to follow with the story of the hermit who spent his years making baskets to burn. But caution prevailed, and he concentrated on willing the pain away.

From the window, he watched Margaret and Kevin making a speedy departure.

As the cars disappeared from sight, Hugh was aware that the pain had gone, completely.

CHAPTER 35

Hugh watched the cars disappearing, and then got up and ambled out to the kitchen. He fed the cat, and put on the kettle. He would shortly have a leisurely cup of tea, and read the paper. But he must think and plan a bit first. There were just a few things he had to think about, and then he could relax.

He went out to the hall and lifted the phone. He dialled Mrs Monks' number.

'Hello, Mr Staunton,' he heard her cheery voice. 'Are you all right? Would you like me to come round?'

'I would, indeed, if it's not too much trouble. And, Mrs Monks?'

'Yes, Mr Staunton?'

'Could John stay over with me tonight?'

He thought of the article in the Sunday paper. It seemed that an ambulance could call at your house, escorted by a guard, with the message that your relatives were having you put in hospital. There would not be any men in white coats, but slick guys in suits and ties, who would talk gently to you, and talk down to you, telling you about the nice place you were going to. There would be a uniformed nurse there, ready to give an injection in case you didn't see eye to eye with them.

'Surely, no problem. I'll make up a bed when I get there.'

'And, Mrs Monks, I know that tomorrow isn't your day for cleaning, but could you come tomorrow anyway?'

Margaret and Kevin had said that they would be back in a few days. But suppose they came tomorrow? Or tonight?

'Certainly. I'll be there tomorrow, from early morning. Look, I'll be over in a few minutes, and we'll talk about what has to be done.'

'Thank you, Mrs Monks.' Hugh hung up, and returned to his armchair. Everything was now in order.

It had been a long and tiring day, quite unpredictable in its outcome. At your age you have to be careful, Margaret had said. Yes, he thought, you certainly do have to be careful. He sat back and closed his eyes. He heard Mrs Monks coming in the front door. And the pain had gone, completely.

'How are you, Mr Staunton?' asked Mrs Monks gently. 'Will I make you a cup of tea?'

'I'll have a whiskey, Mrs Monks,' answered Hugh. 'And bring a glass for yourself. We have a few things to talk about.'

They sat at the fire, in silence, for a few minutes. Then Hugh spoke.

'Angelina and Claire are coming home tomorrow,' he said.

'I know,' she answered. 'Angelina phoned me about an hour ago. They're arriving in Dublin in the afternoon. John's going to meet them.'

'You're very kind, Mrs Monks. You and John, you're both very kind. I can't thank you enough for all your help.'

'Now, don't talk like that. It's nothing, just so long as you always know we'll be here if you want us.'

'I know, I know. Mrs Monks, would you read this?'

He handed her the newspaper article that he had read earlier in the day. While she read it, he glanced through the Irish Times. When she had finished reading, she looked up.

'So you see why I want John to stay over with me tonight?' he asked.

'I do,' she answered. 'And I'll be here from early morning tomorrow. And then Angelina and Claire will be home in the afternoon. Don't worry, between us all, we'll make sure that everything is all right.'

'I knew you would, Mrs Monks,' said Hugh. 'You're a real friend. And now, one other thing. Could you phone Dr O'Neill and ask him if he could call round with me this evening?'

EPILOGUE

Two days later, Angelina woke early, in her own bedroom in Kincade. She woke with a sense of peace. She had come home to stay. There would be no packing up, no tedious journey at the end of a couple of weeks. There would be no need to cajole and placate Claire, who never wanted to leave Kincade.

It was early, just after seven, but she got up, put on her dressing gown, and went out to the kitchen. Her father was already there. He had always been an early riser.

He was frying bacon on the range. He made a pot of tea, and they sat there, enjoying a leisurely breakfast.

'We'll buy a car, Angelina,' he said, after a while.

'Now, don't talk like that, Dad,' she answered. 'Just because I've come home, you needn't think you have to be spending money on me. I'll have to think about finding a job and supporting myself.'

'The money's there, Angelina,' he said. 'Not a lot, I know. And it won't be a great car. But I can get us a small one, second hand. After all, I'll be wanting to get out a bit more than I've been doing of late. So we need a car.'

She smiled happily at him. They always had good times together.

At nine o'clock Mrs Monks arrived. The Irish Times was not in yet, she said, but she'd go back for it later. And there were a few little things to be done around the house, so she'd just make a start.

She swept and hoovered the living room and the porch. She cleaned the windows of the hall and the kitchen. Then, in the little alcove between the kitchen and the living room, she beckoned Angelina over.

'Since you're home to stay, Angelina,' she said, 'we'd better clear out these cupboards. You'll need space for your things.'

The alcove had been the porch of the junior classroom, in the days of the old school. When the building was converted, the door and window of the porch had been walled up, and the area had been fitted with cupboards and shelves. Teresa had used this space for storing things.

Now, as Angelina and Mrs Monks looked in the cupboards, they found them packed tightly with things from the past, Teresa's clothes, Philomena's clothes, Angelina's school uniform, all sorts of things long out of date.

Angelina took one glance, and Mrs Monks understood.

'I know you might find it difficult to sort this lot, love,' she said. 'Would you like me to do it?'

'Please do, Mrs Monks,' Angelina replied. 'I really wouldn't know what to do with all those clothes. Can you give them to a charity shop, or St Vincent de Paul, or something?'

'Of course I will, love,' said Mrs Monks. 'I know it would be upsetting for you.'

****

An hour later, Mrs Monks was in a quandary. She had cleared out cupboards, she had made up bags of clothes and shoes to be given to charity. There were tweed suits that had belonged to Teresa, there were dresses and skirts and cardigans of Philomena's, there were clothes that Angelina had worn as a teenager. She would later ask John to take her into town, where she would give them to a charity shop she knew.

It was the contents of the drawer, the little drawer set far back on a middle shelf, hidden under a pile of old cardigans, that caused her to hesitate.

'There are things in there of your mother's,' she told Angelina. 'Personal things. Maybe you'd like to sort them?'

'I will, certainly, Mrs Monks, thanks,' said Angelina. She lifted out the drawer, which contained a black zipped writing case, packed to overflowing, and a chocolate box, also filled with papers and envelopes. She carried the lot down to her bedroom and emptied everything onto the bed.

For a long time she sat there, going through letters and cards that went back many years. There were postcards, mass cards, memoriam cards, holy pictures. There were lists of addresses of friends and relatives, many long dead. There were old letters, a few that Angelina had written herself, as far back as the first year she was in France. There were letters from Teresa's sister Patricia in Scotland, and from a few other lifelong friends.

Somewhere in the middle of this bundle of correspondence, Angelina found an envelope, dated 1970, in an unfamiliar handwriting. She opened it and read.

The address at the top right was simply Murgintra. The letter began: Dearest Teresa, as time goes on, and I'm getting older, I have decided to make my will. I know you'll understand why I'm leaving everything to

Ellen and the boys. As you know, Ellen is much younger than me, and I want to leave her provided for. The boys have taken over the working of the farm, so I feel it should be left to them. I thought at times that I should leave something to our children, Teresa, but they are all well settled and well off. Also, you know how I love this farm, I would not like to think that it would be sold or divided up. I thought I'd better explain this to you, and I feel sure you'll understand. My best wishes to you, Teresa. Love always, Tim.

For a long time, Angelina sat on the bed, thinking. Then she folded the letter, and put it carefully in the drawer of her bedside table.

Shortly she went back to the kitchen, where Hugh was sitting at the range. She sat down beside him.

'Tell me something, Dad,' she said gently. 'Are you my father?'

Without showing any surprise at the question, Hugh answered.

'I am your father, Angelina,' he said. 'You are my child ---- my only child.'

He explained nothing further, and she asked no further questions.

****

About midday Claire woke up. She was confused at first. She did not hear the familiar roar of city traffic, and she did not see, from the window, the tall grey drab building that faced the Paris flat. And then, with some delight, she remembered her new surroundings, as the clear daylight brightened her room, and she was aware of the silence of the countryside.

Unwilling to waste any time, she quickly got up and dressed. She went through to the living room, where her grandfather was sitting at the fire reading. In the kitchen, Mrs Monks was packing up a lot of old clothes in large black plastic bags. Her mother, Mrs Monks told her, had gone down to the shop to get something for lunch.

Claire made herself some tea and toast, which she was having at the kitchen table when Angelina returned.

'I'll go over and see Donna and Geraldine,' said Claire.

'Not at all, dear,' laughed Angelina. 'They'll be at school. Don't forget, it's Friday. Everyone's not on holidays.'

The previous evening, after Angelina and Claire had arrived home, they had talked at length with Hugh about their future, about what they were going to do. Claire could start school after the Easter holidays. She would go, with her friends Donna and Geraldine, to the school her mother had attended years ago. Angelina would go over one day soon to talk to

190

the headmistress, and Claire would be able to join the exam class for the following year.

Claire was fascinated at the idea of wearing a school uniform. The idea of all the girls at school wearing identical grey skirts and turquoise blouses was great, she thought. She was surprised when her mother told her that most girls hated wearing uniforms.

From the living room, Hugh called Claire.

'Would you open the bottom drawer of my desk, Claire,' he said, 'and take out the radio.'

Claire did as requested, and took out a transistor radio, which she handed to him.

'No, it's for you,' he said. 'I won it in a golf competition years ago. I never use it, I prefer my old radio in the kitchen. So it's yours, Claire. I know that young people like listening to that awful modern music. So there you are, only don't have it up too loud!'

'Oh, thank you, Grandad!' Claire was ecstatic. There was one surprise after another, coming to Ireland to stay, having her own room, going to a school with a uniform, and now her own radio. She rushed off, opening the back of the radio to see what sort of batteries were needed.

****

That afternoon, outside Margaret Gillen's house, there were two cars standing, ready for the journey. Doctor Morris was taking his own car, as he had to go on to a meeting after the visit to Kincade. Margaret was to travel with Doctor Morris, so that she could explain to him fully the problem about her father.

Father Kevin Staunton was to follow in his car, accompanied by Philomena and Father Pius Padden who had been brought along for support. It had been decided that the presence of a priest would lend authority to the proceedings.

As they started the journey, Margaret launched into a description of Hugh's symptoms.

'The first thing, Doctor,' she started, 'was that he didn't know where he was. His mind was wandering. He thought he was in the old school house where we used to live. You know, he was saying that he didn't own the house, and things like that. He's away back in the past.

'And then he was standing at the phone, thinking he was talking to someone. He told us that Angelina had phoned to say she was coming home. Angelina's the youngest, she's away in Paris. She never comes,

191

except in the summer. It's left to Philomena and me to keep an eye on things. And there he was, holding the phone, and coming out with this talk about Angelina coming tomorrow.'

'Would he be hard of hearing?' asked Doctor Morris. 'I mean, could there have been someone else on the phone, and he maybe thought it was Angelina?'

'No, no, there was nobody there. The phone didn't ring. We found him standing holding it, and looking sort of vacant.'

'Now, is he confused like this all the time?' asked Doctor Morris. 'Or is he coherent enough at times?'

'All the time,' answered Margaret. 'The day before yesterday, from the moment we arrived in, he was just rambling. He was going on about socks being a health hazard, whatever that was supposed to mean. And he was raving about ants moving colony. I'd suspect he's drinking a bit. There's this grotty little woman, Mrs Monks, who brings in bottles of whiskey wrapped in brown paper. She's supposed to be his home help, but I don't know what she does, the house is always in a mess, dishes in the sink, books and papers everywhere. I know the kind of her, she'd take advantage of the fact his mind is wandering, to get more money out of him.'

'Would you say he deteriorated rapidly?' asked Doctor Morris. 'The last time you saw him, was he giving any cause for concern?'

'Well, yes, I mean no, he was all right the last time.'

'And how long ago was that?'

'Oh, I can't remember exactly, a few weeks, I suppose .... Tell me, Doctor, do you think you can get him admitted to hospital immediately? It's such a worry to think of him there on his own.'

'We'll see how he is, and take it from there. If he's to be admitted immediately, we need two doctors' reports. After I've seen him, I'll phone his own doctor and see what we can arrange.'

****

In the second car, Kevin and Philomena were engaged in earnest conversation with Father Pius Padden.

'It's like this, Pius,' Kevin was explaining. 'My father is a very obstinate old man. He's gone completely senile, and for years we've been trying to persuade him to go into a home where he'd be properly looked after. But you might as well talk to the wall. And now he's got to the stage when he really needs to be in a psychiatric unit. Knowing him, he'll oppose the idea. So that's where we want your help. You know the way old people would listen to a priest when they won't take any heed of their own family.'

'Surely, surely,' said Father Pius Padden.

'Margaret and I were saying,' added Philomena, 'that maybe you shouldn't talk to him about the move into hospital immediately. If you just chat with him a bit, and get him to feel at home with you, then he'll be more likely to give in if you have to use persuasion. So when we go in first, we'll just sit down and chat for a while. Doctor Morris wants to observe him in his own surroundings, and watch his reactions to people he knows. After that, we'll be able to start the arrangements for getting him moved.'

'All right,' said Father Pius Padden.

****

'Who on earth are those scruffy kids?' said Margaret, as the cars turned into the gateway and she saw two teenage girls walking towards the house. 'Selling tickets, or doing those sponsor sheets or something of that sort, I suppose. Here! You! Come here! What do you want?'

She rolled down the window, as the girls turned round, startled.

'We're going to see Claire,' said one of them.

'Claire? Claire who? There's no Claire here. There's nobody here but an old man, and he's in poor health, and you're not to go knocking the door annoying him!'

The other girl spoke.

'We know Mr Staunton,' she said. 'We were talking to him down the road yesterday, and he told us that Claire Lemoine was coming home.'

'Claire Lemoine is not here,' snapped Margaret. 'It's in the summer that Claire Lemoine comes --- used to come. And she won't be coming back here. Now clear off.'

The two girls, puzzled, turned and went away. Margaret looked meaningfully at Doctor Morris.

'You see?' she said. 'He's got a notion in his head, and he's out talking to everybody. On Wednesday it was Angelina he thought was coming. Now it's Claire, her daughter. What in heaven's name will people be thinking?'

****

Hugh, on hearing the sound of cars arriving, went to the window and looked out. He saw the occupants of the cars getting out, and standing in a group talking urgently.

Incongruously, his thoughts strayed back sixty years, to a time when he used to play skittles with some friends in Scotland. There was a big shed at the back of Herbie Doherty's house. They used to gather there on winter evenings, and set up the wooden skittles at the end of the shed. Then they would take turns to roll the ball, and set about scoring points.

Outside the house, he saw Margaret, Philomena and Kevin, engaged in conversation with two men. One was a priest, and Hugh deduced that the other must be a doctor.

The five figures, standing outside, reminded Hugh of five skittles. He thought again of Herbie Doherty's shed. He thought of the wooden ball, of its texture, its weight. He thought of the technique of rolling it, aiming, if possible, to knock down more than one skittle at a time.

He reared himself up to his still considerable height, and sauntered out the door to greet the visitors.

'Well, now, so you're back again,' he said. He turned enquiringly to the two strangers, waiting for an introduction. Kevin introduced him to Father Pius Padden, while Margaret was deep in conversation with the other man.

'That's the old house over there,' she was saying. 'We all lived there as long as he was teaching. He's been in the bungalow since he retired.'

'Yes,' interrupted Hugh. 'That's the old school residence. A house like this went with the principal's job, in the old days. Though most of them are privately owned now. Tom Kenny there has been principal since I retired. He bought that house some years back.'

Hugh looked at the other man, and then at Margaret, saying, 'And is this a family friend?'

'Hello, Mr Staunton,' Doctor Morris introduced himself. 'Very pleased to meet you. Isn't it a fine day for the time of year?'

'Oh, excuse me,' said Margaret. 'We were so busy talking that I forgot to introduce you. This is Doctor Morris. Remember I told you the other day that we would bring along a doctor, just to give you a wee check up?'

'No need, no need,' said Hugh, as they all went towards the front door. 'I see Doctor O'Neill regularly, he checks the old heart and the blood pressure and all that. He was in here with me just a couple of days ago, and he says I'm in tip top form. As fit as a fiddle, he says, in fact, fitter than most fiddles.'

He did not mention the severe pain that two days ago had alarmed him, the pain that in Doctor O'Neill had diagnosed as almost certainly stress related.

Inside the house, Mrs Monks put on the kettle and called Angelina.

'I think you have visitors,' she said.

Then she looked for Claire, who was in her room, listening to music while she arranged her clothes in the wardrobe.

'Claire, would you ever run down to John,' she said. 'Remind him that he was going to mow Mr Staunton's lawn today.'

By this time the visitors were all in the living room. Hugh, always a courteous host, made sure that everyone was comfortably seated, as Angelina appeared in the doorway.

'Angelina!' exclaimed Margaret. 'What's she doing here?'

'Hello, Margaret,' said Angelina. 'Claire and I have come home to stay. I'm going to look for a job.'

'Didn't I tell you Angelina was coming?' asked Hugh. 'When you were here on Wednesday I told you. I phoned Paris while you were here, do you not remember?'

Margaret was distinctly taken aback. Doctor Morris looked puzzled at first, then irritated.

Mrs Monks arrived in with a tea tray, with scones and chocolate biscuits. Doctor Morris found difficulty in associating this neat little woman, with a smart hairdo and wearing a bright green tracksuit, with the 'grotty little woman' Margaret had talked about.

Everyone sat silently, while Angelina passed round cups of tea, and milk and sugar. There was a general atmosphere of unease, and Hugh was fully aware that he was under close scrutiny.

He broke the silence, and addressed Doctor Morris.

'By your accent, you're not from these parts, Doctor,' he said. 'Further north, I would think?'

'Yes, Mr Staunton, I'm from near Malin, in Donegal, about as far north as you can get.'

'True,' answered Hugh. 'Malin's further north than anywhere in Northern Ireland, and yet it's officially in the south. I knew a fellow from Malin once, Donal Morris, he was called. Any relation of yours? I knew him in the training college in Waterford.'

'You knew Donal? He's my uncle,' answered Doctor Morris. 'He was the principal of a school near Letterkenny for a long time. Like yourself, he's retired now, and like yourself, he's a very active man.'

'It's a small world, isn't it?' said Hugh. 'Though, come to think of it, it's a small country, and I suppose that's why, when you reach my age, often when you meet someone, you will possibly have met one of his friends or relations sometime in the past.'

Hugh and Doctor Morris then became involved in a lively conversation about Donegal, about Sligo, about training college days in Waterford, about schools long ago and schools now, about work and retirement. Doctor Morris was becoming more relaxed. Hugh was happily aware of this.

Margaret was not pleased with the trend of the conversation. She felt that she would need to nudge Doctor Morris back to the purpose of the visit. She leaned over to him and whispered.

'The bottles of whiskey wrapped in brown paper ....'

'Whiskey?' said Hugh. 'It's in the kitchen cupboard. Margaret, if you want to give any of the guests a drink, you know where to find it. None for me, thanks. There's sherry there too, and beer.'

'What was this about ants moving colony?' asked Philomena, acutely aware that things were not going according to plan.

Hugh looked appropriately puzzled. So did everyone else.

Doctor Morris got up.

'I'll have to go,' he said, looking at his watch. 'I've a conference to go to. It was nice meeting you, Mr Staunton. Bye.'

Hugh thought again about the skittles. One down, four to go. He thought of the wooden ball, of the aim, the precision.

Doctor Morris beckoned Margaret out into the hallway, where he gave his opinion of Hugh's state of health.

'There's nothing wrong with him,' he said. 'He's perfectly coherent, and in fine shape. His hearing is perfect, and his reactions are quick. Your young sister has come home to stay, so he won't be alone. He has neighbours who are obviously happy to help out. You seem to have been mistaken about his supposed state of confusion.'

'But, Doctor, he was seriously rambling the other day. Nothing he said made any sense .....'

'I can't agree with you, Margaret. He seems to have been right about Angelina coming home. And he's not at all confused about where he is, he is quite clear about the old house and where he is now.'

'But, Doctor, you've seen him for only a short while. I'm telling you, the other day, he was completely confused, he just talked nonsense the whole time.'

'I can only make a judgement on what I see. But what I do know is that I cannot consider recommending your father to go into hospital. There are lots of seriously ill patients, waiting for a place, and he certainly is not in need of urgent attention. I'm sure you'll find that everything will work out all right. If you still feel concerned, maybe you should have a chat with his own doctor. Don't forget, I'm just here as a family friend. Now, I'm a bit late, I'll really have to go.'

Margaret for once was left speechless. Her carefully laid plans had rapidly crumbled. As Doctor Morris got into his car, John Monks wheeled his lawnmower in the gate, and started to cut the front lawn.

Margaret stood at the front door. She felt furious. As she looked out, she was furious with Doctor Morris, furious at John Monks. Questions flooded into her mind. Why couldn't Doctor Morris have stayed longer? How did her father manage to appear so reasonable today? Why had Angelina come home? What was to be done next?

They would have to find another doctor, she told herself. Her husband Peadar was no use in this particular project. He really infuriated her. A doctor himself, he should have been able to help. But for years he had maintained that she should stop hassling Hugh, that she should not interfere with how or where he wanted to live. Peadar did not even know of today's visit.

She would have to talk to Philomena about the possibility of finding another doctor. Doctor Morris had been a complete disappointment. And time was going on. It was six years now that they had been trying to arrange to have the house sold. Why, she asked herself, should we have to wait any longer for our money? None of us is getting any younger.

And what a waste of time this is, she told herself angrily. Here she was, in Kincade for the second time in three days, and it seemed that she would have to be back again soon, even though she had so much to do at home. Her mind crowded with these thoughts, she walked into the kitchen.

There she found Claire, sitting at the range with the two girls she had sent away earlier.

'Hello, Auntie Margaret,' said Claire, getting up to welcome her aunt.

Without a word, Margaret turned on her heel and stormed out of the kitchen. She was enraged. Not only was Claire bringing all sorts of scruffy hooligans into the house, but those girls had actually come back after she had sent them away.

It looked as if Angelina could be a problem, she thought. What was this talk about coming home and getting a job? She would have to be

197

told that they would be selling the house. Anyway, Angelina, with her city notions, would be more likely to look for a job in Dublin.

She returned to the living room, where Hugh was telling the others about the recent death of his old friend Nicholas Healy.

'Nicholas Healy was the old lawyer fellow, wasn't he?' said Philomena. 'He must have been very old. He was an old man as long as I could remember.'

'He was the same age as me,' said Hugh. 'I had known him for a long time. We used to play golf together from the first year I came to Kincade.'

'It's very sad, very sad, to lose an old friend,' said Pius Padden. 'But it's God's will, and we must accept God's will.' I have to gain his confidence, Pius Padden told himself, especially if I'm going to have to do a bit of persuading later on.

'Who are those girls in the kitchen, Angelina?' asked Margaret.

'Donna and Geraldine. They're Claire's friends. She's known them for years.'

'But you can't let them just run in and out of the house like that,' expostulated Margaret. 'And I had already sent them away, and they just came back. You know, Dad, you're not nearly careful enough about letting people into the house. And that man out there mowing the lawn, John Monks, I suppose?'

'That's right,' said Hugh. 'He always mows the lawn. He's very helpful, a very good neighbour.'

'And how much do you pay him? And you pay that woman to do the cleaning, which she doesn't do at all well, from what I can see. You can't afford to throw money around like that.'

The time has come, thought Hugh. I'm going to sort things out now.

'By the way,' he said, 'there's a bit of family business that I want to sort out with all of you. So, since we're all together, now would be the time. Father Padden, I know you wouldn't mind if we have a family session. You could sit in the kitchen, it's very comfortable in there.'

'Surely, surely,' said Pius Padden, getting up and going towards the door.

A minute later, when Hugh had built up the fire and settled back in his chair, he noticed Kevin and Pius Padden standing in the doorway. Kevin was expostulating about something, Pius Padden was nodding agreement.

'Is the Pious Pudding still here?' muttered Hugh, sotto voce.

'Dad!' exclaimed Margaret incredulously.

Angelina bit her tongue to prevent herself from laughing.

'We've decided that Pius should stay,' said Kevin. 'He could possibly be helpful if there are any difficulties with this family business, whatever it is.'

Hugh got up, and walked towards the door. Taking Pius Padden by the elbow, he steered him in the direction of the kitchen.

'I'm sure you understand, Father,' he said, 'that there are family matters which must be discussed with the family only. If, after our discussion, Kevin wants to tell you what we talk about, he may. We won't be too long. Claire!' he called.

'Yes, Grandad?' said Claire, appearing from the kitchen.

'Could you make Father Padden a cup of coffee? We have things to talk about, so he can sit with you and your friends in the kitchen.'

'Surely, surely,' said Pius Padden.

'OK Grandad,' said Claire, reaching for the kettle.

Back in the living room, Margaret was outraged.

'You can't do this, Dad,' she yapped. 'You can't leave a priest who has come to visit you in the kitchen. And don't call him Pious Pudding. You are so irreverent. Auntie Anne, God rest her, always said that about you, you are so totally irreverent.'

'Margaret,' said Hugh, slowly and deliberately, 'I did not invite Father Padden to my house. I have nothing against him, but I do not like the reason why you have brought him here. If he doesn't like sitting in my kitchen, well, he can go and sit in the shed.'

Two down, three to go, thought Hugh, thinking again of the skittles.

'Well, now we can get down to business,' he said. 'So today's the day you were going to have me committed?'

Angelina was visibly shocked. Kevin and Philomena looked very ill at ease. Only Margaret remained confident.

'Now, you know it's not like that, Dad,' she coaxed. 'You know that at your age you shouldn't be alone.'

'I'm not alone,' said Hugh. 'Angelina's here.'

'But she'll be looking for a job, you heard her saying that, and she won't find any jobs round here, not that she'd stick it round here, a city girl like her will be looking for the bright lights of Dublin, and there you are, back where you started.'

'I'm not going to Dublin, Margaret,' said Angelina. 'I've come home to stay. I've been wanting to do this for ages, but kept putting it off. Claire and I are going to stay with Dad.'

'Well, now, that sounds very smart. But have you thought of the future? Suppose Dad gets ill, has to go to hospital? He won't be here forever, you know. And what'll you do then? The house will have to be sold.'

'No, no, I wouldn't sell the house,' said Angelina, deeply hurt for her father's sake at the turn the conversation was taking. In a moment of lucidity, she lost her awe of the three older members of her family, and realised that they had little concern for him. She had not yet realised what exactly they had in mind, or the lengths to which they were prepared to go.

'What do you mean, you wouldn't sell the house?' snapped Margaret. 'You're just too important of yourself. Do you think the rest of us have no say in this?'

'In a word, no,' said Hugh. 'Now, all three of you are comfortably off, with fine houses, much better houses than this. This, as you know, is not even a modern bungalow. It wouldn't be worth a lot.'

'But that's not the point,' said Margaret. 'You can't have her coming home from France and going on as if she owns the house. Did you hear her? *I* wouldn't sell the house, she said.'

'Angelina owns this house,' said Hugh. 'A few years ago, realising that you three were all well settled, I thought it the obvious thing to make sure that Angelina would have a home when she would come back to live in Ireland. I've known for years that she intended to come back.'

'Do you mean,' said Kevin, in a tone of alarm, 'that you're leaving the house to Angelina in your will?'

'No,' said Hugh. 'I've signed the house and its contents over to her. This house, and all that's in it, belongs to Angelina, and has done for the last five years.'

'You WHAT?' shrieked Philomena. 'I don't believe I'm hearing this!'

'You can't do this!' said Kevin. 'Where do we come into all this?'

'Can I not persuade you,' said Hugh, 'that none of the three of you needs this house, or anything else of my meagre possessions?'

'That's not the point,' said Margaret. 'It's not the value of the house, it's a matter of principle. What about our inheritance?'

'Yes, what about our inheritance?' pursued Kevin. 'It's a well known fact that when a parent dies, the property, whether it's much or little, has to be divided between the family. I know other priests who have done very well out of their parents' wills. In fact, it's customary for the priest in the family to get the lion's share, so to speak.'

Margaret and Philomena did not appear to be entirely in agreement with this point of view.

'And on top of that,' Kevin went on, 'I can't tell you the embarrassment it would be to me if my friends knew that I got nothing.'

'About inheritance,' said Hugh, 'you don't have to discuss my will with your friends. The point that you all seem to have missed is that this house was mine, bought and converted with my money, and I could do what I liked with it. I could have left it to a charity, or, for that matter, to a dogs' home. My final word on this is that Angelina needs a home and none of the rest of you does.'

'It's her!' said Philomena accusingly, pointing to Angelina. 'She talked him into it. But make no mistake, we're not letting it go. We'll see a solicitor, and see what can be done about claiming our rightful inheritance.'

'And another thing,' said Kevin, almost on a note of triumph, 'what about that husband of Angelina's? Just because they've been separated for years doesn't mean that he won't come back. And if he turns up, he'll think he has some claim on the house. I've seen it all in my parish, people who disappear for years, and then come back when there's any word of money or property.'

'Exactly what I was thinking,' said Margaret. 'There are people so greedy you wouldn't believe it. They don't bother with their relations at all, and then suddenly zoom in when there's any talk of money. I agree with you, Kevin, I've known people like that.'

And so have I, thought Hugh, so have I.

'So if that Bernard Lemoine came back,' continued Margaret, 'and found that Angelina owned a house, there's nothing surer than he'd be putting the pressure on to have it sold. And where would you be then, Dad? You hadn't thought of that, had you?'

'I've got an annulment, Margaret,' said Angelina. 'I'm not married to Bernard any more. And he can have no idea where I am. He didn't ever know my home address.'

'An annulment!' Kevin was horrified. 'This just will not do. I'm warning you, Angelina, you're not to be talking that sort of stuff to people round here. If word of this got to my parish, it would be very awkward for me.'

'And have you thought what this means?' said Philomena, wide-eyed with outrage. 'If she thinks she's not married, she could be going with men, and her with a teenage daughter. Flying her kite round Sligo, being an embarrassment to all of us.'

'She'll do nothing of the sort,' said Kevin grimly.

'Dad,' said Margaret, gently, wheedling, coaxing, 'would you not reconsider the whole situation? Can you not see how vulnerable you are? Bernard Lemoine could come and lay claim to our house, or Angelina might get involved with some other man who might make trouble. At your age, you don't need any of this insecurity or hassle.'

'True, true,' said Hugh. 'I don't need any insecurity or hassle.'

'Well, I'll tell you what we'll do. We'll see a solicitor, and we'll see about getting the signing over of the house revoked. And after that ....'

'And after that?' said Hugh, enquiringly.

'And then .... oh, well, we'd see what's best to do ....'

Hugh sat upright in his armchair. He knew that he was about to play his trump card. They just wouldn't stop, they wouldn't accept what he had done. He knew that the time had come to put a stop to their machinations.

From the kitchen came the sound of girlish laughter, as Claire and her friends chatted with Father Padden.

Margaret was visibly annoyed. There was more chatter, accompanied by a loud laugh from Father Padden.

The sound of the lawn mower was just outside the living room window. Mrs Monks knocked the door, and then came in to take away the tea tray.

Everyone sat in silence for a few minutes, a silence that was punctuated by snippets of lively conversation from the kitchen. Now Father Padden was talking, and whatever he was saying sent the girls into gales of laughter.

After a few minutes, Hugh broke the silence.

'If we were to talk from now till morning,' he said, 'we would still be going round in circles, ending up back where we started. So maybe there are a few things we should put straight.

'As I've already explained, this house was mine, to dispose of as I saw fit. But since you are obviously not in agreement, there is something you need to know.'

He paused, as all four looked in his direction, wondering what was to come.

'Angelina is my only child,' he said. 'The rest of you, for reasons I am not prepared to go into, are my brother Timothy's children.'

Kevin went white. Philomena's mouth fell open. Margaret leaped to her feet.

'This just is not true!' said Margaret, in a tone of total disbelief. 'It can't be.'

'It's her! It's Angelina!' squawked Philomena. 'She put him up to this.'

'You're not seriously trying to tell us,' demanded Kevin, 'that we are all ....'

'Precisely,' interrupted Hugh. 'Not that it matters a lot now, you've all gone your various ways, and will continue to do so, and what you now know won't make the slightest difference to anyone. But if you think that you could make trouble about my decision to sign over the house to Angelina, you might make yourselves look rather foolish. And I'll say again what I've said before. All three of you are comfortably well off, with your own homes. Angelina didn't have a home. This house is, as you will all agree, not a very modern house, not a house that would fetch a lot of money. So isn't it reasonable that Angelina should have it?'

He looked round at all of them in turn, waiting for a reaction.

'I just don't believe this,' said Margaret. 'Now, let's all calm down. It doesn't make sense. We'll have to see about proving that it isn't true.'

'Now that you can't do,' said Hugh. 'Where would you start? And I can prove that what I have told you is true. There are documents with my solicitor, and letters in this house that will bear out what I am saying. Margaret, I don't think you'll want to do anything that could make these facts known to anyone outside the family. After all, what would the Gillens think? And Kevin, I would remind you of our conversation the other day, when you expressed strong opinions on the requirements for the priesthood.'

'Philomena! Kevin! We're going home!' said Margaret. 'I'm not standing for any more of this. Come on.'

She got up and went towards the door. The others followed her. Father Padden appeared from the kitchen, asking what everyone was doing.

'We're going now,' said Kevin. They went out to the car without a word between them.

Father Padden got into the front seat beside Kevin. Margaret and Philomena sat in the back. Nobody spoke.

A few miles down the road, Father Padden broke the silence.

'So you're not moving your father?' he asked. 'Not today?'

'No, not today,' said Kevin.

'Ah, well, if you want my help when you do decide to move him, just let me know. I'll be only too pleased to help. A very nice old man he is, I'm sure you all want the best for him.'

'Yes, yes,' said Kevin absently.

'And even though it was, in a way, a sad occasion, I enjoyed the visit. Your niece is a lovely girl, Kevin.'

'My niece?'

'Yes, Claire. And her friends are nice girls too. We were having a good laugh out there in the kitchen. It's good for your father to have young people around to cheer him up.'

He noticed that the other occupants of the car were silent, preoccupied. They must be worried about the old man, he thought. He made one more attempt at conversation.

'Was it anything important, the family business that you had to discuss? I mean, is there anything I can help with?' he asked.

'Family business? Oh, no, nothing at all,' said Kevin.

'No, no, it wasn't important,' said Margaret.

They completed the journey in silence.

****

Hugh stood up, and walked into the hall. He put on his hat, and lifted his walking stick. He took the Irish Times, which he had not yet had a chance to read, and looked round the kitchen door.

'All right, Mr Staunton?' asked Mrs Monks.

'Yes, Mrs Monks, everything all right. I'm going over for a pint. I'll be back in about an hour.'

Claire, with her friends Donna and Geraldine, decided to go out for a cycle.

Angelina sat alone at the fire. She sat there for a long time, thinking.

She thought first over the events of the last hour. She felt very upset as she realised the attitude of the others towards her father. She had always known that they were all a bit too bossy, even intolerant, but it never occurred to her that they would actually arrange to have her father certified so that they could sell the house. Then it dawned on her that their incivility to herself over the years was quite unjustified. When she was younger, she lacked confidence, and felt that somehow she was in the wrong when the others seemed displeased or disapproving, and she would have tried harder to win their approval. But now it was quite clear that they were self-centred, grasping people, with no love or enjoyment in their lives.

She thought about Sister Aine, and felt truly grateful for her good advice. If Sister Aine had not insisted that she would go home, her father would still be subjected to their constant pestering. She realised that it was her presence, the fact that she had returned home to stay, that had made it possible for Hugh to dispense with their unwelcome attentions.

She wondered briefly about her parents, about what was the relationship between her mother and her uncle Timothy. But, whatever it was, it was so long ago that it no longer mattered.

And then she thought about the immediate future. I can't sit around doing nothing, she told herself. I'll have to think about work. The previous evening, when they had been discussing their plans, Hugh had told her that there were courses in the regional technical college that she might find interesting. But that would not be until the autumn.

She was fluent in French. It would soon be the last term of the school year, oral exams would be looming. Leaving cert students might want some last minute coaching. She could place an ad in the local paper, and wait and see what would turn up. It would be worth a try.

Shortly, John Monks, who had finished mowing the lawn, came in for a cup of tea. They sat by the fire, chatting amiably. John told her about a very good folk group that would be playing in one of the local pubs at the weekend, and asked her if she would like to go. She readily accepted, realising how much she had missed the social scene in Ireland during her years away.

Yes, coming home had been the right decision.

In the pub down the road, Hugh carried his pint over to a corner table, sat down and opened his newspaper. But before he started to read, he thought again of the evenings in Herbie Doherty's shed.

All the skittles had been knocked over.